# LASTING SHADOWS

SHADOWS LANDING #3

KATHLEEN BROOKS

❀ Created with Vellum

*Forever Devoted*

*Forever Hunted*

*Forever Guarded*

*Forever Notorious*

*Forever Ventured*

*Forever Freed (coming January 21, 2020)*

*Shadows Landing Series*

*Saving Shadows*

*Sunken Shadows*

*Lasting Shadows*

*Fierce Shadows (coming April/May 2020)*

Women of Power Series

*Chosen for Power*

*Built for Power*

*Fashioned for Power*

*Destined for Power*

*Web of Lies Series*

*Whispered Lies*

*Rogue Lies*

*Shattered Lies*

*Moonshine Hollow Series*

*Moonshine & Murder*

*Moonshine & Malice*

*Moonshine & Mayhem*

# PROLOGUE

*ONE WEEK AGO . . .*

SAVANNAH AMBROSE LOOKED down at the flyer that had been mailed to each Shadows Landing resident. The Daughters of Shadows Landing charitable organization was putting on their annual fundraiser and this year it was to be a bachelor auction.

The flyer posted some pictures of the men up for grabs, but there was only one who grabbed Savannah's attention—Ridge Faulkner. Sure, he grabbed her attention with his masculine looks that were the opposite of her ex-husband's polished, preppy look. Ridge's hair was long, but not overly long. Just long enough to run your fingers through. In the picture his brown hair was pushed behind his ears, framing spring green eyes that seemed to see her even from the picture.

Savannah tore herself away from his image and read the blurb under his picture. *Ridge Faulkner: architect, builder, and*

*owner of Ridge Builders. His work has been featured in*
*magazines all over the world.*

Savannah looked around her house and sighed as the rain dripped inside her living room and into a bucket. She needed help. A lot of it. And she needed someone to teach her how to do it herself because she'd be damned if she were ever dependent on a man again.

SAVANNAH GRIPPED her bidding paddle hard as Ridge's name was announced. He stepped out from behind the curtain and she heard the excited whispers. Apparently, Ridge Faulkner was quite the catch in Shadows Landing. Seeing him in a tux made Savannah think he wasn't just big in Shadows Landing, but in all of South Carolina. Seeing him in a tux brought her closer to a spontaneous orgasm than she'd believed possible. He was raw masculinity encased in formal attire. But this wasn't a date. She needed that man for his hammer. And not the one all the other women were drooling over. Although she had to admit her eyes had drifted down there when he came to stand on the stage.

The reason she needed him was that Savannah had gotten a quote to fix all that was wrong with her house. The quote was over fifty thousand dollars and that would drain the last of her savings. Savannah's ex-husband hadn't left her with much: one year's worth of "salary," if you could call a wife an employee, and the rundown house in Shadows Landing.

She was applying for jobs from here to Charleston, but so far she hadn't gotten anything. "Wife and charity volunteer" weren't what people were looking for on résumés. It didn't matter she'd helped build her ex-husband up to what he was today. She'd hosted all the right parties, invited all the key players, and had catapulted him to the upper echelons of Atlanta society. Again, not what prospective employers considered important.

But if she could win Ridge Faulkner, she could pay a far lower price and get the worst of the repairs fixed on their "date."

"Three thousand dollars," the woman to Savannah's right called out.

"Three thousand one hundred," another woman called.

Oh dear, her limit was five thousand and she'd really hoped the prices would be lower in a small town. However, Savannah knew high society and unless she was mistaken about the small town that was now her home, these were ringers from Charleston society brought in for their disposable income.

"Five thousand dollars," Savannah called out when the price stalled at four thousand seven hundred and fifty dollars.

"Going once, going twice, sold!"

Savannah breathed out a sigh of relief, but then her lungs stopped working as Ridge Faulkner walked straight toward her.

"Hi, I'm guessing you're from Charleston since I don't recognize you. I'm Ridge Faulkner." He held out his hand and Savannah stared at it. His voice was just as sexy as he was and a spontaneous orgasm was becoming more of a possibility by the moment.

She shook her head to clear her thoughts. "Savannah Ambrose. I actually just moved to Shadows Landing. That's why I won you." Savannah shook his hand. It was large, warm, and a little rough. He closed his hand around hers, and she wondered what they'd feel like against her body. Heavens to Betsy, she needed to get her mind back on track.

"Because you're new?"

Savannah dropped his hand and took a small step back to regain her control. "No, because I need some help with my house, and I hear you know what to do with your hammer." Hell's bells, what was wrong with her?

She could see Ridge's lips twitching as he fought not to laugh. But she also saw his eyes glance toward his hammer, which, of course, led her eyes to follow. She swallowed hard and when she looked up she saw Ridge watching her.

"I need help fixing up my house. I'm new here, and I'd love your opinion on it." Savannah was proud that her voice had returned to a somewhat normal tone.

"You don't want a date? Dinner? Romance? Dancing?" Ridge was unreadable as he asked her, and she couldn't tell if he was insulted or relieved.

"I'm sure that would be lovely, but I really need you in my bedroom. To fix a leaking sink," she quickly added. "And on top of me . . . *my* roof. To fix another leak. And then there's . . ." Savannah paused and plastered on her society smile. She didn't want to scare him off with all the work. "Just little things here and there."

Ridge looked over her shoulder at something and Savannah had the feeling she was being dismissed. "Sure. Call me and we'll get it set up. It's nice meeting you, Savannah."

Savannah watched as he walked to join a group of guys. She did it. She had met someone new *and* her house would be fixed. Now if she could only keep her foot out of her mouth around him, all would be well.

# 1

SAVANNAH AMBROSE, formerly Mrs. Penn Benson, grabbed the largest kitchen knife she could find. She raised it above her head and slammed it down. The avocado sliced neatly in half and the knife left an indentation on her cutting board. Still the anger hadn't abated.

Savannah took a deep breath. A breeze blowing from the Shadows River's direction rolled through the screen door on to her back patio. *Do not kill him.* She told herself as she tried to rein in her temper.

"Did you hear me, pet?"

Savannah picked up the knife again, but this time she hit the cutting board so hard the tip of her knife stuck. She looked at the knife wavering from the force of her hit and felt slightly calmer. She imagined it was Penn she was stabbing instead of him being on speakerphone.

"You know I hate that nickname, Penn," Savannah said through clenched teeth. She held out her finger and put it to the hilt of the knife sticking up on the cutting board and pulled it back before letting go. The knife wavered and Savannah tried to take some calming breaths.

Two years ago, she'd walked in on her husband of five years in bed with not one woman, but two. And not just any two women. Two of Savannah's supposed best friends, Ginger and Pepper, from the charity organization she'd help run in Atlanta. Apparently Penn had a thing for spices.

It had been surprising that Penn hadn't tried to stop the divorce. Instead, he had appeared he was all for it. But then he just refused to give her anything she'd asked for. It was a game for him to torture her. He drew it out and didn't let her move on with her life as he enjoyed a veritable buffet of spices. And for the last eighteen months, she'd had to beg for each one of the items they'd agreed to in the divorce settlement. She'd finally gotten out of a low-rent studio apartment in a crime-filled part of Atlanta and into the Shadows Landing house just a couple weeks ago.

"You have the house, what more do you want?" Penn asked, seemingly bored with the conversation, but Savannah knew better. He was enjoying every moment of it.

"You told the judge the house was in perfect condition and didn't need any repairs. I'm faced with fifty thousand dollars worth of repairs! And this house was the least I deserved and you know it," Savannah said in a super-sweet voice. Two could play that game.

"You deserve nothing because you *are* nothing," Penn spat and Savannah yanked the knife from the cutting board and wished, not for the first time, that Penn would be hit by a truck. Or maybe an incurable case of crabs. Or even better, a case of gonorrhea so bad his pecker would rot and fall off.

"You can't talk to me like that," Savannah said, her voice harsh with pain from the names he'd called her over the past two years. It didn't stop him, though. He just doubled his efforts to break her down. Only this time she wasn't going to take it lying down. She was going to give it right back to the asshole.

RIDGE FAULKNER PULLED his large truck to a stop in front of the cottage along the Shadows Landing River. In the front sat a cute sports car and a very overgrown garden lining the large verandah in the front of the house and wrapping all the way around to hide the crawl space the house was built up on to protect it from flooding. The house looked beautiful at first glance, but under his trained eye he saw the paint was chipping, some of the shutter hinges were rusted out, the roof needed fixing, and the chimney needed a lot of masonry work.

Ridge was torn about the Savannah Ambrose project. She'd "bought" him, not for a date but as an all-you-can-get-done-in-a-day worker. He knew women like her. Beautiful women with smooth skin, dangerous curves, and a silk voice who were never seen unless they were dressed to perfection. They were for looking, not touching. Especially by someone who knew how to use a hammer.

Ridge grinned to himself as he thought of a flustered Savannah. Maybe he'd have some fun today after all. Turning her creamy skin pink with impure thoughts was his goal for the day. Ridge reached through the open door of his truck and grabbed his notepad and pencil. Even though he didn't feel like playing handyman, he would do his job and do it well. That was just the kind of guy he was.

Ridge walked to the front of the house, making notes of things that needed to be fixed. A loose handrail, a broken porch spindle, the shutter hinges that needed replacing, and the obvious roof leak in the front left room of the house.

As Ridge walked around the side of the house he noted

that someone had been working on the gardens. If his memory served him right, this was the old Benson cottage. But no one had lived here for twenty years. There used to be a caretaker who would stop by once a month, but it didn't appear anyone had stopped by for quite some time.

"You deserve nothing because you *are* nothing," Ridge heard a man say cruelly.

"You can't talk to me like that," he heard Savannah reply. He heard the hurt in her voice even as she tried to stay brave. Who was the asshole talking to her?

"I'm your husband. I can talk to you anyway I want. I own you, pet."

"You're my *ex*-husband and you never owned me. If you did I would still be in Atlanta with you. Or is that it? You're mad I left your sorry ass so easily?" Ridge grinned and mentally cheered her on.

"Yet here you are calling me because the house isn't perfect. You can't do anything on your own. That's why you're my little pet. I pet you, I feed you, I clothe you, and in return you sit on my lap looking pretty. That's all you're good for," her ex said with satisfaction. "Do you want to come back to my lap like a good girl?"

"*Never*," Savannah swore. "Besides, I'm sitting on someone else's lap. I don't need you anymore, Penn. I never did. You were just too conceited to see that. But what I do expect is for you to live up to the divorce agreement and pay for the repairs to this house."

"What do you mean you're sitting on someone's lap? I shouldn't be surprised. You're nothing but a high-priced prostitute willing to go with anyone who pays."

Savannah laughed, but it was filled with malice. "I wasn't the one caught in bed with two women. And you didn't pay for squat. I made you who you are today, and you have to live with all your cronies wondering where I am. You only got there because they liked me. I think I might make some calls to my dear friends back home today."

"You'll never get a dime out of me, pet. Not even if you beg. Well, maybe if you're on your knees while begging my name over and over again."

"Sorry," Ridge said, opening the screen door and strolling in. His eyes were locked with hers, and he saw Savannah's eyes go wide and her face flush red as she stared open-mouthed at him. She looked ashamed, and it broke his heart. She shouldn't be ashamed. She should be proud of herself for standing up to that asshole. "But Savannah only cries my name over and over again, and she never has to beg for what I give her."

"Ridge," Savannah gasped on a whisper, but it was enough for Penn to hear.

"Who the hell is Ridge? You *whore*. Already moving on to the next man. Watch out, man, she'll take every penny you have," Penn snarled over the phone.

Ridge didn't answer as Penn ranted. Instead he kept his eyes locked with Savannah's as he reached over and ended the call. The phone began to ring again almost immediately, but Ridge sent the call to voicemail and then turned it off. He'd never wanted to hurt someone as badly as he wanted to hurt her ex right then.

Ridge had made up his mind about Savannah, but after hearing that phone call, he was beginning to wonder if he'd jumped to the wrong conclusions. Savannah had *high maintenance* written all over her, even as she stood in jean shorts and a white tank top. But maybe it was just a defense?

"Ridge," she said his name and it shot fire through him. "I'm so embarrassed. I didn't know you were here." She was flustered, and Ridge knew by the blush across her chest and up her neck that she was horrified he'd overheard her. Hearing Penn say those things to her was too much for any gentleman to put up with. Chivalry demanded he come to her aid.

"I'm sorry I interrupted. I know it was a private call. I just can't stand men who treat women like that," Ridge told her as her eyes went to the floor. "Besides, you will be calling my name over and over for what I give you."

Savannah's milk chocolate brown eyes shot up again and her mouth formed an *O* as the blush spread up to her cheeks.

"You're going to love all the improvements I can get done today. I'm pretty sure you'll be so pleased with the way I fix the roof you'll scream out my name and then you should see how I handle my hammer"—her blush turned a deeper shade of red and Ridge grinned—"to fix the porch."

"P-p-porch, right," Savannah smiled and gave a nervous laugh.

"What else would I do with my hammer?" Ridge asked innocently. "Now, do you want to show me the to-do list?" he asked, directing her back to business. He'd have fun teasing her, but he wanted to get this place fit to live in too. She'd done a good job putting lipstick on a pig, but it was still a pig. And a house falling apart was still a house falling apart, even with pretty curtains.

SAVANNAH LET out a breath and nodded. *Stop thinking about his hammer.* "I have a list on the kitchen table." She turned to get it and when she turned back, Ridge was under her sink.

"You have a leak down here," he said from under the counter. His legs stuck out and she had a very good view of his hammer. Savannah sighed with a happy little smile on her face. Oh the things a man with a hammer like that could do. Ridge scooted back out and stood up. "I can fix it pretty easily. I'm going to need a list of things from the hardware store, though. Why don't you show me what else is on that list and I'll run into town before getting to work. Then I can fly through some of these repairs."

"Whatever you say. I'm just so grateful to have you here. Let me show you the living room." Savannah led him into the living room where the bucket was catching the last of the runoff from the morning's quick shower.

"I saw that from outside. Your chimney needs a lot of work. It would cost ten grand to fix, easily. Or do you want me to seal it and waterproof it now and fix it later?"

Ridge was in full professional mode now as he took in the fireplace, the roof, and the floors.

"You can seal it up so it won't leak? I won't use it. I don't have the money to fix it right now," Savannah admitted.

"No problem. I can do that when I fix the roof." She watched as Ridge wrote something down on the pad. He looked up at the lights and wandered off, opening doors until he found the utility room. "I need to upgrade your electrical board to be in code. The wiring actually doesn't look too bad, but I'll test all of it to make sure. You don't want a fire."

"Thank you. That would be great. Does anything else down here need to be fixed?"

"Yeah," Ridge said, but he didn't say more. "Upstairs?"

And so they went, room to room, checking all the plumbing, the walls, the electricity, the flooring, and the roof. "Is there anything else?" Ridge asked and this time Savannah laughed for real.

"Anything else? I'm pretty sure you're building me a new house."

"I love these old houses. They're built to last, that's for sure. The floors are great. There are just a couple boards that need to be replaced because of the leak. When you have time they need to be sanded and refinished. Then they'll look brand new."

Savannah watched Ridge look over the house one more time before tucking his pencil into his back pocket. "I've got my list. I'm guessing it'll be about three to four hundred dollars in supplies. Is that too much?"

"No. Can I write you a check when you get back?"

"Sure thing. If I hurry I can beat the rush at the hardware store and be back within the hour to get to work. With a little love, this house will be back to all its former glory."

"Thank you, Ridge." He nodded and then slipped out the screen door. Savannah looked up at the ceiling and smiled. "Yes, it's getting fixed! Ridge is amazing!" she squealed with delight as she held out her arms and spun.

"I told you you'd be screaming my name," Ridge called from the yard.

Savannah was so happy her house was getting fixed up that she wasn't embarrassed. Instead she closed her eyes and laughed. Finally, something good was happening in her life.

## 2

RIDGE DIDN'T KNOW what to make of Savannah Ambrose. She'd obviously been through a lot with her divorce, but hearing her laugh as he walked around the house had made him smile. He was beginning to think there was a lot more to Savannah than what he originally believed.

Getting into his pickup, he smiled again and realized he hadn't stopped smiling since leaving the house. Savannah had caught his eye the moment she'd bid on him. Now she'd done more than catch his eye. She had his full attention.

IT ONLY TOOK five minutes before he was parked in front of the hardware store. Savannah lived behind a row of tall azalea bushes off Palmetto Drive about a quarter mile down the road from Ridge's cousin Gavin, and just a short drive to town.

The parking lot outside the hardware store was lined with pickups. Some were new, some were old, but they all had tools and a cooler of beer in their truck beds. Half of the owners were inside sitting on old, worn stools at the nail counter sipping coffee and telling tales.

Ridge opened the door and the cowbell overhead rang. "Gentlemen," he said to the usual suspects of older men talking with Squirrel, the owner of the store. Squirrel wasn't his real name, but everyone called him that on account of his squirrel hunting and eating hobby. In fact, Ridge didn't know his real name.

"Howdy, Ridge. Junior's in the back if you need any help," Squirrel said, looking up from where he was hanging out with his buddies. The group of six men were all in their late fifties and sixties who were *fixin'* something at the house and just had to go to the hardware store every morning. They sat at the nail counter in case their wives stopped by, and then they would innocently look up and declare the project could only be completed with a certain nail that they were having trouble finding. The nail counter consisted of old coffee cans filled with a mix of nails from over the years. It was the perfect excuse.

"Thanks, Squirrel," Ridge called out as he waved at the men and headed to say good morning to Squirrel's son, Junior. He'd never really thought about it, but he didn't know if Junior was his real name or a nickname. Maybe it was Squirrel, Jr. "Hey, Junior." Ridge watched as the shorter man tried to hang a hammer on the top peg of a wall full of tools.

"Good morning. What can I do you for?" Junior asked, finally jumping slightly to get the hammer in place.

"I have a list for the old Benson cottage," Ridge said, holding it out for Junior.

"Who's the pretty lady living there now?" Junior asked as he and Ridge began to gather the smaller supplies.

"Savannah Ambrose." Ridge's lips tilted up into a smile at the thought of her.

"Not Benson?"

Ridge shook his head and then tucked a piece of hair behind his ear. "She was married to a Benson, but got the cottage in the divorce."

"That's a shame for her. It's in rough shape."

"I'll take care of it," Ridge replied, knowing instantly this was going to be a lot more than a single charity date kind of relationship. He'd make sure the house was safe and secure for Savannah just to hear her laugh again. And gosh, being a proper gentleman, he'd better take care of it himself instead of sending his construction crew to fix the house. Sure, it would take longer, but then he'd get to see more of the sexy redhead.

Junior snickered. "Sure you will. Pull your truck out back where we can load the shingles."

Thirty minutes after leaving Savannah's house, Ridge was back and unloading his full truck.

"That was fast." Ridge turned to see Savannah leaning against the doorframe of her now open front door. "Do you need any help unloading things?"

"I've got it, thank you." Ridge paused as he dropped the large pack of shingles to the ground. "I do think this will take me two days. Do you mind if I come back tomorrow to finish up?"

"But I didn't pay for two dates," Savannah said suddenly, sounding nervous.

"It'll be part two of our one date."

"Well, then I insist on feeding you while you're here. I want to thank you for helping me fix this place up." Savannah walked down the steps and Ridge saw her carefully avoid the stair with the cracked step. She reached into his truck and pulled out two cans of white paint. "What's this?"

"To paint your deck after I replace the rotted sections."

"I can do that," Savannah said, suddenly excited. "Can I do that?"

"Of course," Ridge said. Her excitement was contagious.

"What do I do first?" Savannah asked as Ridge leapt into the bed of his truck.

"Ever use a pressure washer?"

Savannah's brown eyes widened and Ridge thought she'd renege on her offer to help, but instead she helped him lower it down to the driveway. "Can I use it? Will you show me how?"

"I'll show you anything you want," Ridge promised and had a feeling he wasn't just talking about how to fix things. There was something about Savannah's smile and wide eyes that made him want to show her everything about him—his work, his dreams, his fears. And that was dangerous. Ridge let out a deep breath. He wasn't his cousin Wade. Wade had wanted nothing more than to marry. Ridge had nothing against marriage in general but wasn't about to rush into anything. "I'll show you how to pressure wash and you can do that while I'm fixing the plumbing."

Savannah's smile slipped and she bit her lower lip just slightly. "But, I want to see how you do that too. When I'm out here on my own and something breaks, I want to know how to fix it."

There wasn't anything sexier she could have said to Ridge than that. "Is there anything you want me to fix without you?"

"The electrical. I think that would be pretty boring and too great a risk for me to mess up, but if you could show me what to do if the electricity gets tripped, that would great."

"Right this way then. We'll start with plumbing."

SAVANNAH WAS sure she was having a hot flash—a real back-of-the-hand-to-her-forehead,     fall-down-in-a-case-of-the-vapors hot flash. Right in front of her, Ridge was bent over, hooking the hose into the pressure washer. It had been two years since she'd been with someone in any capacity. After she'd found Penn in bed with Ginger and Pepper, she had thought about revenge sex with some hot guy, but honestly, she'd bailed on the idea after getting to the bar. The idea of getting close to anyone right then didn't sit well with her.

And what she thought would be only a couple weeks turned into a couple of months and now a couple of years. No matter how she tried, she couldn't trust anyone enough to open up to him—body or soul.

Looking at Ridge's butt filling out his pair of jeans, though . . . yup, she was in the middle of a full-blown case of the vapors. The vapors had been building, too. First he taught her how to turn off the water. Then he'd had her crawl under the sink with him to see how he fixed the pipes. Their shoulders were pressed against each other, their hips touched, and Ridge had been so close she could smell him. And he smelled so good she almost swooned under the sink and, well, that would've been embarrassing. Savannah had pulled it together and learned all types of things, but this was too much.

She took a step closer. Her eyes never left his perfect rear end. And his back! The way his muscles moved under his shirt had her reaching to touch him. But then Ridge stood and turned around to face her.

Savannah yanked her hand back and pretended she hadn't been caught ogling him. "Ready for me?"

"Yup," Ridge said, his voice deeper than normal as his eyes trailed down her body. Maybe she wasn't the only one affected. Water sprayed out of the wand, soaking Savannah as she let out a yelp of surprise. "Sorry!"

Savannah looked down at her soaked shorts and shrugged. Well, that chased the moment away. "It's okay. I guess I'm going to be wet anyway."

Ridge dropped the wand. "Crap," he cursed as he picked it up and handed it to her. "Just press the trigger and spray. Sweep side to side and get as much of the dirt and chipped paint off as you can."

"Like this?" Savannah pushed the trigger and water hit the porch and splashed onto her, further drenching her.

Ridge swallowed hard, nodded, and walked inside.

When Savannah looked down to see the area she cleaned, she saw that her white shirt was now see-through. Could Ridge really be as affected by her as she was of him?

RIDGE MADE his way through the electrical and started on the roof. The physical labor of ripping up the rotted shingles and nailing in new ones helped calm him after seeing Savannah in a clinging wet T-shirt. Her breasts were perfectly shaped and sized for his hands. And he wanted to slowly pull up that wet tank top to trace his lips over her stomach.

*Wham*!

Ridge shot a nail into the newly replaced row of shingles. He had at least another three hours on the roof fixing the leaks, but then Savannah would be safe and dry until she could afford to replace the whole roof.

.  .  .

SAVANNAH'S ARMS shook and her back ached, but her porch was clean. She turned off the water and leaned the pressure washer wand against the house. It had taken her three hours but the porch was clean, along with her walkway. And she'd done it herself.

Taking a deep breath and smiling, she looked at what she'd accomplished. Savannah was filled with pride at the brand-new-looking walk and the large verandah ready for paint. Ridge might think she was silly, but she did a little celebratory dance. In her mind, she saw what it would look like tomorrow with a coat of paint and fixed boards. It would be beautiful. Maybe Ridge would teach her how to hammer the boards in place. Maybe he'd even show her how to use a power saw!

With an extra pep in her step, Savannah went inside to change. Inside, the leak in the living room was no more. The electrical was up to code. And when she went into her bathroom, there were no dripping faucets or pipes. On top of that, Ridge had even shown her how to fix a toilet *and* unclog a drain. She was *Woman* and she was ready to roar!

Savannah pulled off her wet clothes and hung them on the shower bar to dry. She noticed that the sunlight coming into her room was dimming. She looked at her bedside clock and cringed. It was after eight and Ridge was still working hard. The least she could do was feed him. And if that meant he stayed with her a little longer, it wasn't anything but good Southern hospitality.

Savannah ran to the shower and jumped in while it was still cold to wash off the dirt from the porch that had sprayed onto her. She hurried out, dried off, and put her wet hair in a bun before pulling on a spaghetti strap sundress and covering it with a sheer, lacy sweater. The nights in South Carolina were still warm, close to seventy degrees in

September, but with the breeze from the river it could be a little chilly.

She slipped her feet into some sandals and skipped down the stairs and into the kitchen. Savannah's phone still lay on the counter where she'd left it when she'd heard Ridge pull up to the front after the hardware store. A whole day without her connection to the world and it had been more fun than she'd had in years.

## 3

RIDGE'S BODY strummed from physical exertion. It had been years since he'd repaired a roof. Now, as the owner and lead architect of his own company, he no longer climbed on rooftops. When he was in high school and college, he did plenty of construction-related jobs. As he nailed in the last shingle, he sat back on his heels and dusted his hands on his jeans. The roof was fixed.

When Ridge made his way down to the ground, he heard music drifting through the open screen door around back. Then he heard something else. An animal in pain? A toddler in a meltdown? Either way it wasn't good. Ridge tossed his equipment into the back of his truck and hurried to the back porch door and froze.

Inside, Savannah was wiggling her hips as she sang along to the music—badly. Very, very badly. However, the excellent smell coming from whatever she was torturing with her singing made it better.

Savannah's little skirt swung as she twirled toward the counter on her right. Mid-twirl she caught sight of him, screamed in surprise, and tripped.

By the time Ridge got to her, she was on her bottom with her head tossed back and laughing. It was a much better sound than her singing.

"Are you okay?" Ridge asked as he offered his hand for her to take.

"I am, thanks." Savannah reached up and took his hand. Ridge pulled her up and didn't stop pulling until she was in his arms once again. He remembered every inch of her body from the one dance they shared just days ago.

"Whatever you're baking smells wonderful." *But not as wonderful as you.*

Savannah grinned up at him, and if he hadn't overheard her with her ex, Ridge would have sworn she was a carefree, happy woman whose whole life had been easy. But she wasn't. She knew pain. She was just choosing joy instead.

"I have a little goodie basket for you. These are my famous peanut butter brownies that I used to make for charity events." The happiness in her voice trailed off as her eyes unfocused. Ridge could tell she was thinking of times gone by.

"They smell very good. You lived in Atlanta?" Ridge asked.

Savannah turned to reach for the basket she'd mentioned and nodded. "Mostly Atlanta, but also Charleston. I knew of this house, vaguely, but when Penn offered it in the divorce settlement, the idea of being in a small town was very appealing to me. I love being around good people."

"Did you work in Atlanta?" Ridge asked as she placed the brownies into the basket.

Her shoulders tensed and then slumped. Her body language answered the question for him. "I was two classes shy of graduating from college when Penn, who was two years older, landed a good job in Atlanta. We met in Charleston where we both went to school." Savannah shook her head at the memory. "I was so naïve. I should have realized then that if he loved me he would have supported my dream of graduating. But he gave me an ultimatum. If I loved him, I would go with him. If I didn't go with him, I didn't love him and we needed to break up. I stupidly dropped out of college my last semester and followed him. I became the perfect stay-at-home wife, just like my mom had been before she and my dad passed away. I was trying to make her proud when I should have been making myself proud." Savannah shook her head and took a deep breath. "But that's all in the past. I'm looking at finishing my last classes to get my degree."

"Is that what you want?" Ridge asked, leaning against the countertop.

"It is."

"Then you should do it."

Savannah turned to him with a question. "You don't think it's strange for a twenty-eight-year-old to be going back to school?"

Ridge kept his eyes locked with hers so she knew he meant what he said. "No. I think it's brave to go after what you want."

Savannah's lips tilted up into a slow smile as she handed him the basket of brownies. "Well, right now I want to take you to dinner. I bought you for a date, and it's about time I lived up to it."

SAVANNAH THANKED Ridge as he opened the passenger door of his truck for her. He backed out of her driveway and headed the short drive to the Pink Pig BBQ. The gigantic rotating pig was lit up with a spotlight as they pulled into the parking lot.

When they went inside, a girl of about sixteen smiled past Savannah at Ridge. "Evenin', Ridge. Two?" Her dark brown eyes landed curiously on Savannah.

"Yes, please. Tamika, this is Savannah Ambrose. She's new here. Savannah, this is Tamika Foster. Her grandfather, Darius, owns the Pink Pig."

"Nice to meet you," Savannah told the girl who grabbed two menus and led them to a table.

"You too."

Tamika set the menus down, took their drink orders, and strode off to the kitchen. The menu was small but full of delicious dishes. And Tamika was quick with their food and drinks.

"You know all about my life now. What about yours?" Savannah asked after taking a bite of her BBQ sandwich.

"Grew up in Shadows Landing. My parents, aunts, and uncles all left for Florida after we graduated from high school. They bought a small resort and run it now. I have a sister, Tinsley, who's an artist. She has a gallery right up the street. I'm also very close to my cousins who are more like siblings to me. Recently we've become close with our extended family in Keeneston, Kentucky," Ridge explained as they ate. She remembered some of the other Faulkners— such as Wade—who was now on his honeymoon with Darcy Delmar-Faulkner. Savannah hoped to get a job at Darcy's museum in Shadows Landing.

"I think I saw some of them at the auction and the museum opening."

Ridge nodded. "We do travel in packs," he said, laughing. And their pack had gotten much larger with the

Davies family from Keeneston coming down for all weddings and sometimes to just hang out.

"I read that you were an architect in Charleston before starting your own company," Savannah said.

"I was. I love designing. It's actually my favorite thing to do. I just got tired of builders messing up my projects. I also got tired of sitting in an office. So, I went old-school. Back to when architects were on site and knew every inch of a building because they were there, helping build it. I'm much happier now." Ridge looked at her and held her stare. "You should take risks to find your happiness. It might be scary, but if you never take risks, how do you know what you can accomplish?"

It was rhetorical, but Savannah felt as if Ridge was speaking to her heart. It was time for her to take a risk to find happiness. The first risk was to enroll in college. She was done hiding. Done playing it safe. She was ready to go after what she wanted.

Ridge insisted on paying for dinner and stood up from the booth when they were done. He reached down and held out his hand to help her from the booth. Savannah placed her hand in his, and just like every time they touched, she felt excitement from the tips of her fingers into the deepest part of her heart. She was expecting him to let go of her hand, but he didn't. Instead, Ridge held her hand as they left the Pink Pig. While she didn't know most of the people there, she knew they were all going to be talking about her. Judging from the whispers and stares, Ridge didn't take many women out on dates. The idea of that made her smile and her heart soar as they left the restaurant.

.  .  .

RIDGE WAS ENJOYING himself more than he'd ever dreamed. He had fun talking with Savannah. She was kind, funny, witty, and completely down to earth. She wasn't anything like he'd originally thought, and he chided himself for prejudging her. He also noticed she hadn't pulled her hand away from his as they drove down Main Street. It excited him to hold her hand. Something he hadn't felt before. When he turned left onto Palmetto Drive, though, Ridge suddenly went rigid.

"Is that smoke?" Savannah asked.

"Call 911," Ridge told her in answer. There was smoke filling the night air as he sped toward her home.

"My house is on fire!" Savannah gasped, panicking as she gave the address to dispatch.

Ridge parked a house down from hers on the grass and together they ran toward the flames and smoke now visible above her azalea bushes.

Savannah gasped when they rounded the hedge and saw that the kitchen was in flames. "Move your car so the fire truck can get in here," Ridge ordered as he ran straight for the fire.

By the time he heard the first siren in the distance, Ridge had the hose hooked up and was spraying down the house around the kitchen to try to contain the fire. Flames licked the porch door. The screen door he was so fond of eavesdropping from had melted.

Ridge was able to get inside a ways after spraying down the door and battled the flames back, but only a foot or so. The smoke was thick and choked him as he made his way farther inside. He wasn't going to last long. He wanted to spray the walls leading to the dining room and the living room to make it harder for the fire to spread.

"We got it, Ridge!"

Ridge felt Granger, the sheriff of Shadows Landing and

one of his family's closest friends, tap him on the shoulder. Ridge backed out, letting Granger pull him from the smoke as the volunteer firefighters set up lines and began to douse the fire with water, way more water than the puny garden hose had been capable of producing.

Ridge was coughing, his lungs were burning, and his eyes watered as Granger and the fire department attacked the fire. "Ridge!" Savannah called out as she ran toward him. Tears were rolling down her pale face as she looked between the fire and his face. "Are you okay?"

"It's only in your kitchen. Your house should be able to be saved," Ridge told her between coughing fits.

"I'm not worried about the house. I have insurance. I was worried about *you*. What were you thinking running into the house? You could have died!"

Ridge blinked as Savannah pulled off her sweater and poured a bottle of water over it. She pressed it to his eyes and Ridge felt relief. The cool water felt so good after the stinging smoke.

"I'm fine, although a garden hose isn't much of a weapon. I wanted to save the house for you," Ridge admitted.

Savannah's worried frown softened, and she reached for his hand. Suddenly she tensed and looked behind him. "Ridge. Something isn't right here."

# 4

SAVANNAH SHIVERED as the fire in her kitchen raged on. It felt as if the devil were dancing a jig on her grave, fingers of unease prickled their way down her spine as she narrowed her eyes.

"Ridge, something isn't right here."

From where they stood off to the side of the house, she could see around back. Her eyes landed on the path that led toward the river. She'd been weeding and slowly cleaning up the yard and hedges since she moved in. The row of azaleas in the front of the house was now pristine. After that, she'd cleared the brush and trimmed the shrubs along the back of the house so she could have a good view of the river. It had been movement from the shrubs that had seemed out of place.

Savannah started walking in that direction and Ridge followed. Feeling him behind her gave her the courage to continue toward the shadows.

"What is it?" Ridge asked quietly as she stopped at the entrance to the path leading to the river. There was a six-foot hedgerow of boxwoods on each side of her property leading toward the river. Across the back of her property was a smaller hedge made up of rosebushes against a white picket fence. In the middle of the fence was an arbor lined with multiple colors and varieties of clematis.

"Part of the arbor is broken," Savannah told Ridge as she realized what felt out of place.

"Okay," he said slowly and Savannah knew he didn't understand why it was giving her the heebie-jeebies. "I can fix that in less than a minute," he said, looking at the small white wooden piece of the arbor hanging loose.

"I finished trimming this all back just a couple days ago. I look at this arbor all the time. This piece wasn't broken when we left for dinner," Savannah told him.

"So?"

"Miss Ambrose!" Savannah turned around and saw the sheriff walking their way with a fireman next to him.

"Yes?"

"We haven't met yet. I'm Granger Fox, the sheriff. And this is Chief Lambert of the fire department."

"Savannah Ambrose," she replied automatically as she shook their hands. "Thank you for saving my house."

"That's why we're here," Chief Lambert said. Where Granger was in his thirties and had the chiseled look of an athlete, Chief Lambert looked to be in his early fifties with a big white mustache and a big pot belly. However, there was no doubt in her mind that Chief Lambert would be able to carry her or anybody else out of harm's way. His shoulders were wider than a barn door. "The fire was started because the gas stovetop was left on. A dishtowel was partially on the stove and caught fire. It caused the old cabinets to go up like kindling. It was a good thing you caught it early or the house would be a total loss."

Savannah knew her mouth gaped because what he said

wasn't true. "You're wrong. I *never* leave the stovetop on. Not only that, but I haven't used it today. I only baked and used the oven, not the stovetop."

"I'm sure it was just an oversight," Granger said, trying to placate her, but she wouldn't be pacified.

"You're wrong," she said again, crossing her arms over her chest in defiance.

"I assure you, it's a clear-cut accident," Chief Lambert said, backing up the sheriff.

"No, it's not." Savannah bit off the words as she felt her heart beating in her chest.

"Granger, Chief," Ridge said, getting involved. "I was there, and the stove was not on."

Both men looked at them disbelievingly. "We'll show you," Chief Lambert said as he turned and led them back toward the house. "We were able to save the house. The kitchen will need to be gutted and there's some minor smoke damage, but nothing a good cleaning and airing out won't fix. The house is livable, just not the kitchen."

Savannah was both thankful and annoyed. "Thank you for saving the house, Chief, but I swear on my life, that stove was not used today. Then the whole arbor thing . . . I think someone set the fire on purpose."

"Arbor?" Granger asked.

"That's what we were looking at," Savannah explained. "There was a broken lattice in the arbor that wasn't there just hours ago."

Chief and Granger shared a look and Savannah knew exactly what it meant. It meant they thought she was being an unreasonable female. Penn had given her that same look many times.

"I'll look into it," Granger said in a way Savannah was sure meant he wouldn't.

Well, if no one was going to look into it, she would.

"ARE you really going to look into it?" Ridge asked Granger as he examined the broken lattice.

"I told you I was. Have I ever lied?" Granger used his flashlight to look around the arbor area and Ridge felt bad for insulting him. However, neither Granger nor Lambert seemed to believe the stove had not been on when they'd left for dinner. So much so, Ridge started to doubt himself.

"No. You never lie. Or at least not well."

Granger chuckled as he walked in the backyard, but then his flashlight suddenly stopped sweeping the yard. "Does Miss Ambrose have a boat?"

"I don't know, why?" Ridge asked.

"Just wondering," Granger said in a way Ridge knew he was lying. "Is anyone staying here tonight?"

"Something *is* wrong! We aren't crazy."

Granger shook his head. "I don't know yet. But if it wasn't an accident . . ."

Granger didn't need to finish his sentence. Ridge already knew the answer. "I'll see if she'll let me stay with her."

"I'm sure you would make the sacrifice," Granger said teasingly as they made their way back to the house. The fire crew was cleaning up, and Savannah was curled up on a chair on the porch with a big blanket, drinking a large glass of wine.

"Miss Ambrose," Granger said in his cop voice.

"Please, call me Savannah," she said with a sigh.

"Savannah, I see what you mean about the arbor. Do you have a boat?"

"No, why?"

Ridge listened but didn't talk. He had the same question as Savannah.

"It's hard to tell because the tide is coming in, but I think a boat pulled up to your yard. The grass is indented as if it were kayak-sized or a small rowboat pulled ashore. Now, it could also be an alligator. Goodness knows Bubba is big enough to cause the same marks."

"Bubba?" Savannah asked with her brow crinkled.

"He's a very large gator that is known to wander around the houses here. If you see him, Gator can catch and move him," Granger explained.

"I'm confused," Savannah said, gripping the bridge of her nose with her fingers. "If I see a gator named Bubba, I'm supposed to call another gator so he'll move?"

Ridge snickered and Savannah shot him a dirty look. "I'm sorry. The alligator is named Bubba. Gator is a person who removes gators. So if you see Bubba the gator, you call Gator the person to remove him. Is that as clear as mud now?"

"I think I've had too much to drink because that somehow makes sense."

"Either way, it would make me feel better if you had someone here tonight," Granger finished.

"Sheriff," a young firefighter called out near them. "I'm going to stay tonight to make sure the fire is completely out."

Ridge looked to Savannah who shrugged. "I'm going to sit out here for a while. I have fans running through the house and all the windows open. The bedrooms don't smell too bad, so I'll be okay here. Thank you."

Ridge wanted to see what Granger came up with. The idea that someone set the fire on purpose didn't seem likely. Sure, there were questionable people in Shadows Landing, maybe a few drunk pirate re-enactors, but not arsonists.

"I can stay if you'd like," Ridge offered, but Savannah just shook her head.

"I'm fine, but that's very nice of you to offer. I'm pretty sure that date I bought is all over. You've been a huge help, thank you."

"I'll be here early in the morning with my crew. We'll get your kitchen back to right in no time."

SAVANNAH LOOKED up at Ridge and felt herself take a deep breath. She was trying to be brave, but it felt good to know that Ridge would be back soon. "Thank you. I emailed my insurance agent who said he'll be here tomorrow."

"I'll see you in a couple of hours. I'll draw up some plans for you to consider. In the meantime, here's my phone number." Savannah reached up and took the business card from Ridge. "Please call me if you need anything at all."

"Thank you, Ridge," Savannah said, meaning it more than she could ever tell him. "I'll see you in the morning."

Savannah watched as Granger and Ridge walked off together. Their heads bent toward each other as they talked and she wondered what they were saying. But all too soon Ridge left, then Granger, then Chief Lambert, and soon she was all alone with a rookie firefighter who sat in her kitchen, making sure all the embers were out.

Savannah poured a glass of white wine from the bottle that the rookie had rescued from her refrigerator. This house didn't feel like hers. She'd never owned anything of her own. Everything had been Penn's. Since the divorce, she'd gotten her first place all by herself. She'd taken title to her little convertible and had driven away, hoping to never look back. Then Penn had delayed in deeding this cottage over to her. When she finally got here, she was a different person from who she'd been when she'd signed the divorce papers.She was free.And she was in charge of her future. Something she had never been with Penn.

Now she could get her degree. She could have her own career. She could find love. The kind that wasn't one-sided. Savannah's lips turned up as she thought of Ridge. What would it be like to be loved by him?

## 5

"THANK YOU," Savannah said to Chief Lambert as he handed her a brown paper bag from Stomping Grounds Diner. Savannah had fallen asleep on the front porch couch and only woken up when she heard a vehicle coming down her gravel driveway.

When she'd awoken, she'd found that the rookie had put a blanket around her, her shoes had been taken off, and the wine was back in the fridge. The rookie had done well and she'd told Chief Lambert that when she first saw him get out of the truck. But then he'd handed her breakfast and she almost broke out in tears. It was overwhelming. She thought he'd written her off the night before and here he was, bringing her breakfast at six in the morning.

"I thought you'd be hungry without having a working kitchen."

"That's very kind of you, Chief."

"Shadows Landing is a small town, and we look after our own here. Besides, I have been thinking about what you said. There was no question in your mind that you didn't use the stove. I want to look around and see if I can find anything else. I have to make a determination for your insurance company. Even if it was arson, it'll be hard to prove. It's not like the gas line was yanked free or gasoline spread across the house."

"Thank you for looking again," Savannah said as they made their way to the charred kitchen.

"Granger called me and told me about the broken arbor and signs there may have been a boat pulled up on the property." Chief Lambert began to look around the kitchen. His mustache sank low as he frowned the longer he looked around. "I think I'm going to have to rule it inconclusive. I'm sorry I can't find the answer for you."

"Thank you for your work, Chief. I'll send you my award-winning cobbler when my kitchen is operational."

His mustache wiggled as he smiled. "Well, I won't turn that down. I don't think there's anything a firefighter likes more than food. Good day, Miss Ambrose. Please let me know if I can help you in any way."

Pickup trucks began to roll in as Chief Lambert left. They were weighted down with wood, tools, and contraptions Savannah couldn't identify. Last to pull in was Ridge. He got out of his truck and his eyes instantly went to hers.

He didn't look like an architect. No suit and perfect hair. Instead, he was in jeans that hugged all the right places and his hair looked as if he'd run his hand through it in frustration several times already.

"How are you?" Ridge asked, and she felt the meaning in his words. It wasn't a simple greeting. He cared.

"I fell asleep on the couch outside, but I slept all night."

"I brought some plans. My crew will start the cleanup

while you pick the design you'd like. And if you don't like anything here, I can draw up new plans according to your desires."

Oh, Savannah had desires but pen and paper weren't involved. Soon the sounds of construction filled the air as Ridge laid out different plans to her. The first one was nice, but the second one, well, it was perfection. The window she loved to look through over the sink was blown out into French doors and a small kitchen table could fit there while the appliances had been moved to the other side of the kitchen.

"This one," Savannah practically gasped as she envisioned sitting and drinking her coffee while looking out over the gardens to the river.

"I'll get the guys right on it." Ridge stood for a moment and Savannah began to wonder if there was more to the plans.

"I was wondering if you'd like to have dinner with me tonight. My cousin Harper runs Shadows Bar in town, and she's having a live band. I thought we could eat at Lowcountry Smokehouse and then head down to the bar."

Savannah had held her breath while he was talking for fear of missing what he was saying, but now she almost shivered with excitement. "I'd really like that."

"I can pick you up at seven?" Ridge asked. Savannah shook her head.

"I want to go into Charleston this afternoon to look at some things for the house. I'll let you know when I leave for home, and then we can decide if seven or seven-thirty is better. Does that work?"

.　.　.

"It does," Ridge smiled with relief and excitement as Savannah accepted his invitation. They'd had such a good time yesterday, and he wasn't ready for it to end. "I need to talk to the guys and show them the plans. We'll be here working every day for the next three weeks."

"Thank you for moving me to the front of the list. I know you must have other clients."

He did. In fact, after he talked to his crew, he had to call who was supposed to be next. The plans were all drawn up and Ridge would share that with him to keep him satisfied over for the next month. His client's wife had an interior decorating hobby so sharing the plans now would probably save him a month of no work. The wife was known to pick and prod at things until they were exactly how she wanted them. Strangely, they usually ended up almost exactly where Ridge's original plans had started.

Ridge had designed a lake house for them before. The woman had spent two weeks moving the sockets around until they were "perfect." Perfect had been exactly where Ridge had put them in the plans. But if it made his client happy, he feigned surprise at how good they looked there.

"It's nothing that can't wait. Besides, they already have a place to live. You need this fixed now so you have a place to live with a kitchen."

"Thank you, Ridge," Savannah said as she placed her hand on his arm and gave it a little squeeze. Ridge would have sworn she'd touched someplace a lot more intimate than his arm by the way his body reacted.

"Have fun shopping. I'll see you tonight."

Ridge watched as Savannah headed inside. Okay, it was time to get his head into the game and focus on work . . . at least for the next twelve hours.

. . .

"GREAT DAY OF WORK, GUYS," Ridge said as the men packed up their tools. Savannah had left Charleston already, and Granger had just texted him to stop by the station. After he talked to the sheriff, it would be time to get ready for his date.

"See you tomorrow, Ridge," a worker called out as they left for the day.

Ridge waited until everyone was gone before making sure the house was secure. Then he got into his truck and headed to Granger.

"Where is everyone?" Ridge called out as he entered the sheriff's department. Normally Brenda Baker, the sweet woman in her fifties who was the gatekeeper of the department, was sitting out front, guarding the office. But she wasn't there. And if she wasn't there, usually one of the other part-time deputies was there. Even Deputy Kordell King's office was dark.

"I'm in my office," Granger called out through the empty department.

Ridge waited until he heard the buzz of the door on the far side of the counter and then he opened the door and entered the police department. Ridge walked down the small hall, past the rows of filing cabinets, the messy desks the two part-time deputies used, and the large oval meeting table.

"What happened to the dry erase board . . . oh," Ridge asked as the question had been answered as soon as he walked into Granger's office. His desk was covered with papers, and the dry erase board that was normally in the main area was crammed into his office. Granger's short sun-streaked brown hair was sticking out as if he'd just been caught in a storm, and the room didn't look much better. "What's going on here?"

"I talked to Chief Lambert who told me he couldn't rule one way or the other on Miss Ambrose's house fire. It also bugged me about the grass down by the river, so I asked Gator about Bubba or any other large alligators in the area."

"And?" Ridge asked, suddenly feeling as if there were rocks in the bottom of his stomach weighing him down.

"Did you know she went through a nasty divorce?" Granger asked as he pointed to the dry erase board where there was a picture of a man straight out of reality television central casting. Underneath, it read "Penn Benson" followed by bullet points of the things that came up during the divorce.

"Yes. I know about some of it," Ridge told him as he looked over the board. There were newspaper clippings from the divorce. There were legal documents highlighted. And then there were Granger's own notes. "Do you think he had something to do with the fire?"

"I thought it was possible so I looked into him further, but I found pictures of him at a charity event in Charleston last night. Apparently he's here for the week for some venture capitalist conference. Last night he was the emcee of the event. I even called Ellery and got Tibbie's phone number to check to see if Penn was there all night."

"I think Gavin and Ellery might've been there, too. Ellery can run in those circles if she chooses," Ridge said of his cousin and his new wife. Ellery was the head of an art gallery in Charleston and had the right pedigree for Charleston's elite social scene.

"They went but only stayed an hour. She gave me her friend's number. And as you know, as the grande dame of society, Mrs. Elijah F. Cummings knows everyone and everything."

"Did you call her Tibbie?" Ridge asked, his lips

twitching with amusement. Only those incredibly close to the octogenarian would dare be so informal. Ellery and Gavin had been given that honor.

"Lord no. I'm not stupid."

"And since you're not pleased, it appears she provided an alibi for Penn."

Granger nodded. "Not only that, but I suddenly have a new deputy. She wheedled the truth out of me faster than a Spec Ops interrogator. Now she's determined to find out everything she can about Penn Benson."

Ridge thought for a second. "That's not entirely bad. She has access to things we would never have access to. Even Ryker can't get into the sewing circles, book clubs, or charity brunches." Ridge's cousin Ryker was a shipping magnate based out of Charleston. His family knew the real Ryker— the one who laughed and played as a child. To the outside world, though, his glacial stares left people quaking. He was famous for his ruthlessness in business. No one messed with Ryker and survived in the business to tell about it. His vast wealth and political influence got him access to a world they were not born into. The trouble was that in the South the men might be powerful forces in business, but it was the women who ran the town.

"I thought that, too, which is why I didn't argue with her," Granger told him. "I must admit I am at a loss. By all accounts, Savannah was the perfect wife. She is described as being highly intelligent and can maneuver in society as if she were Tibbie herself. I heard of no one other than her husband holding a grudge against her."

"What about the former friends who were having an affair with Penn?" Ridge asked, looking over the dry erase board.

"I set Tibbie on them. They may be Atlanta society, but

from what I have learned from Tibbie, Charleston society is by far more elite. Something to do with tracing roots back further. I don't pretend to know, but Tibbie said she was on it."

Ridge looked at his watch. "I'm having dinner with Savannah in an hour. I'll see what I can find out."

Granger smiled, something his friend needed to do more of. Granger had been in a terrible car accident in his early twenties. His girlfriend at the time had told him she was pregnant. When he lost his football career, she suddenly wasn't with child and had moved on to the next athlete, but not before telling Granger how grotesque his scars were from the accident. He had a foot-long scar down his side and another slightly smaller jagged one down his thigh. Cousin Wade's new wife, Darcy Delmar-Faulkner, had given Granger a pep talk. She'd forced him to show her his scars and told him that yes, they were there, but they were not grotesque. Any woman with "more brains that boobs" wouldn't care at all. Since then, Granger hadn't dated a soul. Well, not that Granger ever *dated*. Ever since the accident he had a string of one-night stands. However, now he was smiling a little more and those one-night stands were fewer and farther between. He even went fishing with the guys last week. He left his shirt on, but he actually wore board shorts. Usually he was never seen in shorts. All the Faulkner cousins were thrilled to see the slow changes Granger was making and encouraged him as much as possible.

"I was hoping you'd ask her. She might be more likely to tell you things she wouldn't tell me," Granger told him. "I have Kord watching her house tonight just in case the fire was arson."

Granger's phone rang and Ridge turned to review the board. Would Savannah's ex-husband really try to kill her? And if it wasn't Penn—and it looked like it wasn't with his alibi—then who would want to hurt someone trying to start her life over in a new town?

## 6

SAVANNAH HAD PICKED out her new cabinets and appliances. They were being ordered and would be ready to be installed whenever Ridge's crew was ready for them.

Savannah turned onto South Cypress Road as she began the final ten miles home from Charleston. The roads went from city, to suburban, and then to rural. Savannah let her hair fly wild in the wind as the perfect fall air blew off the river and engulfed her in the smell of pluff mud. She was still getting used to its strong smell at low tide as she followed the curves of the river.

River turned to swamp as she headed slightly away from the main river to enter the west side of Shadows Landing. Savannah turned up the radio as her favorite song came on. This was happiness. It had been so long since she felt it.

*BAM!*

Savannah heard the explosion, saw the fire leaping out from under her hood as she approached a sharp turn. Her singing turned to screams as she stomped frantically on the brake pedal and nothing happened. She fought the steering wheel, but it didn't move. She was going to crash into the swamp and there was nothing she could do to stop it.

"MISSY, ARE YOU ALIVE?"

The thick country twang permeated the darkness.

"Don't matter, Gator."

"Gator? Save me from the gator!" Savannah whispered, her eyes still shut as the darkness began to drag her back.

"Bubba, no! Get back, boy," she heard someone yell. "Turtle, get the truck," the same voice ordered.

"Turtles can't drive trucks," Savannah muttered as her mind battled the darkness.

"Skeeter, hold her neck steady. We have to get her out of the car before it blows. I can smell the gas and the fire's spreadin'."

Hands wrapped around her neck and Savannah wanted to battle them, but she couldn't move. Then she heard a slicing noise and her body fell to the side. She was caught by large hands as her seatbelt was cut off. Then she moved, struggling to open her eyes as she felt herself being eased down on something hard. Ropes were tied around her, pinning her to the hard board.

"Get Bubba out of here," the voice ordered again. She heard yelling, a splash, and then she felt herself being lifted up and set down again.

"He's gone now, and we better be too."

"Drive faster than the wind, Turtle," the one who was giving orders yelled.

"Hold on, missy. We'll get you to the hospital in a jiffy," the first voice she'd heard said. Someone held her hand as tires spun and whatever vehicle she was in took off.

Savannah moaned as they bounced over uneven ground.

She was outside. The wind was hitting her, but she was strapped down. She must have been in the back of a pickup truck.

"There she blows," the man giving orders said a second before a loud explosion rocked the truck.

"Sorry about your car, missy."

That was the last thing Savannah heard as the blackness took her. She dreamed then of talking alligators and turtles driving race cars.

"RIDGE, WAIT," Granger said seriously as he put his hand over the phone, but he didn't wait to see if Ridge listened before talking into the phone once again. "What's her status?"

Ridge felt his stomach plummet. Something bad had happened and he knew it happened to Savannah.

"I'll send Kord and Lambert to the scene and meet y'all at the hospital," Granger said with tight lips and cold eyes. He hung up the phone and was already grabbing his brown cowboy hat as he spoke to Ridge. "Savannah's been in a car accident. She's unconscious, but she talked to Gator when they got her out of the car before it exploded. Turtle is driving them to the hospital with Gator and Skeeter in the back, taking care of her."

"Her car exploded?" Ridge asked as they jogged out of the sheriff's station.

"Strange, isn't it? First the house and then her car."

Ridge was already thinking the same thing.

"Follow me," Granger ordered. "And try to keep up."

Ridge had no trouble keeping up. His body was a bundle of frayed nerves. Seeing the flaming wreckage didn't help either. Kord and the volunteer fire department were seconds behind him, but Granger and Ridge didn't stop. They headed straight for Charleston Memorial Hospital.

"Gavin," Ridge said into the pickup's Bluetooth.

"Hey, cuz. What's going on?"

"Savannah is heading to Charleston Memorial. She's been in a bad car accident. Turtle, Gator, and Skeeter are driving her straight there instead of waiting for the ambulance."

"Who's Savannah?" Gavin asked, flipping instantly into doctor mode.

"She bought me at the auction, and it was her house that had the fire down the road from you."

"The redhead. Gotcha. Do you know her injuries?"

Ridge took a deep breath to calm himself. "I only know that she talked a little and is now unconscious."

"Full name and age?"

"Savannah Ambrose. Twenty-eight."

"Are you on your way there? I hear sirens." Gavin was taking notes. Ridge could tell by the way he spoke.

"I'm following Granger. We're worried that these accidents haven't been accidents."

"Two accidents in a matter of days sure is suspicious," Gavin agreed. "I'll call the hospital and give them a heads-up. Do you want me to meet you there and take primary on the case?"

"Yes, I'd feel better if you were there. You could at least translate what's going on for me and help me make any decisions if she's unable to do so herself."

"I'll be right there."

Ridge pressed the hang-up button on the steering wheel and stuck to Granger like a tick to a deer as they sped toward Charleston.

.  .  .

Savannah came around slowly. It wasn't a quick gasp and suddenly she was awake. It was subtler than that. She was first aware of the beeping noise. Then she felt oxygen blowing up her nose. She heard hushed whispers of someone in the room. She was in the hospital. That she knew. How she got here she didn't know. In a flash the car accident came back to her. Then things went fuzzy. Surely an ambulance brought her to the hospital, not the alligator and turtle from her dream. The voice grew louder as she was brought more into the present.

"I know, baby, I miss you too." She must be hurt more than she thought because Savannah knew she was hallucinating. "Don't sass me. I'll give you something to do with that mouth as soon as I get to the hotel." There was a chuckle. "I'll do everything your husband won't and then more."

Savannah's eyes popped open because this nightmare wasn't going away. The beeping on the monitor sped up as she took in her ex-husband standing at the end of the bed, talking dirty to someone's wife. His back was to her, but concussed or not, Savannah knew it was him.

"This won't take long. I just have to tell them to pull the plug," Penn chuckled as if he said something clever. "Be in my room and be naked by the time I get back or I'll have to punish you."

Savannah rolled her eyes and groaned. Her head was throbbing. She slammed her eyes closed to stop the pain. No eye rolls. Got it. It might be hard with Penn in the room though.

"Savannah? Are you awake, pet?"

Savannah groaned again. That asshole knew she hated that name. She heard a sliding door open and then the hushed voice of a female.

"You are so good at your job. I know you have a real big . . . heart," Penn said all slimy.

"Mr. Benson, your wife," she giggled.

"Oh, we're not married. Savannah doesn't know how to handle a man. But I bet you do. What's your name, pet?"

Savannah groaned again as she rolled her eyes behind her eyelids.

"Mrs. Benson?" the woman asked as Savannah felt a hand touching her forehead and prying open her eyes. "I'm a physician's assistant. My name is Randi."

"Of course it is," Savannah said as a bright light was flashed in one eye and then the other. "And don't ever call me Mrs. Benson again."

"Mrs. Benson," Randi said sternly as Savannah squinted up at the curvy PA who had to be around Savannah's own age.

"Get out. Both of you," Savannah groaned.

"Mrs. Benson," Randi said seriously. "You have been in an accident."

"I know I was, Randi. And if you can't follow the simple instruction to never call me Mrs. Benson, then I need someone else to look at me. I will not allow that man in this room. Now leave. Both of you."

"Mrs.—"

"Hand of God, Randi. If you finish that next word, I will lose it. Get out!" Savannah screamed even though it caused her head to pound.

"Now, pet . . ." Penn said severely.

"Out!"

The door burst open and three men raced in looking ready to fight. One was massive and of indiscernible age. He was wearing denim overalls and was shirtless underneath. On his head, covering part of his face, was a South Carolina

Gamecocks ball cap pulled low that read "COCKS" in giant letters. Another one was skinny as a rail with a dirty T-shirt that was at least four sizes too large and torn jeans. The third had a ball cap on backwards and a T-shirt with a turtle on it. The sleeves of the shirt had been cut out so that the sides of his ribs were exposed.

"You all right, missy?" Oversized Shirt asked.

The big man in overalls crossed some rather large arms across his chest. "And just who are you?" asked the man who ordered all the others around in her dreams. He was real.

"The better question is, who the hell are you?" Penn asked, assuming his *I'm superior* pose. The three men didn't seem to care.

In fact, Turtle Shirt chuckled. "If you want to measure peckers, you should know mine's so strong I've had a snapping turtle hang from it."

Penn blinked. Randi blinked. Savannah giggled. Turtle Shirt winked at her.

"You want him to leave, ma'am?" COCKS Hat asked her.

"Yes, please," Savannah smiled sweetly at the men. "Would you be dears and remove this man from my room?"

Penn scoffed at her. "They have no authority to do that."

"Sure thing, missy." Oversized Shirt lifted his droopy hem for the first time and exposed a massive hunting knife strapped to his waist.

"It would be our pleasure, ma'am," COCKS Hat said with a smirk as he flexed his muscles.

"Don't you dare touch me!" Penn raised his voice. "Security!"

Randi was pulling out her phone and calling someone.

A security officer ran into the room as the three men started to walk toward Penn, who had darted around her bed to gain distance from them.

"Thank goodness," Randi said breathlessly. "These men were about to assault Mr. Benson."

"These men are a menace and should be arrested. They are a danger to myself and my wife," Penn said, full of bravado since a security guard was in the room.

"*I am not your wife!*" Savannah yelled even though it caused her head to explode. But at least it stopped everyone from talking.

## 7

RIDGE AND GRANGER took off at a run when they heard Savannah scream. Granger flashed his badge at the nurse and practically leapt over an orderly. Ridge's heart raced, but at least he knew Savannah was awake. And by the stream of curse words being yelled, she was feeling strong enough to fight.

"I'll hold him!" Savannah was yelling to Gator, Turtle, and Skeeter as she had a vise grip on some guy's wrist—a guy Ridge instantly recognized as her ex-husband, Penn Benson. "You grab him," Savannah ordered as Skeeter distracted the security guard, Turtle winked at the PA, and Gator grabbed Penn.

"Sheriff's department," Granger said calmly as he took in the room.

"Thank goodness!" everyone in the room exclaimed and began talking at once.

Ridge ignored them and went straight to Savannah. She held out her hand and he took it instantly. "Are you hurt?"

"I don't know yet. I woke up to Penn in my room, and he won't leave."

"Is that right, sir? You won't leave after Miss Ambrose asked you to?" Granger asked, zeroing in on Penn with narrowed eyes.

"Those men are the ones who need to leave. I'm her husband."

Ridge could feel the anger pulsating from Savannah's hand. Her mouth opened, but Ridge spoke up first. "Ex-husband for over a year now, isn't it?"

"It doesn't matter. I'm her emergency contact."

"Well, now she's awake. Miss Ambrose, is it your desire for Mr. Benson to leave?"

"Yes, thank you, Sheriff Fox." Ridge felt Savannah relax.

Penn was about to argue when a doctor came into the room. His head was down as he walked and read her chart at the same time. "Mrs.—"

"*Miss*," Savannah corrected through clenched teeth.

The doctor looked up for the first time and noticed the room was packed. He shrugged and looked back down at the file. "You have a concussion and some bruising on your knees, but luckily nothing is broken. There's a burn mark on your neck and bruising on your chest consistent with injuries from your seatbelt. Good thing you were wearing it. You might be able to go home tonight after we get a CT scan to make sure there's no bleeding around your brain. You just need someone to stay with you for the next twenty-four hours."

"I'll do it," Ridge said at the same time Penn did. Ridge looked over to Penn who was staring daggers at him.

"I'll give these instructions to the discharge nurse and let you sort this all out. A tech will be here shortly to take you to get the CT."

"Thank you, William."

Ridge turned and saw Gavin standing calmly by the

door. "I'll be monitoring Miss Ambrose from here on out," Gavin nodded to Ridge who nodded back.

"Gavin, wonderful. Miss Ambrose, you'll be in excellent hands with Dr. Faulkner." The two men stepped out to the hall and looked over the file together as an orderly came to wheel Savannah to get her CT.

"Thank you all," Savannah said with a little wave to Gator, Turtle, and Skeeter. "I don't even know your names."

"I'm Gator," COCKS Hat said with a smile.

"And I'm Turtle," Turtle Shirt said with a wink.

"I'm Skeeter, missy," Oversized Shirt said before shooting a glare that promised he wasn't done with Penn yet.

"They're the ones who pulled you out of the car and brought you here," Granger told her.

"You all saved my life. I don't know how to repay you," Savannah said, choking up a little.

"A round or two at Shadows Bar when you're all better sounds good to me," Skeeter told her as they all nodded.

"That can be arranged. And I make a mean dessert I know you'll love. When my kitchen is done, you can count on that too." Ridge squeezed her hand before letting go as Savannah was wheeled out. "Sheriff Fox?" she called out.

"Yes?" Granger asked.

"Can you make sure he's gone by the time I get back?"

"Yes, ma'am."

Everyone was quiet for a moment as the doctors and the PA all walked off together. Penn was seething. The boys were closing in on him. Apparently they disliked him as much as Ridge did.

"Gentlemen," Granger said calmly. "Thank you for your help. You saved Savannah's life."

"It was a right pleasure. She's good people," Gator said to Granger before narrowing his eyes at Penn. "Unlike others."

"I'll take it from here." Granger shook their hands and stared them down until they left with distinctly unhappy grunts.

Ridge thanked them and promised them all a gift as well. He figured he could buy a keg and have Harper put it on tap for just them at the bar. They'd get a kick out of it.

"Not so fast, Mr. Benson. I'd like to have a word with you," Granger said calmly.

Ridge watched as Penn puffed himself up again.

"Why didn't you arrest those rednecks? One of them had a knife, and they threatened me. I'd like to file charges."

"From what I saw, you were asked to leave and refused. I'd like to know why." Granger eyed him cautiously.

"Why what?"

"Why you refused to leave when your ex-wife, whom you cheated on and then denied most of the joint assets in a nasty divorce, asked you to." Granger was so casual in his stance it seemed clear Penn thought he could huff and puff his way out of this.

"That's none of your concern," Penn snapped. He tried to walk by Granger, and Ridge stepped up to block the door.

"It *is* my concern," Granger said. Standing up tall, he suddenly didn't look so casual anymore. "See, I think someone is trying to hurt Miss Ambrose, and I think that someone might be you."

"Hurt her? She was in a car accident! She's always been a horrible driver. How could I have anything to do what that?" Penn practically rolled his eyes at Granger.

"Where were you at six tonight?" Granger asked.

"I was in the middle of an awards dinner at a table of the top financial men in America. There were a thousand people there who can tell you I was there until I got a phone call from the hospital."

"Where are you staying while in Charleston," Granger asked, "in case I have more questions for you?"

"I'm staying at the hotel where the conference is. It's one of the best. I should know since Savannah and I were regularly in Charleston. In fact, she's even been to this hospital once when she got a cut from a shell on the bottom of her foot and needed stitches. If you need me, Savannah knows how to get in touch with me. Is there anything else?"

"Nope. We're all good."

Ridge watched Penn strut out of the room, wink at the PA lurking in the hallway, and disappear down the hall.

"He didn't seem very concerned that someone was trying to hurt his wife," Ridge said as they watched him leave the ER.

"He has a solid alibi, and I think he didn't believe me. I think he thought it was an accident," Granger said with a little frustration.

"What does that mean?"

"It means he might not be our guy."

Ridge tightened his jaw. He didn't like Penn, but Granger had a point. "Or that these two accidents were just that. Accidents."

## 8

AS RIDGE DROVE past Savannah's house and onto the larger, newly built homes on Palmetto Drive, Savannah couldn't help but feel cold as she saw her house. She could only see it for a second between the azalea hedges. She saw a police car parked outside next to a dumpster that was filled with charred debris. The harsh realities of the past twenty-four hours hit her like a punch to the gut. The fire. The accident. Penn. It was all too much.

"Where is your house?" she asked.

"I built a house in the subdivision near Bell Plantation."

Savannah watched as the small cottages turned into larger houses on the riverside. On the opposite side, the small lots turned into larger ones with houses far from the road and lots filled with old trees.

Ridge turned left into a small neighborhood with extra-large lots and two-story homes. There were beach houses, traditional houses, and then a beautiful contemporary that seemed to blend into the heavily treed lot. And it was at this house that Ridge pulled into the driveway.

"It's beautiful," she said, looking up at the large windows.

"Thank you. I finished it last year. It was a design I had been working on since I was a teenager. It just morphed, grew, and matured as I did. Then this five-acre lot came up a couple years ago and I grabbed it. I built the house in my spare time."

"It looks as if it should be in a magazine."

"It has been," Ridge said, pulling into the garage and closing the door. He helped her from the car and escorted her into a mudroom before leading her down a small hall and into the kitchen. "My cousin Trent built most of my furniture."

Savannah was blown away by the custom pieces, but then they walked into the living room. There was a large fireplace with the most beautiful piece of art she'd ever seen hanging over it. "The art work you have is stunning."

"My sister, Tinsley, is a painter. These are some of her works."

Savannah knew that name. Her mind was moving just a little slowly. "You told me about her. She has the gallery downtown. I actually remember I know of her work. She donated a piece to one of the charities I was involved with when I was in Atlanta."

Ridge suddenly swept her off her feet and into his arms.

"Ridge!"

"You don't need to be walking so much after being banged up. Let me take you up to your room." Ridge began to carry her up the floating staircase that looked as if she were walking up freshly cut trees. The stairs were raw-cut wood with a layer of shine to preserve them. The handrail was thin and metal so that nothing blocked her view of the gardens surrounding the back and sides of the house.

"Oh, Ridge, I can't wait to see your gardens in the light of day."

"We'll take a walk after Gavin clears you. He'll be here in the morning to check on you." Ridge walked into a room and set her down. The room was ivory and chocolate. It was masculine yet inviting at the same time. More importantly, the bed looked like a cloud and suddenly she felt very tired. "You'll have a nice view of the garden from here when the sun comes up. I thought you could get comfortable and I'll bring you some dinner."

"You'll cook for me?" Savannah blurted out of surprise. Penn wouldn't even call for delivery.

Ridge looked at her as if she were slightly crazy. "Of course. I don't want you running all around the house after your injuries. Get settled and I'll see what I can whip up."

"Thank you, Ridge. You didn't have to do this. I know you don't even know me . . ."

"I want to know you, Savannah. I want to know you a lot better." Ridge paused after the admission and then gave her a warm smile. The kind where his eyes shone a little brighter, and she was pretty sure she was going to melt on the spot. "I'll be back with some food in no time."

Savannah sighed as she sat down on the bed. She could hear Ridge walking down the stairs as she thought about what he'd said. Right now there wasn't anything she'd like more than to get to know him better too.

Savannah forced herself up from the heavenly bed and looked around the room. She found the closet and then the bathroom. Inside was a shower with a rain feature and six body sprays. Pure bliss. This was enough to make a woman moan in pleasure just by looking at it.

Savannah was growing stiff as the stronger pain meds were wearing off. She undressed and stepped into the orgasmic shower. Sure enough, she moaned again as the warm water sprayed her body. She wanted to spend the whole night in the shower, but she also didn't want Ridge coming up and finding her there.

"I'll see you in the morning, sexy," Savannah told the shower as she wrapped a towel around her.

"Savannah?"

Busted. "Um, yeah?" Savannah called out from behind the mostly closed door.

"I brought you some of my sweats and a T-shirt. I thought you might want some clean clothes. I put them on the bed. I'm going to run down and get your dinner now."

"Thanks, Ridge." Her face flamed red with embarrassment. She knew Ridge had heard her talking to the shower. But the lure of clean clothes and food had her changing quickly.

There was a light knock on the door and then Ridge opened it, carrying in a tray. "Hop in bed and I'll put the tray over your lap."

"It smells good. What is it?"

"I whipped up some shrimp and put them over angel hair pasta with pesto and sun-dried tomatoes. Is that okay? I can make something else if you'd like."

Something else? Was he kidding? "No, it's perfect. Thank you so much." Her stomach rumbled, but Ridge was nice enough to ignore it.

"How are you feeling?" he asked as she climbed into the bed.

"Tired. And sore. And a little worried," she finally admitted. "Does Granger think Penn did this to me?"

Ridge set the tray over her lap and then surprised her by climbing into the bed next to her. "We don't know. Penn has an alibi, a very public one, for tonight and also for the fire at your house. The trouble comes with two accidents so close together . . . it seems too coincidental."

Savannah felt that heavy weight on her once again. It was the same feeling she'd gotten when she saw the broken arbor. "And what did Granger find?"

Ridge frowned. "Nothing. As of right now, it appears to be nothing but coincidence."

It should have made her feel better, but it didn't. Because deep down Savannah worried that it was anything but coincidence.

THEY'D SPENT dinner talking about Shadows Landing and Ridge's family. Savannah didn't bring up her family and she was glad that Ridge didn't ask any questions about them either. Dinner was wonderful, but the more she ate, the more tired she became.

"I'll take this downstairs," Ridge said softly as her eyes began to close.

"Don't leave me," Savannah whispered as she pulled the fluffy chocolate comforter up to her chin. "I don't believe in coincidences, Ridge."

"I don't either," Ridge admitted. "I'll clean up the kitchen and be right back up. Okay?"

"Okay," Savannah said, feeling weak. She didn't like that feeling, but she needed to know she was safe. And she felt safe with Ridge.

The question: why was she in danger to begin with? It didn't make sense. The door opened quietly in the darkened room. Savannah noticed that Ridge had changed into a T-shirt and athletic shorts as he walked in. She felt the bed dip slightly as he got in and she rolled over to face him.

"Thank you," she said quietly as she slid her hands under her pillow.

"You're welcome."

"I'm scared, Ridge." Savannah admitted.

"You don't need to be scared tonight. I've got you."

His hand touched her waist and pulled her to him. Savannah curled up against him and, with the warmth of his arms around her, she fell asleep.

## 9

RIDGE WOKE to the early morning light. He was spooning Savannah, and he'd love nothing more than to give in to the urges his body was experiencing. Only it wasn't the right time. It especially wasn't the right time when the doorbell rang. Savannah sat upright instantly. Her head turned to the right and then the left before she looked behind her and saw him in bed with her. Her whole body relaxed as soon as she saw him.

"I think we have company," Ridge told her as he ran a hand down her back. "Are you up for it?"

"Depends. Who is it?"

The bell rang again and Ridge pulled out his phone and opened the app that allowed him to see his security camera. He pressed a button and spoke into his phone. "Morning, Gavin. I'll be right down."

"Your cousin is here?" Savannah asked, trying to remember if Gavin was the doctor or the cousin or both.

"Yes. He and his wife, Ellery, are here. He'll want to make sure you're recovering well. And Ellery is really nice. She runs an art gallery in Charleston."

Ridge got up and used the tray to shield the excitement that waking up with Savannah curled into him caused. "I'll go let them in. They can come up here if you don't feel like doing the stairs."

"I'll come down. Just give me a minute. I remember him from the hospital. He was the reason they discharged me, right?"

Ridge nodded. "Take your time and just yell if you need any help," he said before he hurried from the room. By the time he was downstairs he had himself under control. He set the tray down in the kitchen and then opened the door to find that the number of people at his door had multiplied.

"You brought the whole family," Ridge said with a roll of his eyes to Gavin.

"It's not our whole family," Gavin said, before looking behind him and cringing. "Okay, it's our whole family who are in town."

"Come on in. Savannah is getting ready."

Gavin and Ellery walked in and headed straight for the kitchen.

"Morning, sis," Ridge said, leaning down and kissing Tinsley's cheek.

"I brought fresh biscuits and apple honey butter," his little sister said. Tins was "little" in age and build. She only came up to his shoulder, but for what she lacked in size, she made up for in talent. She was the best painter he knew.

"Well, you're allowed in. You, I'm not so sure about," he said, looking at his cousin Trent. Trent flipped him off as he walked in.

"Here I build most of the furniture in the house and I have to bring something. Ungrateful pup."

Ridge laughed at Trent. Trent was all of three months older than Ridge, but he never let him forget it.

"I brought Bloody Marys," Harper said, holding a cooler.

"You're definitely allowed in." Ridge looked behind him and saw Savannah walking toward them.

"I knew I liked you," Harper said with a wink to Savannah as she walked inside.

Ridge looked back to the door and saw Ryker looking at him with one eyebrow slightly raised. "Last time I brought something y'all bitched nonstop."

"It was caviar, and it was disgusting," Ridge reminded him.

"*It* was a gift from the president of France," Ryker said yet again. Ridge had heard the whole spiel at Wade's bachelor party.

"It was still gross," Ridge told his uptight cousin. Although, Ryker hadn't always been uptight. Everything had changed one night in high school.

"Don't worry, I wouldn't offend your palate with the world's best food. I'm just on my way to Charleston and wanted to know if you needed anything. I might not bring food, but I can hire personal protection or a lawyer before you can blink."

"Can I arrest myself just to have that smoking-hot Olivia Townsend represent me?"

"Kordell," Ryker said formally to the deputy.

"Mr. Faulkner," Kord said mockingly back. "Don't tell me you're still upset I spit out that caviar, are you?"

"You spit it out *on me*!" Ryker said, finally snapping over the caviar.

"It was really disgusting. The taste, the texture. Be happy I didn't vomit on you," Kord told him, slapping him on the back before walking past him and into the house. "Biscuits, yum!"

Ridge just shook his head at Ryker. "Come on in and meet Savannah."

"I'm right here." Ridge turned to see Savannah walking from the kitchen toward the front door. "Hi. I'm Savannah Ambrose."

Ryker shook her outstretched hand. "I'm Ryker Faulkner."

"Of Faulkner Shipping. My ex-husband tried to land your account. He was quite pissed off when he didn't get it. For that alone, I thank you."

Ryker's lips quivered as if they thought about smiling. "Who was your husband?"

"Penn Benson."

"You made the right decision leaving him. There was something shady about him that I didn't trust. I certainly wasn't going to turn five million dollars over to him for a venture I didn't think he completely understood."

Ridge blinked. That was the first time Ryker ever mentioned money. They all knew he'd made a killing at shipping but no one knew just how wealthy he'd become. Mainly because they just didn't care. Ryker was family and that mattered more than how much money he had. Ridge was pretty sure no one had ever bothered to ask him.

"Well, you made the right choice in not investing with him. It was some tech startup, if I recall. I wonder what ever happened to it?" Savannah asked not really expecting an answer.

"I bought it."

"Oh," Savannah said with as much surprise as Ridge did.

"You own a tech company?" Ridge finally asked.

"I own a lot of companies," Ryker said with a shrug.

"Why didn't you tell us?" Ridge asked his cousin.

"You never asked."

Well, that answered that.

"I'm sorry we don't ask about your business more." Ridge felt bad now. He thought Ryker didn't want to be bothered with business when he was finally home. The man lived and breathed work. When the cousins finally got him to relax, the last thing they thought he'd want to talk about was work.

"It's okay. It's all pretty boring. But what isn't boring is what's happening to Miss Ambrose." Ridge let Ryker steer the conversation away from himself. "I have to get going, but if you need anything, my cousin knows how to get in touch with me. It was nice meeting you."

"You too, Mr. Faulkner," Savannah said with a little smile that made Ridge know she was teasing Ryker's stiffness just a little. "I appreciate your offer. It's very nice of you."

"There's nothing nice about me. That's why I can get you anything you need."

Ridge wanted to roll his eyes and defend Ryker to himself. Ryker had been a sweet child. Until that night. But even after that, he was always there for his family. Mean people didn't care enough about their family to send a lawyer in the middle of the night to defend a girl he didn't know simply because a cousin had asked for help. And Ryker always helped. He was always there, for not only the family, but for Shadows Landing.

"You, sir, are a liar. If you weren't nice you wouldn't be offering to help me. So take the compliment and say, 'thank you, Savannah.'"

"Thank you, Savannah." Ryker almost looked like he was going to smile.

"You're welcome. And I happen to love caviar, so

anytime you want to indulge I have some caviar recipes that will make your mouth water. I'd be happy to make them for you."

Ryker smiled at Savannah. She'd just won him over. "I'd like that. It's nice to meet someone with a sophisticated palate. I'll see you soon, Savannah. And Ridge, let me know when you're done with the plans for my international office and I'll secure the funding."

"You'll have it in a couple weeks. I made all the changes you asked for and now I'm waiting on the availability of some of the materials."

"Good. Can't wait to see some of them that you were telling me about. I'll talk to you soon."

Ridge watched Ryker walk to the car that cost more than Ridge probably realized.

"Your whole family is so nice."

"Yes, they are."

Ridge and Savannah walked into the kitchen where his family sat around the giant table eating and drinking together. As everyone talked about the fire and the accident, Gavin took Savannah aside for ten minutes. When they came back, he declared she was on the road to a full recovery.

"Excuse me," Kord said after congratulating Savannah on feeling better.

Ridge watched Kord as he stepped away from the table to take a call. He began to pace while on the phone and a bad feeling came over Ridge. He knew he was right when Kord hung up and turned around. His face was no longer smiling and carefree. His lips were in a thin line and his face looked harsh. "Savannah, Ridge, a moment."

"What is it?" Savannah asked as soon as they stepped into the living room.

"That was Granger. He just got off the phone with Chief Lambert. Your car accident wasn't an accident. They found a device in your car. One they think caused the wreck."

Someone had tried to kill Savannah. That meant the fire wasn't an accident either.

"I want you to stay here," Ridge said into the silence. "You're not safe at home."

"I'm beginning to think you're right." Savannah's voice shook as he reached out to wrap his arm around her waist. He pulled her against his side to offer his silent support.

"Can you think of anyone who would want to kill you?" Kord asked.

"No, I can't. The only person I could think of was Penn, but he was so surprised to see me hurt and didn't know anything about the fire at the house. And he had an solid alibi for both incidents."

"These started after you went out on your date," Kord mentioned as gently as he could. "Ridge, could this have anything to do with you? Or Savannah, could you have a stalker?"

"Me?" Ridge asked in surprise. "I guess it could, but I don't know who or why. But you are right about the timing."

Ridge looked to Savannah to gauge what she was thinking.

"I had felt like someone was watching me in Atlanta. It was one of the reasons I was so happy to leave. Surely someone wasn't stalking me, were they?"

"Those are just two possibilities. Unfortunately, we don't know which one it is or if it's one we haven't thought of yet," Kord told them.

"Now I don't know where to go or what to do." Savannah let out a little sigh and her shoulders slumped in defeat.

Ridge squeezed her hip, trying to let her know she wasn't alone. "You'll stay with me until we can get this figured out."

Savannah nodded and they both thanked Kord, who grabbed another biscuit before leaving. She was noticeably quieter as his family talked. Harper invited them to her bar, Trent offered to help with any furniture Savannah might need, and Gavin promised to check back in with her tomorrow morning.

"If you feel up to it, you can come to my office. If not, just have Ridge call me and I'll come to you."

"Thank you, Gavin." Savannah then hugged Ellery and promised they'd get together soon.

Ridge turned to the only one left, his sister. "Tinsley," Ridge said, stopping his sister from cleaning up his kitchen. "I've got this. Would you mind staying for a little while? I need to run over to Savannah's house to check on my crew."

"I can stay by myself," Savannah protested. Ridge was concerned about leaving Tinsley there too. It wasn't that long ago she'd been viciously attacked for harboring their family friend, Edie Greene Wecker. But he knew there was safety in numbers.

"I'd be happy to," Tinsley said brightly as she went back to loading his dishwasher. Tinsley was never happy sitting still. "And don't worry. I have Tina with me."

"Tina?" Savannah asked.

"My gun," Tinsley said cheerfully as she pulled out a gun that looked as if it had been covered in paint splatter. "I decorated it myself."

"Do you even know how to use that?" Ridge asked, suddenly worried about his sister. He knew she's taken self-defense classes in Charleston and a class here in Shadows Landing after the attack, but a gun? His sister wasn't exactly the shoot 'em up type.

"Aunt Paige, Cousin Greer, and Aunt Annie taught me. I'm a very good shot. And Cousin Sophie had the gun made just for me. It was my Christmas present," Tinsley said as if showing off a new bracelet.

"It's very you," Savannah said with a real smile. Well, if she was comfortable with Tinsley packing a paint splattered gun, he would make himself be as well.

"I'm going to check on the demo and then come back. It might take a couple of hours, though," Ridge told them.

"Can you pack me some things?" Savannah suddenly looked embarrassed. "I can get a hotel or even move back to my place if it's too much trouble having me here."

"No. I want you here and safe until we figure out what's going on." Ridge stepped forward and placed a quick kiss on her cheek. "I'll be back as soon as I can."

As Ridge drove off, he looked back and saw his sister and Savannah waving to him. It wasn't a bad feeling, knowing he had someone waiting for him when he got home. In fact, he found that he quite liked it.

## 10

SAVANNAH WAS sure Tinsley must be her long-lost sister. They laughed, they giggled, and they painted while drinking iced tea and lemonade mix-ups, affectionately known as Arnold Palmers. Tinsley never pushed her to talk about her life, and in return, Savannah never pushed about the attack Tinsley had survived. Instead, they talked about books, art, movies, and, of course, Ridge.

"That magnolia bloom is beautiful," Tinsley told her as she helped touch up the paint on some of the greenery around it. "There."

"It's going to look so pretty in my kitchen. Do you have any stencils to use?" Savannah asked as she cleaned off the brushes.

"Of course, but I always free-hand it. What do you want it to say?"

Savannah looked at the giant magnolia flower surrounded by green leaves. "In pink I want it to read *Savannah's Kitchen*."

"No problem. I'll come back tomorrow after it's dry and put that on for you."

Savannah spontaneously hugged Tinsley. The woman was even shorter than she was. She was probably no more than five foot two. "This has been so much fun. Thank you for teaching me."

Tinsley laughed sweetly. "I think you already knew a lot more than you thought. It's been a lot of fun."

"You should host a wine and painting party. So many people are doing that in Charleston and Atlanta. You're a way better teacher than they were."

"That would be a lot of fun. I have a large art show in Paris next month. Maybe when I get back from that, I'll do one," Tinsley said as she began to clean up the paints.

"Paris! That's wonderful, Tinsley."

Tinsley looked slightly embarrassed as she turned away and carried some brushes to the sink. "Thanks. I don't expect much from it. I'm not a famous painter or anything."

"You are in the South. I know everyone in Charleston has heard of you, and your work was all over Atlanta when I left," Savannah said, hoping she conveyed the respect she and others had for Tinsley's artwork.

Tinsley turned around and gave her a little smile. "It is exciting to hear that people besides my family actually put up my work," she laughed. "What about you? What do you enjoy doing?"

"I've always wanted to go into interior design. But for right now, I'm hoping to run the Delmar-Faulkner Museum. I love history, and goodness knows I've raised millions for charity. It seems like the perfect job for starting over in Shadows Landing."

"I'm sure by the time my cousin Wade and Darcy get back from their honeymoon, he'll have messages from all of us to hire you," Tinsley teased. Savannah laughed and Tinsley shook her head. "No, really. I'm sure he will."

Then the two of them broke out laughing again.

"Has it been hard moving from Atlanta to Shadows Landing?" Tinsley asked after they cleaned up.

Savannah poured more drinks and handed one to Tinsley as they made their way out onto the verandah overlooking the gardens. "Yes and no. After the constant pressure of high society, it's nice to just be me. It took me a while to find myself again. My ex had cut me off from a lot of my old friends and I realized the only friends I had were through him. When the divorce hit I had no one, no support. So it took a little time to learn to be independent again. To figure out what I liked and didn't like. To just be me. I've found that here in Shadows Landing."

"And you found my brother," Tinsley said slyly before wiggling her eyebrows, causing them both to break out into another fit of giggles.

RIDGE LOOKED AT HIS WATCH. It was almost five in the afternoon. He'd called and checked on Savannah twice already. He was thinking of doing it again when Tinsley texted a picture of her and Savannah curled up in his hammock together. Ridge let the tension from his shoulders roll off him. They'd run into problems with the electrical lines while doing demo. The house was old and the wiring in the walls was shot. It was a miracle it hadn't caused a fire on its own. It turned out Ridge was gone most of the day. Even though he was less than ten minutes away, it still felt as if they were a world apart.

"We've got it all grounded now and hooked up to the new wiring and box you did," the electrician reported as the men began to clean up. The day was done and Ridge couldn't wait to get home.

*Can you get two seafood delights from Stomping Grounds?*

Ridge read his sister's text message and wrote back that he'd be home soon with dinner.

"See you guys tomorrow. Thanks for all your hard work," Ridge called out as the guys headed to their trucks.

After they all left, Ridge walked around the site, checking everything one last time before going upstairs and packing a bag for Savannah. He didn't know what she'd want or need so he grabbed a little of everything and ending up moving up to a giant suitcase. He tried not to think about how intimate it was to pack for her, but he couldn't help it as he added her toiletries to the suitcase.

Wade and Gavin had told him they had fallen hard and fast for their wives. Great-Uncle Jake and Great-Aunt Marcy Davies told him the same of their children and grandchildren in Keeneston, Kentucky. When they knew, they knew.

It wasn't taking Ridge long to realize it was happening to him. There was just something about Savannah that made him happy. Suddenly images of their future together flashed through his mind. Drinking coffee together in the mornings. Coming home to each other in the evenings. Sharing in the joys of life together.

After making sure the house was secure, Ridge turned left out of the driveway and headed toward town. He'd already called in their order and pulled to the curb across the street from the courthouse.

"Ridge!" Granger called out as Ridge was about to open the door to Stomping Grounds.

Granger jogged across the street to meet him on the sidewalk. "How's Savannah?"

"Tinsley is with her. Seems as if the two of them had a great day. And Gavin said she's healing well," Ridge told him. "Have you found anything?"

"Nothing. It's frustrating. Every lead is neatly wrapped up leading nowhere. Kord told me he mentioned our theory about you being the target. What do you think about that?" Ridge saw that his friend hated to ask him that. But if it was the only possibility left, he had to accept that maybe he *was* the target.

"I can't think of anyone. I mean, I have ex-girlfriends, but I can't imagine any of them would be so possessive as to try to take out my . . . friend."

Granger's eyebrow rose as if to challenge Ridge's terminology.

"Would any of them know about Savannah?"

"A couple of them were at the auction." Ridge hoped this wasn't the case. If Savannah was in danger because of him, Ridge didn't know what he'd do.

"I need their names."

Granger handed him a pad of paper and a pen. Ridge wrote down their names, numbers, and addresses.

"I'll get this out and let you know what I find."

"Thanks," Ridge said weakly as he watched Granger jog back across the street and into the courthouse.

Ridge turned and opened the door to Stomping Grounds. Mary Jane had dinner all ready to go for him, and in minutes he was headed back down Main Street. He turned left onto Palmetto when suddenly he was thrown. His seatbelt caught him as a large black truck T-boned him in the driver-side door.

Ridge slammed on the brakes, but the truck revved its engine and pushed him into the swampy part of Shadows Park. Ridge tried to get control of his truck, but the other vehicle was much larger than his. He looked into the tinted window as the truck backed up. The engine revved again and Ridge didn't have time to take in anything other than a shadowy outline of a person as the truck charged toward him.

Ridge unbuckled his seatbelt and lunged for the far side of the cab just as the black truck's reinforced grill rammed into the driver's door again. Ridge was thrown against the window as his truck was lifted up with the force and suspended on two wheels before it lost its battle with gravity and flipped the rest of the way over onto the roof. Ridge landed with a thud as his truck began to sink into the loose mud. It was high tide and water lapped at his busted window and began to trickle in.

"Ridge!" He heard his name being shouted over the engine of the truck that had hit him. Then there was gunfire, the distant sound of sirens, and the roar of the engine revving again.

Ridge didn't wait to see if he'd survive the hit. He scrambled back to the driver's side window, now the farthest window from the attacker's truck. He used his booted foot to kick out the rest of the broken window and climbed out. He was bruised and bleeding, but adrenaline had him keeping low as he dove into the marsh waters. Snakes and gators were the least of his concern as the truck slammed into his again, sending it sliding deeper into the mud, grasses, and water.

Ridge swam for his life until he knew he was safe and took cover behind the thick spartina grass. The attacking truck spun its tires, sending mud and sand flying as people raced toward it. Gil from Gil's Grub and Gas wielded a large tire iron and Darius Foster, owner of the Pink Pig, carried a massive butcher's knife.

Ridge could see that black truck had no license plate on it as sped right for the group running to Ridge's aid. "Look out!" Ridge yelled as he began to slog his way through the marsh.

Gil and Darius leapt out of the way as the truck barreled past them, clipped Granger's SUV, sending it spinning, and sped off down Main Street. Granger spun his tires and took off after truck.

"Ridge!" Gil and Darius shouted as they both hurried toward him.

"Savannah! I have to see if she's hurt." All thoughts of himself had vanished the second the truck began to race away.

"We're on it!" Gil yelled as he pulled out his phone and began running as fast as he could toward the intersection.

Seconds later, Miss Ruby's old tank of a sedan skidded as it took the corner of Main Street and Palmetto practically on two tires.

"Are you okay, sonny?" Darius called out as he hurried into the marsh and reached out to help Ridge. Mud and muck were pulling on his feet as if he were walking in wet cement.

"I think so. I know I'm banged up, but I don't think it was anything worse than that. I managed to not hit my head." Ridge grabbed Darius's hand and Darius yanked him free from the marsh.

Ridge looked down at his feet. One of his work boots had been sucked off and would forevermore live in the marsh. "I saw Kordell take off after Granger. And here comes your cousin," Darius told him.

Ridge looked up and saw Gavin's car coming to a sliding stop at the park entrance where Gil was waving him down. His door was flung open and Gavin shot forward with his medical bag in hand. "Are you hurt? What happened? Good God," he said all at once.

"My truck is shot. I have to check on Savannah!" Ridge yelled as he began an uneven run toward his cousin.

"You shouldn't be running. Let me check you out first."

"Gavin," Ridge warned.

"Right, Savannah first." Gavin turned directions, got back in the car and drove it through the playground and right up to where Ridge was running. "At least I can restrain you from running."

Ridge looked down at himself covered in smelly mud. "I can't ride—"

"Get in," Gavin ordered as he spread a medical journal on the seat. Ridge ripped off his shirt, kicked off his other shoe, and sat on the medical journal.

Gavin peppered him with medical questions as he raced down Palmetto Drive toward Ridge's house.

"Are you sure you didn't hit your head?"

"I'm sure. Now hurry up." Gavin did as Ridge ordered. He was going so fast he almost missed the turn. Neighbors walking dogs and pushing strollers yelled as Gavin flew by them through the quiet neighborhood streets.

Miss Ruby's sedan was in his front yard. She'd jumped the driveway, drove through the front yard, and parked at the steps leading up to his front door.

Before Gavin had completely stopped, Ridge was out the door and running up the front steps. He twisted the door handle and then banged on the door when he found it locked. "Savannah!"

His keys were still in his truck and he couldn't unlock the front door. "I've got it!" Gavin called as he ran up with Ridge's spare key. Everyone had keys to each other's houses. Ryker's was a black key and a complex security code specific to each cousin. Tinsley's was a deep purple. Everyone else's were the standard hardware store key so it took Gavin a couple tries until he got the right key.

"Savannah! Where are you?" Ridge yelled again as he unlocked the door. He went to open it and it only opened an inch before it slammed against something heavy and wouldn't open farther.

"Savannah! Tinsley! Anyone here?"

"Ridge?"

"Miss Winnie?" Ridge asked when he heard the elderly Southern voice. "I thought Miss Ruby was here."

"You bet your biscuits I'm here too." He heard Miss Ruby then. "But how do we know you're Ridge?"

"Excuse me? You've known me my whole life."

"That's right, but you could be some impostor here to hurt Savannah and our Tinsley. Gil called us and said she was in danger and not to let anyone in the house."

"Ruby," Ridge groaned, now at least feeling the relief of knowing Savannah was safe. "You always slipped me candy in church. I built a doll house for your granddaughter."

"Oh, do me, do me."

Gavin snickered next to him at Miss Winnie's voice coming through the crack.

"You smacked my hands with a Bible when I acted up in church, causing Miss Ruby to feel bad and give me the candy. What you didn't know was I knew that, so I acted up to get the candy."

There were some grunting noises and then Miss Ruby's rounded face came into view. "We can't move this. I'll open the garage door. Welcome home."

## 11

Savannah and Tinsley were huddled in the pantry. They were smashed together as Savannah used a hand towel wrapped around the door handle to try to prevent the doors from being opened. She tightened her grip on her towel and kept it pulled tightly. Tinsley had her gun out and the safety off. Neither of them spoke. Savannah was pretty sure neither of them even breathed. Her heart had stopped as soon as she'd learned Ridge had been run off the road.

A softly rounded, elderly black woman in a yellow dress and a pale elderly white woman who resembled a chicken had burst into the house yelling that someone had tried to kill Ridge and they were in danger.

The women ordered Tinsley and Savannah to move large pieces of furniture across the front and back doors and then had literally shoved them into the pantry when there was banging on the front door. Everyone paused except the chicken-like woman who had shoved them into the pantry. "We've got this," she had told them. "Ruby brought the cutlass from the church." She gave them a wink and shut the door on them.

Next to her, Tinsley's knees might have been shaking but her aim was steady as she held the gun pointed at the door. There was more of a commotion but Savannah couldn't make out the words.

They heard footsteps coming toward them and then, "Yoo-hoo! It's safe to come out now."

Tinsley didn't drop the gun, though. "Open the door slowly," she told Savannah. Savannah let go of the towel and slowly turned the knob. Her heart was beating, yet it felt as if all the blood had left her body.

The door opened slowly. "Ridge is home," the chicken lady said with a smile as she reached out her hand for Savannah. "I'm Winnie."

"Savannah Ambrose," Savannah said automatically as she shook her hand. "Does your friend really have a cutlass?"

"Sure do. I'm Ruby," the woman who was softly rounded and resembled the ideal, iconic granny image said, and sure enough, she was holding a cutlass.

"Savannah!"

Savannah turned to see Ridge and Gavin shoving their way in through the garage door. "Ridge! Oh my gosh! Are you hurt? Why are you covered in mud?"

Savannah ran into his arms. She was so relieved he was there that she didn't care about the muck or the smell. She was too busy trying to check for wounds.

"I will explain everything," Gavin said calmly as he took control. "While I do, Ridge, go take a shower and use this antiseptic wash. Then I want to examine you both."

Savannah began to pull away, but Ridge wouldn't let her go. "Not yet," he whispered. "I was so scared you were hurt."

"No one was here except Miss Winnie and Miss Ruby." Savannah leaned around Ridge's shoulder to look at the two old women who didn't seem the least bit upset. "Thank you for rushing to protect us."

"Anytime, dear. We were at the church for our women's group and Mildred was droning on and on. You did us a favor," Miss Ruby turned to Miss Winnie. "Are you having a craving for apple pie?"

"You know I am," Miss Winnie said, nodding her head. "I might even slip that sexy Mr. Gann a piece tonight. Do you know he sat me on his lap for the after-church rush to lunch? His scooter with the custom-built engine zoomed past everyone. He even let me hold his cane to knock the fast ones out of the way so we could be first in line."

"Now that's a gentleman," Miss Ruby decisively said as she picked up a purse that had to weigh thirty pounds. "Y'all call us if you need us. We'll drop by with some pie real soon and a welcome basket for you, hon."

"Thank you. That's very kind of you." Savannah might have been in danger, but there was no place she rather be. Good manners didn't go away just because of an attack or two. Shadows Landing was everything she dreamed of. Well, as soon as they caught the person after her . . . or was the person after Ridge?

"YOU'RE BOTH IN GOOD SHAPE." Gavin closed up his bag and Savannah finally relaxed. She wasn't worried for herself, but for Ridge. He was starting to bruise, but other than a couple scrapes and bruises, he was going to be fine. Gavin turned his head and looked out the window. "Looks like Granger and Kord are here."

"I'll let them in," Tinsley said as she carried her cup of tea with her. She was acting tough, but Savannah wouldn't soon forget the way Tinsley's body shook with fear.

Ridge reached his hand out across the kitchen table and covered Savannah's as they waited for Granger and Kord to join them. It didn't take long, but when they walked into the kitchen Ridge didn't let go of her hand. His large, warm, callused hand covered hers as if he were protecting it.

"Did you catch him?" Ridge asked. Savannah heard the tension and worry in his voice and also saw the way both men frowned and knew the answer before it was said.

"No. When he rammed me, it blew my tire. I was able to give chase but then it exploded and I spun out," Granger told him. "Kord found the truck in an empty field off the main road behind a row of bushes. He only found it because it was on fire. Whoever had been driving, and I honestly couldn't tell if it was a he or a she, was long gone."

"Dammit." Ridge said as he squeezed her hand and clenched his jaw. "What do we do now?"

"Now I'm inclined to think this has something to do with you," Granger told Ridge. Savannah didn't know whether she felt relieved or not. What she did feel was helpless, and she didn't like that one bit.

"Well, whatever it is, I want to help." Savannah looked at Ridge and knew that she'd do anything for him. Here was a man who lifted her up, not held her down. She wanted to do the same for him.

"I think it might be wise for you to go home tonight. If I am the target, I need you safe." Savannah began to shake her head, but Ridge looked so torn up that she stopped.

"If you think that's best. I want you focused on finding this person. I want a another date." Savannah tried to lighten the mood and it worked. Ridge leaned forward and kissed her quickly on the lips. It was so fast she didn't have time to register it, but as soon as he pulled back, her fingers went to her lips. She could tell

Ridge hadn't planned that kiss because he stood looking nervously at her. "I take it that's a yes to a date?"

Ridge's look of nervousness faded into a smile. "Yes. I would be honored to take you out on a date."

"Now we have that scheduled," Granger said with a smirk, "let Kord take you home, Savannah. We'll have a deputy outside your house tonight just in case."

"That's nice and all, but what about Ridge? Isn't he in more danger than I am?" Savannah asked worriedly.

"Ridge gets to have me spend the night. Not as romantic as you, but I do make a good spaghetti dinner." Savannah laughed as Granger slapped Ridge's back. "And I refuse to cuddle."

Ridge spun and grabbed Granger in a tight hug. "But I love to cuddle!"

Savannah and Kord busted out laughing. The laughter chased away the darkness of the fear. She refused to give into the fear. This was her fresh start and she was going to take it.

"You're right," Ridge said later that night. "You do make a good spaghetti dinner."

"I'm still not cuddling you," Granger warned as he looked at his phone. "Ellery delivered her dinner and stayed for an hour before leaving. Now Savannah is in bed," Granger reported.

"I got the same report from Savannah with a little more detail." Granger had kept it light tonight. They joked about old times, but there was still underlying tension.

Ridge sat down on the couch and turned on the sports

channel. He'd finally found a woman he wanted to have a serious relationship with and all of this happened.

"Have you found anything out on the names I gave you?" Ridge asked.

"Cleared Delight. I still can't believe you dated a girl named Delight and more shockingly, she wasn't a stripper," Granger said, disappointed as he shook his head.

"You probably have too. You just don't care enough to remember their names." Granger was a one-night–and-done kind of guy.

"I'm pretty sure I would remember Bunny. That's worse than Delight."

"Did you find anything about Bunny?" Ridge asked.

"Not yet."

"Are you seeing anyone right now?" Ridge asked, suddenly feeling like a teenager at a sleepover as they talked about girls.

"You know better than that. I don't see women for longer than twelve hours." Granger let out a sigh and leaned back on the couch. "Did Wade tell you what Darcy did to me?"

Yes. They all knew. "No. What could little Darcy do to big tough Granger Fox?"

Granger was quiet for a moment. "She told me the scars were scars, but they weren't grotesque. She said I should show them more. That the women I should be dating are the ones who won't care about the scars."

Ridge pretended to think about what Granger had told him. He was actually surprised Granger had admitted that conversation had ever taken place. "I think she has a good point. You could try it out and see if it works."

Ridge kept his eyes on the television just like Granger was. "Maybe."

Ridge wanted to pump his fist in the air. If anyone

deserved to be loved for who he was, it was Granger. "You know what I'm good at? Dessert." Ridge changed the subject knowing that was all Granger was going to say. He got up and went into the kitchen. While he was there, he texted Savannah goodnight.

*Can't wait to see you tomorrow. Goodnight. Sweet dreams.*

Yup, he was a teenager all over again because reading that text from her made him feel on top of the world. Ridge reached into the freezer, pulled out two pints of ice cream and headed back into the living room.

Granger looked up and rolled his eyes. "What a chef! I'll take the chocolate caramel turtle."

And because Ridge was a good friend, he handed his favorite ice cream over to Granger as they settled in for the night.

## 12

"Good morning, cupcake."

Ridge blinked his eyes open and looked up into Granger's smiling face.

"What time is it?" Ridge asked, wiping the sleep from his eyes. He glanced at the window and confirmed his suspicion that it was really early as the sun had yet to come up.

"Four forty-five. And I have news."

"What news?" Ridge asked, sitting up in bed.

"Whoa," Granger said, blocking his eyes. "Get dressed and we'll talk over coffee. I told you no cuddling and that includes naked snuggles."

Granger spun around and left the room with the door still wide open. Ridge shoved off the remaining sheets and stepped into a pair of black athletic pants and tugged on a T-shirt for the Atlanta Vultures football team as he rushed down the hall toward the stairs.

Ridge could already smell the coffee and was thankful for that. All in all, Granger was a pretty good roommate. He cooked dinner and made morning coffee. When Ridge came into the kitchen, he also found that Granger had brought in the newspaper. "Do you want to move in with me?"

Granger's lip curled in disgust. "No way. You sleep late and you can't cook."

"I can cook. I'm great at grilling *and* I can do laundry," Ridge said defensively.

"That is a plus," Granger admitted, taking a seat at the kitchen table and sipping his coffee. "But I think you'd rather have a certain green-eyed beauty in your house than me."

"I can't argue with that," Ridge joked as he poured his own cup of coffee and took a seat across from Granger. "So, what's the news?"

"I think I've tracked down the person responsible for the attacks against you and Savannah."

"What?! Who?"

"You won't believe it, but I think it's bachelorette number two, Bunny."

Ridge shook his head. "No way. Bunny is a bubbling blonde bimbo. She's not going to set fire to the house of a girl I'm seeing or ram me from the road."

"Bunny was your last serious girlfriend, right?" Granger asked, already knowing the answer.

"Yeah, but so what?"

"So, when I was interviewing Trisha, the girl you went out with just a couple of times after Bunny," Granger said as if Ridge didn't remember his girlfriends.

"I'm not like you. I remember the girls I date."

"Whatever," Granger dismissed before continuing. "Trisha says otherwise. She said Bunny warned her that you two were still together. Then when Trisha came home from your last date, you two kissed by the front door. Do you remember?"

"Yes, we made out a little. So?"

"Well, when she woke up the next morning, she walked out to get her newspaper and found that her car had been keyed and the word *SLUT* had been spray-painted all over the front of her house in huge letters," Granger told him.

This was the first he was hearing this, but now it made sense. "Trisha called me and told me that while she had fun, she wasn't ready to take things further and wished me all the best. And you think Bunny is still holding on to our relationship? It's been over nine months since we were together."

"She's avoiding me and won't take my calls after hanging up on me the first time she answered. I asked Charleston PD for some help and guess who they can't find right now?"

"Bunny," Ridge said on a shocked whisper.

"She tried to scare off Savannah and look what happened," Granger told him. "You moved her into your house. In these stalker cases, when it's clearly no longer the other person's fault, they turn into their obsession. It was no longer Savannah's fault you and Bunny weren't together. It was yours. You moved a woman into Bunny's house. That how she sees it. You finally betrayed her."

"And then she went after me with the truck."

"Exactly," Granger said, taking another sip of his coffee. "Charleston PD and the state police are helping me look for her. She's currently wanted for questioning."

Ridge let out a long breath. He had a name and a face to put with the danger. And now it didn't seem as dangerous. Facing Bunny was a lot better than facing an unknown.

"Do you think she's still in Shadows Landing?"

Granger shrugged. "I don't know. We know she was here for the auction. She was the losing bid to Savannah. But I'm putting out feelers with my informants."

Ridge chuckled. "You mean the town."

"Informants," Granger said, doubling down.

"Mary Jane at Stomping Grounds and Gil from the gas station aren't informants."

"They inform me of what's going on in town. That's the definition of an informant."

Ridge shook his head and hid his smile behind his coffee cup. "What should I do about work today?"

"I think you're good to go as long as you stay visible. It might even be worth putting on a breakup scene just in case Bunny is watching. It could draw her out."

"Break up with the woman I'm not even officially dating. Sounds like a plan."

"Yeah, but then there's make-up sex," Granger pointed out.

"That does make the plan more interesting," Ridge agreed.

"I'm off to work. Do you need a deputy to trail you?" Granger asked as he scooted the chair back and stood up.

"Nah. I can handle Bunny. Especially if she thinks I'm no longer with Savannah. She'll want to get back together. And I'll call you first thing if I see her."

Granger nodded. "I'll still check in on you." He grabbed his cowboy hat from the table and headed for the front door. "Make sure to lock the door after me."

"Yes, dear!" Ridge called out.

It was pretty hot for a fall day. Savannah had slipped on a tank top and shorts and attacked housecleaning with a vengeance. Ridge had called and woken her with news on the case. The woman who had bid against Savannah for Ridge at the charity auction was behind it all.

The woman had seemed determined, but Savannah had pushed higher with the bids. However, now the glares and narrowed-eye stares Bunny had given her at the auction made sense. And Savannah was positive she'd seen her around town later that night and the next morning. Strange for someone who lived in Charleston to be in Shadows Landing so often.

Ridge and his workers showed up at seven, and knowing who she was up against had calmed Savannah's nerves. It was time to focus on the future. Clean the house, finish unpacking, go on a date with Ridge, stage a breakup, catch the psycho Bunny, and then . . . Savannah smiled at the then. Then she could be with Ridge, start her college classes in the new term, and, hopefully, get a job she loved.

"Savannah?"

Surprised, Savannah dropped the stripper she was using on the walls as she worked sections of decades old wallpaper from the wall. She'd been lost in thought and hadn't heard anyone approaching.

"Oh hi, Trent." Savannah smiled at the man who was easily identifiable as a relative of Ridge. The cousins had that same masculine look. The only differences between Ridge and Trent was that Trent's hair was a darker brown and his eyes a little greener. He was about the same height as Ridge but just a smidge shorter. And they both smelled of fresh wood and ocean breezes.

"Ridge asked me to stop by to see if there's anything you haven't gotten yet that you might want me to build." Trent leaned down and picked up a spare scraper and began to help strip the wallpaper from the wall.

"I have everything for the kitchen ordered. But, there is

something I've always wanted. It has nothing to do with the fire, so I totally understand if you don't have time," Savannah told him. "It's nice enough that you're helping me strip wallpaper for a couple of minutes."

Trent chuckled. His hair was shorter than Ridge's and pushed back from his face. "It's not a problem. As long as it's not a big project, I can work on it at night after I stop working on my clients' furniture. What is it you're wanting?"

Ridge.

"I once saw in a magazine a porch swing that was a swinging bed. Not a king- sized bed but around a double. And it had this amazing woodwork along the back."

Trent nodded. "Was that in *Southern Times*?"

Savannah stopped scraping and turned to him. "Yes! You saw it too?"

Trent chuckled. "I made it."

Savannah looked at the man scraping wallpaper in jeans and a T-shirt next to her. "You're . . . I can't remember the company name they used."

"TAF Designs," Trent said casually, all the while continuing to work.

"You're TAF?"

"Trent Ansell Faulkner."

"You're renowned," Savannah sputtered.

"I'm just a furniture maker. Ridge is renowned."

"Your whole family is," Savannah said in sudden realization. "You with your furniture, Ridge with his homes, and Tinsley with her art."

Trent nodded. "We're pretty evenly split. The three of us are right side brain dominant, and Gavin, Ryker, Harper, and Wade are left side dominant. Gavin told us that when we were just kids. Ridge, Tinsley, and I always wanted to build or color while the others wanted to figure out mysteries and puzzles."

"Who won out?" Savannah asked as she felt as if she really understood the family better now.

"We all did. We did two activities. Just don't ask Ryker to paint for you. It's not pretty. However, I've definitely had him give me a hand with my business."

"You all supported each other's strengths." No wonder the family was so close.

"That's what family does," Trent said, stripping a sheet of wallpaper from the wall. "I'll get that swing made over the next couple of weeks."

"Thank you, Trent. That will be so special."

Together they worked as the wallpaper came down. Sometimes they talked, and other times they worked together in silence until Ridge entered.

"Do you need any more help?" Ridge asked as he came over and rubbed her aching shoulder muscles.

"I think we've just finished. Whatever you do, don't stop," Savannah groaned as he worked out the sore, tight muscles.

"My turn next," Trent said, picking up the tarp covered with wallpaper remnants.

"Thank you for helping out," Ridge said to his cousin. "Now, are you ready to have a romantic date and break up?"

"Oh, I want to see that," Trent said with a grin. "You have to throw your drink on him."

"Hey, now." Ridge turned to his cousin as he shook his head. "We can have a fight without throwing things at each other and still be convincing. I was just going to break up with her on the porch."

Trent looked horrified. "You can't do that. Who is going to see? There won't be any gossip about it that way."

"But if Bunny is here, she'd follow us back and she'd see it," Ridge explained.

"Nope. You need to have dinner at Lowcountry tonight and sit out on the front sidewalk. Everyone will see you."

Savannah thought about it and actually, it was a good idea. "That does make more sense. She'd probably see us. And if she listens to the local gossip, she'll hear about it. We'll just have to be careful not to be seen together for a little while afterward." And that part broke her heart. She loved the excitement she got when she knew she would see Ridge and the way her heart seemed to beat a little faster. However, she would do anything to keep him safe. That included not seeing him for a while.

"Then let's get ready to break up. Want to meet there so you'll have your own car to drive home?" Ridge asked.

"Sounds like a plan. Let's give the town something to talk about."

## 13

RIDGE WALKED into Lowcountry Smokehouse and got a table front and center on the sidewalk. Everyone who was out strolling on this beautiful fall night would see and hear them.

Ridge ordered a beer while he waited. As soon as it was placed in front of him, he went to take a sip and saw his whole family casually walking by. There was no chance they were going to keep walking by.

"Ridge!" Harper said, sounding surprised to see him. "What are you doing here?"

"I have a date with Savannah, remember?" He loved his family. He did. But this was something he dreaded having to do. The last thing he ever wanted to say to Savannah was something mean. And he was going to have to tonight.

"I'm surprised after that fight you had at her house today," Trent said so smoothly Ridge thought he was telling the truth.

"We're going to talk about our relationship and see if we have any future," Ridge said through gritted teeth. This was supposed to be a two-person show, not a whole theater troupe.

"Good luck," Harper told him as they started to head inside.

"Who's covering the bar for you, Harper?" Ridge asked just to put her on the spot.

"Skeeter," Harper said as she shot a smile over her shoulder at him.

"I thought you were going to hire a full-time bartender." Ridge broke character because Harper had said she was going to do that instead of working all the time. With Darcy's help, Harper had found a massive emerald that had once belonged to the Shadows Landing pirate Black Law. It was worth more than Harper ever dreamed of making and she had intended to use that money to hire help at her bar.

Harper shrugged. "I'll get around to it. In the meantime, Skeeter said he'd like to fill in here and there. I pay him in beer. It works."

"Please tell me you actually pay him and you report it on your taxes," Ryker groaned.

"Yeah, yeah, I did everything your stuffy accountant told me to do." Harper rolled her eyes and shoved through the heavy wooden door into the inside of the restaurant. "I've never seen a man so proud of his bow tie collection. It's a little weird," Ridge heard her saying as they disappeared inside.

Ridge slumped back in his chair. He loved his family, but sometimes they were a little overwhelming.

*Fake breakup to protect your potential girlfriend from an ex-girlfriend? And Bunny, really? You dated a woman named Bunny?*

Ridge groaned at his cousin Ryan's text. Ryan was from

the Davies side of the family that lived in Keeneston, Kentucky. He was also the head of their local FBI office, but it wasn't investigative work that got Ryan the gossip from Shadows Landing.

*Who told you?* Ridge texted back.

Ryan quickly replied back to him. *Gavin told me, Ellery told my wife, Ryker told Dylan, Harper told Sophie, Tinsley told Piper, Trent told Wyatt, and even though he's on his honeymoon, Wade texted Walker to see if you were okay.*

Ridge blinked at the text message. He loved his family. They were helping because they loved him.

*I'm good. I've got it all handled.*

Ridge took a deep breath. He did have it handled. They had a plan, and by this time next week, he and Savannah would be together again publicly, once Bunny was caught.

*Let us know if you need any help Bunny hunting,* Ryan offered. And while Ridge felt overwhelmed with the strong family presence, it said a lot that his cousins were so concerned. Ryan had helped them in the past. Cousin Layne had saved their best friend, Walker. They'd married and were now happily uniting the two family branches that had been separated out of spite a few generations back.

*Thank you. I will. Give my love to the family.*

"Sorry to keep you waiting." Ridge looked up to find Savannah looking gorgeous. Her hair was down, she was in sandals and a sundress, and she'd never looked so beautiful. And he had to be a jerk in public to her.

"You should really get a watch. What could possibly take you so long to get ready?" Ridge complained loud enough for the patrons around them to turn to look at them.

Savannah pulled out her chair and sat down. Her eyes were narrowed and she looked pissed. "You don't have to be such a jerk about it." More heads turned.

"I guess I'm just the jerk then. I don't see why you can't simply get ready on time. You do this every time we go out."

Savannah slammed her hand on the table and now even people from inside were staring out the windows at them. "It's always just about you, isn't it? Only Ridge's time matters. Only what Ridge wants matters."

Ridge felt his heart tearing in two. It was all fake, but he had a feeling Savannah had said these words before and he never wanted her to feel anything like that again. Instead of hurling insults, he was going to end it swiftly. And dramatically.

Ridge got up and threw the napkin on the table along with a twenty for the waitress. "I'm over it. It's clear you and I don't mesh well together."

Savannah stood up and glared across the table at him. "I never should have bought you!"

"Why? You buy everything else," Ridge snapped. Suddenly water was splashed in his face and Savannah stormed away. Ridge didn't hang around to listen to the gossip. He strode away in the opposite direction.

SAVANNAH LET out a long breath as she leaned back against the driver's seat of her rental car. That hit close to home. Way too close to home. Her body shook and tears pressed against her eyes. This wasn't Penn. This wasn't real.

*I'm sorry I had to do that. Call me when you get home.*

Savannah looked down at the phone and read Ridge's text. She was sorry too,

THOUGH IT WOULD BE worth it if they caught Bunny. Emotions were still high as Savannah drove home. She was lost in the past—the anger, the fights, the affairs. She'd tried to be the peacemaker, and that worked for the first couple years of her marriage. But as Penn grew more successful, the worse his demands became. She had to be perfect all of the time. The ironic part was she was the one who helped make him successful.

Savannah parked her car and took a moment to sit in the garden overlooking the river. Although her garden didn't compare to Ridge's, it was still peaceful. Ridge was supporting, understanding, caring, and after seeing Penn fake those things, it was easy to spot the real deal. Ridge was the real deal.

Savannah's frown finally lifted. She was ready to call Ridge. She pulled out her phone as she unlocked the front door. She reached for the light switch and her head was snapped back by a savage punch to the face.

Savannah screamed. Her flight-or-fight instincts kicked in, and she turned away from the figure in a ski mask to bolt out the door. "Help!" she screamed frantically as her arm was grabbed and she was yanked back inside.

Her eyes were desperate as she looked for an escape. The man had her by the neck and began to squeeze. Savannah went wild. She scratched at his face and arms. She struggled with all her might as she felt the helplessness come over her as he squeezed the life out of her.

"Miss Ambrose?" She heard someone calling from outside.

The man turned his head and Savannah used all her strength to kick him. He dropped her and the elation of being able to take in a deep breath was cut short as the back of her head hit the brick fireplace and everything went black.

· · ·

RIDGE HADN'T GONE straight home from the scene at the restaurant. Instead he'd gone to the park and looked out over the river. His gut was twisted as he thought about how cruel he'd been to Savannah. It wasn't in him to act that way.

As he sat on the bench, he hoped Bunny had heard it. It's why he'd left his car and walked to the park. He hoped she'd find him and confront him. Then he could detain her and call Granger or Kord. The two of them were stationed around downtown keeping a lookout for Bunny.

A twig snapped behind him. "Bunny?" he asked as he turned around.

It wasn't Bunny.

A man in a ski mask stood directly behind him. As soon as Ridge turned, the man reached out and raked his nails across Ridge's arm. "What the hell?"

And then it was on. The man leapt at him and Ridge threw a punch. The man kept attacking. A swipe of his nails down Ridge's other arm. A shove. A punch to the stomach.

Ridge fought back. He punched the man three times in a row, getting him to back up a little more with each punch. Even through the shock of the attack, Ridge noticed the man wasn't trying to block the punches. Finally Ridge swung hard and connected to the man's chin. The man stumbled back weaving. But instead of falling down, he turned and ran.

Ridge gave chase, but the man was faster. They approached the road and the man jumped into a running car and drove off. He must have had it waiting for him. But none of this made sense. Why had he walked into the park and attacked Ridge?

Sirens sounded and Ridge began pacing as he saw Kord's cruiser heading straight toward him. What the hell had just happened?

Kord got out of the car slowly. He took a look at Ridge and his hand went to his gun.

"Don't worry. It's over," Ridge said with a huff as the adrenaline finally began to die down. He leaned against the hood of the cruiser and looked at the scratches on his arms.

"Why'd you do it, Ridge?" Kord asked with shock in his voice.

"I had to. The attack came out of nowhere."

Kord came to stand in front of him and pulled out his cuffs. "I'm sorry, but . . . Ridge Faulkner, you're under arrest for assault and battery."

Ridge felt his mouth drop open in surprise. "I was the one attacked. I was just defending myself."

"And Savannah is the one found barely conscious. Let's go."

The earth fell out from under Ridge. "*Savannah*? What happened to Savanah?"

"Ridge, I advise you not to say another word until you have a lawyer. It's not looking good for you. Granger is with her now."

"Savannah said I attacked her? That doesn't make sense. Wait, Kord, something is wrong," Ridge said as the cuffs were closed around his wrists. They hung heavy even though he knew they weren't.

"Savannah was attacked. She was hit and then choked. She punched the face and scratched the arms of the man attacking her. I was to look for anyone with matching defensive wounds. Your wounds match those described, exactly. Your knuckles are bloody, your face is bruised, and you have scratch marks down your arms."

Kord grabbed a stunned Ridge by his shoulder and pulled him up. "Can you call Ryker for me?"

"Sure thing, Ridge. I'm sorry, but you have the right to remain silent," Kord said as he read Ridge his rights.

## 14

GAVIN FINISHED EXAMINING Savannah's injuries and set about cleaning the cut on the back of her head as Ellery brought her some hot tea for her bruised throat. Savannah sat quietly as everyone now discussed her as if she weren't there.

Her neighbor had heard her scream and had run over with a shotgun. The man who attacked her had fled out the back and disappeared. Granger had arrived shortly after and immediately called Gavin for emergency medical attention.

Savannah hadn't been knocked out for long. She had woken up with her neighbor bent over her. As soon as Gavin arrived, he had questioned her. Savannah had told him about the intruder and about how she had fought back. How she kicked, punched, and scratched the man attacking her. Granger then called Kord and started a manhunt.

And now Granger was whispering to Gavin who was shaking his head. Savannah was starting to get annoyed at being left out of the conversation. She was tired, she was hurt, and she was pissed. Savannah was ready for some Bunny stew.

"No. That's not possible," Gavin said as his voice rose in anger.

Granger purposely avoided Savannah's gaze as he tried to calm Gavin down. Ellery joined them and Savannah's anger rose as she saw Ellery's arms moving rapidly as she whispered urgently at Granger.

"That's it!" Savannah shouted as she ignored the pain it caused her throat. "Stop talking as if I'm not here. I was the one attacked, and I should be the one you're talking to if you have news."

Granger cleared his throat and stuck his hands on his hips. His face was completely unreadable as he stared her down. "We found your attacker."

"Great!" Savannah said with relief. It was if her whole body turned to jelly. The fear was gone, and she knew he wouldn't come after her again.

Savannah closed her eyes and took a deep breath. When she opened her eyes, no one else was looking as relieved as she was. Gavin's lips were pressed so tightly together there was nothing left but a white line. Ellery's face, which normally had a kind smile on it, was cold. Her lips were downturned, her eyes filled with anger, and they were all looking at her.

"What's going on?" Savannah asked and felt her anger begin to boil as no one said anything. "You said you caught the guy. What's the problem?"

"It's Ridge," Granger said in a complete monotone voice.

"Is he okay?" Savannah asked as she stood up so quickly she became dizzy. "Is he hurt? What happened to him?" No one answered her, but Gavin had crossed the room to steady her. "Dammit! Someone tell me what's going on right now or I'll have a hissy fit that will leave you curled up on the ground in tears!"

Granger stepped forward and looked down into her face. "Ridge has been arrested. He was the one who attacked you."

Savannah's whole world came to a screeching halt as she took in Granger's serious words. Then, like a record on double time, her brain caught up and processed the information. "You're wrong."

Granger shook his head as his cop face never changed. Savannah was staring him down as Ellery came to join her for silent support.

"I'm sorry, Savannah. You know I don't want to believe it. But his face is bruised and he has defensive scratches on his arms. Just like you told me you gave your attacker."

Savannah shook her head over and over again. "No."

"I'm sorry," Granger began to say, but Savannah wasn't listening. She was replaying the incident over and over again in her head.

"A watch."

"What?" Granger asked as Savannah's focus snapped back up to him.

"Was Ridge wearing a watch when he was arrested?" Savannah asked calmly. She knew the answer and she knew it was only a matter of time before Ridge was freed.

"I don't know, why?" Granger asked as Gavin was nodding his head. He knew exactly what Savannah was talking about.

"My attacker was wearing a watch. Plus, how tall are you?" she asked Granger.

"Around six one. Again, why?" Granger asked in his steady voice.

"Is Ridge taller or shorter than you?" Savannah saw a tic

by Granger's eye. He didn't like these questions. He wanted to get to the point. And she would.

"A little taller. Again, why?"

"Because the attacker had on a watch and when he faced me to choke me, I was looking right at his nose." Savannah pointed to where her eyes reached on Granger. "On you, who is a little shorter than Ridge, my eyes come to your upper chest."

"Well, let's see if Ridge is wearing a watch," Granger said, opening the front door. "Savannah, you can ride with me."

Savannah headed for the passenger door of his SUV and waited for him to unlock it. Gavin and Ellery were on the phone and Savannah knew the family well enough to know that by the time they arrived at the jail, half the family, if not the entire crew, would already be there.

"You know I have to be harder on Ridge and demand more evidence than I would someone else, right?" Granger asked as he started his SUV.

"Why? He's your friend." Savannah let him clearly hear her frustration.

"That's exactly why. Anyone we arrest after Ridge will use him to create reasonable doubt. I have to clear him with more evidence than I would anyone else or a good defense attorney will say I played favorites with my buddy. Suddenly a jury thinks I'm not being truthful and the real bad guy walks."

Oh gosh, he was right. "I'm sorry. I didn't think about that. I just want Ridge cleared. The townspeople are going to think the worst of him. They saw that public fight and then he's arrested for assault. It could ruin his reputation."

"I'm sure Kord will make sure the very last thing we do is any kind of paperwork. We'll give him time to get an attorney there . . . what the hell?"

Granger stopped the SUV as a helicopter landed ahead of them on the corner of Main Street and South Cypress Lane. The door opened and out stepped Ryker.

"Ryker has a helicopter?" Savannah asked in surprise. Then Ryker turned back to the helicopter and held out his hand. A slim arm in a ruby red suit handed him a briefcase that Ryker shifted to his other hand before holding his hand up to the woman.

Slowly, slim legs in designer high heels appeared, then a smooth face that seemed to be made of porcelain and blonde hair in a ballerina bun at the base of her neck came into view. "Who's that?"

"Well, Kord is going to be useless now," Granger grumbled. He drove closer as the helicopter pulled up, hovered, and took off low over Shadows Landing. "That's Olivia Townsend, one of Ryker's lawyers. She's the one who helped Darcy get the rights to the Black Law treasure."

"What does she have to do with Kord?" Savannah asked, so relieved that Ryker had brought an attorney that she wanted to kiss him.

"You'll see," Granger said, finally grinning as he pulled to a stop in front of the courthouse.

Savannah had her door open and was already halfway around the car before Granger caught up to her. "You may not believe me, but it's really best if I do the talking. Just answer my questions. Don't elaborate. This will be on the record and one thing I've learned as a cop is people can talk themselves into trouble faster than green grass through a goose."

"Okay," Savannah said, but she didn't slow down, and she wouldn't until she saw Ridge.

Granger opened the door to the courthouse and they walked through the empty hallway a short distance until they reached the sheriff's department. Granger opened the door and Savannah's breath hitched. Through the front desk opening she could see Ridge talking to Ryker and Olivia Townsend.

"Ridge!"

Granger was entering a code to unlock the door when Ridge's head snapped.

"Savannah, I di—"

Olivia's hand slapped over his mouth, and she turned with a sweet smile such as a great white shark might have before eating a seal and looked at Savannah. "I am Mr. Faulkner's attorney. My name is Olivia Townsend. I'm sorry, but at this time my client is not to have any communication with you." She turned to Kord and smiled a kinder smile. "Would you be a dear and get us a private room?"

"Right this way, Miss Townsend," he said as he gave her a wink.

Savannah rolled her eyes.

"It's just a flirtation. Even Kord couldn't handle a woman like Olivia," Granger told her as he led her back to interrogation.

"Should I have a lawyer with me?" Savannah asked as Granger pulled out the chair for her.

"This is an victim interview. You can have one if you like, but it's not necessary."

Savannah took a deep breath and reined in her emotions. "Can I have a glass of water for my throat?"

Having the room to herself gave her a moment to think without pressure. The faster she could prove Ridge was innocent, the faster Ridge would be released. She could do this.

Granger walked in and set the water down. "Would you like to call an attorney?"

Savannah shook her head. "I'm ready to give my statement."

Granger pushed the recording device. "This is Sheriff Granger Fox with victim Savannah Ambrose."

"RIDGE, YOU NEED TO CALM DOWN," Ryker said, seated calmly in the office with his legs crossed as he flicked invisible lint from his tie.

"How can I be calm? Did you see the marks on her neck? I could see them from across the room!" Ridge continued to pace. His blood pressure was through the roof. He felt the blood pumping in his ears.

"Mr. Faulkner," Olivia said just as calmly as Ryker. "Sit down and shut up.

Please."

Ridge stopped pacing and took a deep breath. "I'm sorry," he said as he pulled out a chair and finally sat down. Although he was not calm. He was worried to death about Savannah, and his leg was bouncing so fast it was shaking the table.

"Now," Olivia said, sounding calm and even, "is there a reason for Ryker to leave the room? I don't want to know what it is, but Ryker can break confidentiality and I need you to lay it all on the table."

Ridge stopped bouncing his knee. "No. I never touched Savannah. I would never touch a woman in anger. I was at the park when I was attacked."

Olivia looked at him and slowly leaned back and crossed her legs. "Tell me everything and don't leave out a single detail."

## 15

SAVANNAH STOOD in front of the tape measure and pointed to where her direct line of sight fell on the man who attacked her. Then she added where the top of his head was. The man clearly wasn't Ridge. This man was around five foot nine whereas Ridge was a good five inches taller. Not something easily confused or concealed.

"I have your report," Granger finally said, turning off the recording equipment. "I need to talk to Ridge. Kord will be in, and he can take you home if you'd like."

"I'm not going anywhere until Ridge is able to leave with me." Savannah crossed her arms and sat back in the chair. When Granger opened the door, Savannah was accosted by the sounds of people filling the front entrance and yelling for Granger.

Granger groaned as the entire Faulkner family looked pissed off. Gavin had clearly told them what had happened.

"Oh, Savannah," Tinsley gasped, catching sight of her looking down the hall at them. "You poor thing. What can I do?" Sweet Tinsley then narrowed her gaze on Granger and pointed at him. "You better unlock this door right now or I swear I will jump the desk and take you down."

Granger pressed a button and the door unlocked. "No need for threats, Tins. I was coming to let you in. You can see Savannah, but I have to talk to Ridge without you all."

"There's no way I am letting you near my brother without a lawyer." Tinsley marched up to him and poked him in the chest. The top of her head barely reached his chest, but she was fierce.

"Ryker brought Olivia Townsend."

"Oh," Tinsley said as her finger froze in midair. "Good. Then things are in hand." She pushed past Granger and headed straight for Savannah, her face filled with worry. Tinsley didn't say anything. She just wrapped her arms around Savannah and Savannah felt all the love this small person had packed in her.

"It's okay, Savannah. I have you," she whispered and Savannah felt her body go weak as the strength she had finally wore out. Giant sobs that hurt her bruised throat escaped as tears ran down her face. More arms were around her as Savannah smelled Ellery's light floral perfume.

Savannah wasn't sure how long she stood there being held by Tinsley and Ellery as she cried. But finally the fear, the realization she had almost died, and the anger finally escaped through her tears. She sniffled and opened her eyes to find boots standing behind Tinsley.

"I don't do crying. I do this. Drink." Harper handed her a bottle of vodka and Savannah laughed as Ellery and Tinsley released their hold on her. "I got you the fruity flavored stuff."

Savannah sniffed and then smiled. It was hard not to laugh at Harper's obvious discomfort. She looked like Trent and Gavin, who stood just inside the door with pained expressions.

"Thank you. You got the right stuff." Savannah took a sip and any remaining tears dried as the vodka burned on the way down and then warmed her belly. The men approached cautiously and Trent pulled out chairs for everyone.

Savannah took another drink from the bottle and felt herself calming. She sat with Tinsley on one side and Ellery on the other. Trent awkwardly patted her shoulder. "I'm not good at this, but it'll be okay. You're not alone in this."

No matter how hard Savannah tried to stop them, the tears started again.


"You have my client's statement, Sheriff. Are you going to arrest him or let him go?" Olivia demanded.

"I'd like to measure your client's height for the record," Granger told them stone-faced. His face had been a mask of indifference since he walked into the room. Ridge wanted to beg and plead with him to know how Savannah was. Ridge wanted to know Granger believed him when he said he'd never hurt Savannah or any woman. Just the thought of harming a woman went against everything in him.

"For what purpose?" Olivia asked.

"A lineup of sorts," Granger said, not giving anything away.

Olivia leaned forward and placed her hand next to his ear so Granger and the video camera recording the interrogation couldn't see her lips moving. "One last time, do you have anything to hide?"

Ridge barely shook his head and Olivia leaned back. "On the condition that it's off the record," she said, glancing at the camera.

"No," Granger said simply, but then he turned his eyes to Ridge. The look he gave practically begged Ridge to do it. The camera was to Granger's back so his face couldn't be seen. But Ridge saw it.

"I'll do it," Ridge said, pushing back from his chair and standing up.

"Mr. Faulkner, I strongly urge you not to comply unless it's off the record," Olivia said with so much disapproval he almost sat down. But there was just something in Granger's look that prompted him to continue.

"I understand, Miss Townsend. I'm going to do it anyway."

Granger stood up and pulled a tape measure from his pocket. "Please stand against the far wall so that I can mark it for the camera."

Ridge followed the instructions. He felt as if he were a child having his height measured to see how much he'd grown in the last year. Only this time it mattered a whole lot more for a reason Ridge didn't know yet.

Granger used a green sticky note to mark the top of Ridge's head and had Ridge go sit down. He measured to the top of the sticky note and wrote in a black marker 6' 2".

"Mr. Faulkner, you said you were attacked in the park and that is how you sustained these injuries. Could you tell me, how tall was your alleged attacker?"

Ridge blinked, wondering why he would ask and then it hit him. He was systematically working to clear Ridge's name. Ridge took a deep breath and shook his head. "He was shorter than me by several inches."

"Did you stand face to face with him?" Granger asked, his cool professional tone still in place.

"Yes, and he came up to here," Ridge said, holding out his hand to indicate the height of his attacker.

"Can you take this sticky note and put it on the wall to represent the height of your attacker?" Granger handed him a blank blue sticky note.

Ridge took it and slowly walked to the wall. He stood and reached out with his hands, remembering where he punched. When he had a clear mental picture of his attacker, he placed the sticky note on the wall and sat back down.

"What is this all about?" Olivia demanded, needing to know.

"I'll show you," Granger said as he measured the height and marked the blue sticky note with 5' 9 ½ ". Ridge watched as Granger walked back to the table and opened up the file that had been sitting there. Inside was a pink sticky note with 5' 9". Granger walked back to the wall and measured out the height and stuck the pink sticky note right next to Ridge's blue one before going back to his chair.

"It appears it's impossible that your client attacked Miss Ambrose. In fact, I now believe they are both victims of the same attacker. The pink sticky note is the height of the man who tried to kill Miss Ambrose. It is a nearly identical match to your client's description of his attacker," Granger stood up then. "You're free to go, Mr. Faulkner. I have your report of the attacker and will add it into Miss Ambrose's report as I believe you're both victims of assault. No charges will be filed against you at this time." Granger turned to Olivia and held out his hand to shake hers. "I'll call your office if I have any more questions for your client."

"Thank you," Olivia said as if the interview hadn't just done a one-eighty.

Granger turned off the camera and let out a deep breath.

"What the hell was that about?" Ridge asked with the full anger of having just been interrogated.

"I had to prove you couldn't have done it or a good defense attorney would have created reasonable doubt," Granger said, running his hand through his hair, showing just how stressed he was, too.

"I'm impressed," Olivia told Granger as he nodded. "You accomplished just that."

"Can I see Savannah now?" Ridge was tired and impatient to see her. He wouldn't feel better until he had her in his arms.

"Go ahead."

Ridge was out the door in a heartbeat. Savannah was sitting among his family members, but as soon as she saw him she let out a little sob and jumped up from her chair. His arms came around her—he could finally breathe again.

"Are you okay? What did that bastard do to you?"

"He tried to kill me. I think he only left because I hit my head and blacked out momentarily. He must have thought I was dead and didn't check when my neighbor came running in with a shotgun."

"And then he found me in the park and attacked me," Ridge told them. "It wouldn't have taken him long to get to me. Especially if he had a car nearby."

"But why?" Tinsley asked, clearly upset.

"Because he thought he killed Savannah, and he wanted to blame Ridge for it. Make it look like a domestic violence incident. After all, you two put on a very public fight just before," Granger said as he joined them with Olivia and Ryker.

"I don't understand," Savannah said, feeling frustrated.

"I don't either, except all of these incidents were made to look like accidents. Right? The towel left on the stove. The car wreck. A fight gone too far," Ridge explained.

"So, someone *is* trying to kill me," Savannah said as

Ridge pulled her tightly against his side as if he could protect her from the answer.

"Maybe. Or they're trying to punish Ridge. Making him sit in jail for arson or a murder he didn't commit seems rather evil," Granger replied.

"Surely this is beyond Bunny wanting to get back together with me." Ridge was positive Bunny couldn't pull this off. But if it wasn't her, who was it?

"I'm getting a court order tomorrow to track her down through her credit cards and phone," Granger said, clearly upset about the matter. "I'm just relieved Savannah noticed so much about her attacker so we could clear you."

"You did a good job, Sheriff," Olivia told him as she briefly rested her hand on his arm.

"I did a good job too, right?" Kord asked, sending her a wink.

Olivia laughed and Ridge rolled his eyes. Kord was so infatuated, and it was clear Olivia enjoyed it, but she didn't feel the same. For that matter, Ridge wasn't all the way sure Kord cared one way or the other.

"Let me walk you to your helicopter." Kord held out his arm for her to take and Olivia linked her arm through before turning back to the group. "Please keep me updated and let me know if I can help in any way. Ryker, are you coming back to the city tonight?"

"I'll be right there. I'll call the pilot." Ryker sent a text as Kord escorted Olivia outside. "She'll eat him alive," Ryker told them as he watched Kord and Olivia head outside.

"How old is Kord?" Savannah whispered to Ridge.

"Not that age matters, but she's in her early thirties and he's twenty-seven."

Savannah nodded. "It seems as if they're in two different places in their lives. The timing is all wrong for them." She paused and looked at him with sadness. "I'm afraid it's all wrong for us too."

Ridge felt as much fear as he had when he'd heard Savannah was hurt. "Don't say that. Nothing has ever felt so right."

He could see the sheen in her eyes as if Savannah was battling back tears. "Someone is trying to hurt us to keep us apart. That doesn't sound like good timing to me."

"The only thing that matters to me is if you want to be with me. If you don't, I'll step back. I'll never step away from you unless that's what *you* want."

Savannah threw her arms around his waist and squeezed. "I already know what I want, and it's to be with you."

"Then that's what we'll do. Screw pretending to break up. Someone call Reverend Winston and tell him what's going on. He'll spread the word and everyone will be on the lookout for Bunny. Instead of hiding, it's time to face this together," Ridge said before kissing the top of her head as she hugged him.

"As a family," Tinsley said, stepping up to join them.

"And friends," Granger added. "Go home. I'll get the word out."

"I'll get my security team out here as soon as possible. They're at my office in China right now, so it'll be two days tops. I'll have them set up both houses with state-of-the-art security," Ryker told them as he patted Ridge's shoulder. "I'll call you when I talk to them and give you a better time frame. In the meantime, you can use my house if you need."

"Thank you, Ryker," Ridge said, shaking his cousin's hand. "For everything. For flying your attorney out here for me, for setting up security, for just being there for me."

Ridge almost laughed at Ryker's expression of extreme

discomfort. "That's what family does. I'll let you know when the security team will be here." And then Ryker practically ran from the room.

"Ridge?" Savannah asked in Ryker's wake.

"Yes?"

"Take me home."

## 16

RIDGE WAS TORN as to what to do. Savannah had gone upstairs to get ready for bed after they had eaten some sandwiches and cuddled on the couch. It had been peaceful, intimate, and wonderful.

It felt as if they were a couple. Ridge loved it. If only Bunny could be caught, then he wouldn't be torn in the least. Right now there was nothing he'd rather do than spend as much time as possible with Savannah. He wanted to pick her up for dates. He wanted to take her to his favorite places. He wanted to discover all the things that made her happy. He wanted to find out her favorite foods, her hobbies, and her interests. He wanted to talk to her, hear her opinions, hear her thoughts, and then there was the constant need to touch her. To feel Savannah's lips on his. To feel the heat of her body under his hands.

However, he wasn't free to follow his desires. Not yet. Now he was stuck in some kind of relationship purgatory. To move forward would distract him from keeping her safe from Bunny. To move back would risk losing her forever. What Ridge needed was a sign. Preferably one that said

*Savannah is safe now*. Then he could put his whole heart into showing her the love she deserved.

"Ridge?"

Savannah's quiet, unsure voice had him turning to look up the stairs. She stood at the railing to the open second floor looking down at him. Her face was free of makeup. Her hair was brushed and hanging around her shoulders, and she was in a nightgown that made him instantly hard.

Ridge had to take several deep breaths to calm down. It wasn't like he was a teenager, but seeing her so fresh and at home and wearing that little strappy, thigh-length white nightie had scrambled his brain cells.

"Yes, sweetheart?" The term of endearment slipped out and Ridge hoped Savannah didn't notice, but by the way she sucked in her breath she did. Ridge practically groaned because when she breathed deeply it did amazing things to that nightgown.

"Will you sleep with me tonight?"

Ridge knew it wasn't in a sexual way. And he knew by the way she shifted from foot to foot she was nervous to ask him and that saddened him. She should never feel bad for asking him for anything. Especially something that made her feel safe.

"Of course. I'll be up in just a minute."

Savannah began to turn from the railing, but turned back and gave him an embarrassed smile. "Thank you."

Savannah then headed into her room. Ridge got up from the couch and made the rounds to close all the blinds, lock all the doors, and make sure no one was lurking in the yard before heading upstairs and into his room. He went through the motions of getting ready for bed and at the last minute stopped and pulled a heavy metal case from his nightstand. Inside was a handgun he'd gotten years ago when he and his cousins had taken up target practice.

He put his shirt over it and carried it into Savannah's room. She was in bed with the television news on low volume. Ridge set the gun case next to his side of the bed and climbed under the covers. He sat up with his back against the fabric covered headboard and began listening to the latest news out of Charleston.

"Are you sure you don't mind staying with me tonight?" Savannah asked quietly during a commercial.

Ridge turned to her and realized Penn probably would have minded. He was the kind of dick to put only his needs first and not recognize anyone else's. "I never mind spending time with you. In fact, I look forward to every moment we have together. Always know you can ask me anything. It'll never bother me. I want to make you happy, Savannah. To do that I need to know what you think, what you want, and what you need."

Savannah slid closer to him and took a deep breath. "Then will you hold me?"

Ridge smiled and opened his arm for her. "There is nothing else I'd rather do."

"Nothing?" Savannah asked in such a way he knew she'd just taken things *there*.

"Well, there's nothing I'd rather do that doesn't involve you naked and underneath me. Or on top." Ridge paused as if he were thinking. "Or sitting, bent over, standing up."

"Okay, okay," Savannah giggled. "I get it."

"Are you sure?" Ridge asked sincerely. "I could draw diagrams if you aren't sure."

Savannah's giggles turned into laughter, and she playfully slapped her hand against his bare chest. Then she stopped laughing as she ran her hand over his muscles.

Ridge felt his heart beating under her hand, and he wasn't laughing anymore either. Especially not when Savannah leaned forward and placed a kiss right over his heart.

"Where were you all my life?" she whispered.

"Right here, waiting for you."

"You don't have to wait anymore," Savannah said, lowering her head and placing another kiss on his chest. She kissed her way up his neck and across his jaw. Ridge had the sheets fisted in his hands as he allowed Savannah to take the lead. Her kisses set him on fire, but he felt the nervous flutter of her fingertips on his shoulder as she moved to face him more fully.

Ridge finally let go of the sheet and ran his hand gently through her hair. He'd show her what she meant to them, but he wasn't going to make love to her tonight. Not when they were beaten and sore. Not when they were still in danger. But he'd show her love.

SAVANNAH WOKE to the feel of her stomach growling as the smell of sausage and biscuits entered her room. She didn't bother putting on clothes or brushing her hair. While they hadn't had sex last night, they were certainly on intimate terms now. If he saw her during those intimate moments, he could see her like this.

She shoved off the sheets and followed the smells into the kitchen. Ridge was in an old college shirt and athletic shorts as he cut the biscuits in half and placed them in a shallow bowl.

"Good morning," he said to her as he looked up from the bowls. He leaned across the island and placed a quick kiss on her lips. "I hope you like biscuits and sausage gravy."

Who didn't? "I love it. It's actually my favorite." Savannah got two napkins and poured two cups of coffee. "How do you like your coffee?" she asked, suddenly realizing there were so many things about him she didn't know. She wanted to know his favorite things and what he liked to do for fun. Then maybe she could plan some dates for them in the future. Her happy thoughts faded as she realized they wouldn't have fun dates until this mess was over. Last night someone had tried to kill her and put Ridge in jail for it.

For the first time in Savannah's life, she stopped behaving as she thought she *should* behave. She was angry. Furiously angry. And she took another step toward expressing her real feelings. She said it. Out loud. Just how angry she was and with lots of cursing. Creative cursing, at that.

Ridge looked up from where he was smothering the biscuits with thick sausage gravy. "What did the poor duckbilled platypus ever do to you?"

Savannah stopped her rant and began to laugh. "I'm just angry," she admitted. And it felt good to say it out loud. "I know I'm supposed to take everything with good grace, but I'm angry that someone torched my kitchen. I'm angry that someone caused my wreck. I'm angry that someone tried to kill me. And I'm angry that someone tried to hurt you." She slammed the silverware onto the table and took a deep breath.

"Feel better?"

"Actually I do," Savannah said as she sat down at the table and primly put the napkin across her lap. "Coffee?" she asked, handing Ridge the cup she had poured.

"I think I might have something that will make you feel better. You mentioned that you didn't like the wall dividing the kitchen from the living room. Well, my guys just called and it's not a weight-bearing wall. It can easily come down. And I might have a present for you. Give me one second."

Savannah sipped her coffee as Ridge disappeared into the garage. She heard the banging of drawers and then some grunts of approval. The door opened and in came Ridge holding a sledgehammer with the handle covered in red duct tape. "To match your pretty hair," he said with a grin.

Savannah's eyes went as wide as her smile. "This is for me?"

"Your very own sledgehammer. I have it on good authority when you're angry it feels really good to smash something with it."

Savannah jumped up and hugged him before taking the heavy sledgehammer into her hands. "Let's do it."

## 17

SAVANNAH'S ARMS ACHED. Her back hurt. Her hands were probably raw under the gloves. But she felt *good*. Damn good. She stepped back and looked through the kitchen and into her living room. The wall was gone and she'd helped destroy it.

"You have a future home improvement reality show in store for you," Ridge joked as he took her sledgehammer from her.

"I can't believe how big this looks!"

"With some minor changes throughout the rest of the house, you could turn the inside into a contemporary home," Ridge told her.

"Cottage on the outside, contemporary on the inside. I like it," Savannah declared.

Ridge looked at his watch. "It's lunchtime. Want to go into town and get something?"

"Sure. I can pick up some pies from the diner for the guys to thank them for their hard work."

Cheers went up on the side porch where they were eating and Savannah knew this was what real happiness felt like. She was making friends, had a supportive man in her life, and had gone out of her comfort zone and demolished a wall. She felt great.

Ridge's phone rang and he grimaced. "I have to take this. It's a really big potential client."

"Go ahead. I'm going to run up to my room and clean up a little."

"Hello," Ridge said into the phone as Savannah walked through the now nonexistent wall space and into her living room before going upstairs.

It was strange, Savannah thought as she looked around. The house she was so proud to finally have didn't feel as if it were hers anymore. Not that it ever had been. It was still Penn's. She was excited to paint it and to update it but when she thought of going home, she thought of being curled up on the couch in Ridge's house with his arm around her. It clearly wasn't her house, but she felt more at home there than she did here. Probably because Ridge had welcomed her into his home. Here she still felt like the intruder since she wrestled it away from Penn in the divorce.

Reality home improvement show . . . she could just go ahead and flip this house. She wanted to be an interior designer and she could show that off. Then she would sell it for a profit and buy a house in Shadows Landing that was her own. Savannah took a deep breath. Yes. It felt so right. Giving a little squeal of delight, Savannah hurried down the hall and into her bedroom.

She looked out the window and saw Ridge pulling out papers from his truck. With a smile and a renewed sense of determination, she opened up her closet and grabbed an old sundress. She'd put her dirty clothes back on after she ate.

Savannah stepped into her en suite bathroom and

pulled off her sweaty, dusty T-shirt. She tossed it over the edge of the bathtub and her shorts quickly followed. She wet a hand towel and did a quick once-over on her body before pulling on her dress.

When she looked in the mirror she felt cleaner, but goodness gracious, her hair was a mess! How Ridge found her attractive she didn't know, but she knew he did. And the feeling of being desired no matter what you looked like was freeing. She opened the mirrored medicine cabinet over the sink and pulled out her brush and some hairspray.

She flipped her head over and began brushing the underside of her hair. Chunks of drywall went tumbling to ground along with a white cloud of dust. Booted feet entered her line of vision and she laughed as she used one hand to ruffle her hair, sending more dust flying.

"Can you believe this? No wonder so many of your guys have shaved heads."

Savannah flipped her hair up ready to tackle the outside of it when she realized the boots weren't Ridge's. Fear shot through her as she froze with the brush still in her hair. She swallowed hard and turned to face the man in a black ski mask holding a gun right at her head.

"You are quite the problem," he said. His voice was as steady as the gun he was holding—completely still.

Savannah grasped the sink with one hand to steady herself as the brush fell to the floor. She was going to die. She felt the blood drain from her body as it rushed straight for her big toe. She wavered and leaned against the sink for stability, turning her head to the left to see the man.

"Why are you doing this?" she asked as tears ran down her face. Her body was shaking so hard her teeth were chattering.

"It's just a job, lady. But you've been a real pain in my ass. No more accidents. I'm getting this over with."

Savannah's shaking stopped. The blood rushed from her toe back up to her face as anger overcame her. "A job! Killing me is a fucking job?"

"It's a good job, and almost always easy," he told her, keeping the gun aimed at her. "Make it look like an accident, they said. It'll be easy, they said. Well, I'm afraid it won't look like an accident, but I'll still get my twenty grand."

"Twenty thousand dollars is all my life is worth?" Savannah gasped.

"I know, I would have charged double if I knew you had nine freaking lives."

The man rolled his eyes and Savannah moved. Her thumb flicked the top off the hairspray as she raised it and sprayed it right into his eyes.

"You were right, I'm worth way more!" Savannah shouted as the man's arms flailed, trying to wipe the pain from his eyes.

Savannah charged him as she screamed at the top of her lungs. They went down hard, and he hit his head on the door, slamming it shut. Shit. Now they were trapped in the bathroom as she let out two years of anger on him. At least the gun had fallen somewhere out of reach.

Savannah breathed hard as her blood boiled. Normally her flight-or-fight response told her to run, but not today. He'd pissed her off something fierce. Savannah fisted her hands and let loose.

"YES, SIR," Ridge said into the phone yet again. This was a high-profile client and would be a massive deal for Ridge, but the man enjoyed talking to "normal" people. If only

Ridge's client knew there was nothing normal about him or his family.

"I'm so glad you liked the plans. I can meet with you as soon as I finish my current job. That will give you time to see if there's anything else you'd like changed or added to your beach house," Ridge said patiently.

Ridge was ready to be with Savannah. They'd had so much fun together through the day. They were connecting on a level he never knew existed before. Ridge was beginning to understand what his married cousins were all talking about when they discussed their wives. They lived their own lives, had their own interests, but each said there was nothing better than learning something new about his wife or coming home to her.

"Great, I'll call you in a couple of weeks and set up a time to meet," Ridge said as his client finally got off the phone.

Ridge turned to walk back inside when he heard a bloodcurdling scream filled with rage. He and his men raced for the house. *No no no* was all that was going through his mind. It couldn't be Savannah. She had to be safe. She just had to be.

"TAKE your twenty grand and choke on it!" Savannah screamed as she slammed her fists one after the other into the man's face over and over again. He'd tried to fight her off but Savannah was too lost in the blood thirst to notice the punches he'd gotten in as she straddled his chest, letting all her anger out on him. She truly understood the phrase "seeing red" now.

"Damn mask," she muttered ripping it off and looking at a man she'd never seen before. His eyes were wide with shock. His nose and lip were bleeding as he wrestled with her. He looked to be in his late thirties. His hair was a dirty blond, and he looked like a surfer dude. A murderous asshole surfer dude.

He tried to reach for her, but Savannah leaned back out of his reach. The man tried to dislodge her by kicking his legs, but she caged his arms to his side with her knees, and she wasn't letting go. "Sorry, dude, but society life is a bitch. To survive I've had over six years of daily Pilates. I can make your little head explode with these thighs."

"You're crazy!" he yelled at her as he struggled to free himself.

"Wrong thing to say," she said as she stuffed the mask into his mouth. "Choke on this. Twenty grand my ass," she muttered when she felt the house shake as booted feet stomped up the stairs.

"Savannah!"

RIDGE HEARD Savannah screaming about twenty grand and her ass. The bathroom door was closed and there were muffled screams coming from inside. Ridge's heart beat hard against his chest and there was no way he'd been able to take a deep breath since he heard her scream.

Not bothering to knock he turned the knob and opened the door. Only it wouldn't open more than a fraction of an inch. "Savannah! Are you okay? Open the door!"

SAVANNAH SHOOK her head as the man screamed for help, but it sounded more like *hmmmmmmpf*! The red faded and Savannah was now stuck. If she let go of him, he'd be able to attack her.

"I can't move or he'll be free," Savannah called out as she heard Ridge ordering his men to break down the door.

In seconds, the whole door was suddenly gone as it was lifted off the hinges and tossed into the bedroom.

"What the hell?" Ridge muttered as the man beneath her looked pleadingly up at Ridge. "Brady, get in there and grab him as soon as Savannah gets up."

Ridge's foreman squeezed into the small bathroom, and Savannah could finally let go of the man. As she shoved herself back toward the tub, Brady hauled the man up to his feet. The man yanked the mask from his mouth. "Thank you," he said to Brady before turning to see Ridge.

Savannah saw the look of recognition on the man's face in the mirror. "You bastard!" Savannah jumped up, her legs shaking, as she lunged at the man who tried to hide behind Brady.

"Savannah, what are you doing?" Ridge asked as he tried to keep her away from him. "Look at his arms. Roll up his sleeves. I bet this is the man who attacked us."

Ridge went stiff next to her as he ordered Brady to hold him still. The man tried to hide his arms, but Ridge was able to pull one sleeve up. There was the evidence she knew would be there. Long nail marks down his forearm.

"Take him outside and tie him up. I'm calling Granger," Ridge said with barely contained anger. He should let it go. Savannah felt remarkably better after beating the crap out of her assailant.

"Granger, that man tried to attack Savannah again. He's the same guy who attacked both of us," Ridge was explaining as Brady shoved the man through the tunnel of workers and into the bedroom.

Suddenly the man twisted. Brady hollered and his crew blocked the door. The man's eyes were wild and Savannah saw red again. She screamed at the top of her lungs and charged. The man turned and ran straight through the closed window.

Glass shattered and some of the crew took off down the stairs to give chase. Ridge, Savannah, and Brady hurried to the window and looked out. "Asshole. He squashed my rhododendron," Savannah said in a huff. "Where is he? I'm going to kill him."

Men burst out the front door as Brady stepped onto the porch roof and looked over. "I don't think you'll need to kill him, ma'am."

All of Savannah's bravado fled as her shaky legs carried her downstairs so fast she jumped the bottom three stairs. Ridge and the rest of his men were right behind her. She went out the front door and down the steps and over to where her window was. Three crewmen stood staring at her rhododendron bush. Through their legs she saw the man's legs, and they weren't moving.

Savannah skidded to a stop and looked down at her attacker. "Oh my god, I killed him!"

## 18

RIDGE STARED down at the body of the man who had attempted to murder both him and Savannah. His neck was at a bad angle and a rhododendron branch stuck partially up his pant leg.

"Looks like he hit the bush and it messed up his jump. Basically tripped him in the air and sent him diving headfirst for the ground," Granger said with his hands on his hips.

"Do we need to call Olivia?" Ridge wondered out loud. Savannah was on the porch swing and his crew had turned into a group of mother hens when the first tear fell. Not that Ridge didn't feel the same way, but he could better help Savannah by dealing with the fallout of this man's death.

"No."

"Yes," Kord called out at the same time Granger answered.

Granger probably rolled his eyes behind the mirrored glasses. "There're so many witnesses who will say he jumped on his own that we don't need Olivia. But if you feel better about it, by all means call her," Granger said, turning to find the coroner from Charleston arriving. He talked to Granger for a moment before beginning to process the body.

"What I can't figure out is if someone is after you or her or both?" Granger told Ridge as he joined him again.

Ridge watched the coroner begin to work as Kord answered any questions that came up. "It has to be her. The man said he was paid to make her death look like an accident."

"Then where is Bunny and why is she missing?" Granger asked.

"You haven't had any luck with the credit cards?" Ridge knew the answer was no. Granger would have told him if there'd been a hit.

"No. Took forever to get the request in and she hasn't used them since the morning after the auction. She'd stayed at Bell Plantation, paid for her room, had breakfast at Stomping Grounds, got gas at Gil's, and hasn't been heard from since."

"Let me ask for some help. If we can find her and determine she's not responsible, then we can cross her off the list of suspects," Ridge said as he was already sending a text to Ryan.

*How legal do you want this search?* Ryan texted back.

*Faster would be better than legal,* Ridge told his cousin.

*I'll have our friend Kale do it then. You just won't be able to use it for evidence. Or tell anyone how you got it.*

"Ryan is having a friend look for Bunny. He said it'll be fast but not necessarily court-friendly." Ridge saw Granger's lips tighten. Granger liked everything to be legal, but he knew when it was better not to ask, and this was one of those times.

A text from a number Ridge didn't know with an 859 area code popped up after two minutes. It must be Kale.

*She's on a yacht with this guy. They're currently in the Bahamas. Do you need the exact coordinates? – Kale Mueez*

"Ask him how long she's been there," Granger asked, having read the text over Ridge's shoulder. Ridge tapped on the picture of a topless Bunny on a yacht with a man. "Isn't he that creep on that Southern reality show?"

Ridge nodded and then asked Kale how long they'd been on the yacht.

*They left Charleston at three in the afternoon the day after the bachelor auction. There's been no suspicious financial activity.* And attached was a time-stamped photo from the Charleston marina.

Granger shook his head. "I don't want to know how he got that."

*I hacked it, duh.*

Ridge and Granger stared at the text message from Kale that popped up.

"You're listening to us?" Ridge asked even as he felt stupid for doing so. Kale was in Kentucky. He couldn't be listening to them.

*Makes it easy to know what you want. Besides, everyone is listening to you. Social media, the government, even companies who want to data mine all your conversations to sell you that television you mentioned you wanted. It's not like it's hard to do. By the way, the girl's cute. Is she the one Walker was telling us about?*

"He's watching us too," Granger whispered, now completely weirded out.

"Yeah, that's her," Ridge replied.

*Let me know if you need anything else. I'm sure I'll meet you at the next Keeneston wedding. Peace out.*

"Who the hell was that?" Granger stated slowly as he covered the phone.

Ridge chuckled and shook his head. "You never know with my cousin. If he's a friend of the family, he's good."

"I wonder if he can get me things legally?" Granger asked with a shake of his head.

*Anytime. You have my number.*

Ridge laughed at Granger leaping back as if Kale were reaching through the phone to grab him. "That's just wrong," Granger said as he turned off his cell phone.

"Don't you need your phone?" Ridge asked as he tried to stop laughing at how freaked out Granger was.

"They can call me on the radio."

Ridge looked back at Savannah and the laughter stopped. The woman he was falling for was in trouble. "Do you think this will be the end of it?" Ridge asked Granger. Not only was Granger the sheriff, but he was Ridge's friend. And right now Ridge needed his friend the sheriff to be honest with him.

Granger's jaw tightened and Ridge was worried he had his answer. "Here's what I'm worried about. Who is after Savannah? Why? And will they realize this guy failed and send someone else after her?"

"Are you sure I'm not involved?"

Granger's lips thinned, and behind the mirrored sunglasses, Ridge was sure Granger's eyes were narrowed. "No. At this moment I'm not sure about anything."


SAVANNAH FINALLY STOPPED SHAKING. Brady and the guys on the crew were doing a good job of trying to distract her. The hot tea the guys had made for her helped too. But right now she felt dizzy, exhausted, and she couldn't stop trembling. All she really wanted was Ridge.

Savannah took a deep breath. She'd fought for her life, and she was still standing. The guys, the coroner, Kord, and Granger all told her she didn't kill that man. She didn't believe them. And right now she couldn't decide how she felt about that. The rage, the hurt, and the pure shock of hearing her life was only worth twenty thousand dollars had made her lose control. She'd never gone after a person like that before in her life, much less an assassin.

And why in hell would an assassin be after her? She was an unemployed ex-housewife with a small bank account, living in a small town. It wasn't as if she had life insurance that Penn wanted to get his grubby hands on. Was this Bunny crazed enough to kill her because she and Ridge were dating? Well, kinda. Savannah let out a long breath as she imagined the headline, "Killer Bunny on the Loose."

If this was all because some spoiled brat lost out on a man . . . well, this time Savannah was older and wiser. She knew the difference between men like Penn and Ridge. Ridge was worth fighting for.

Savannah watched Granger step away from Ridge as he pulled out his phone. There was lots of nodding and then he hung up and turned to her. Their eyes met immediately. As much as Savannah had wanted to be in his arms, as much as she had wanted to have all of his attention to herself, as much as she wished it was just the two of them, she knew she had to stay put and let him do his thing. He was taking care of her in his own way. Plus, Savannah had seen the look of utter desperation and fear on his face when the bathroom door had been ripped off.

The only thing Savannah worried about was if Ridge liked her for her or because she needed rescuing. Although, she smiled to herself, she rescued herself today. While her body trembled in the aftermath, she was proud of herself. The feelings she had for Ridge were different. She didn't think eighteen months would change things, but they had. She felt like a new person after the divorce. She was older, wiser, more mature, and focused on what really mattered in a relationship—love, trust, dependability, partnership, mutual respect, and support. She had that with Ridge. She knew it deep down to the bone. She still felt strong when he was away from her. She felt in charge. She wasn't afraid of messing up. She wanted to take chances. Because when it came down to it, this person she'd known for a week was more supportive and encouraging than Penn had ever been. And the knowledge that someone had your back was, well, freeing.

Savannah took a deep breath and stood up as Ridge began to walk over to her. She took the steps down to the grass and waited for him to reach her. "Thank you for handling the police for me."

Ridge didn't say anything. Instead, he simply opened his arms and wrapped her in them. Savannah let out a deep breath as she rested her cheek on his shoulder and hugged him back.

"That was the most terrifying moment of my life," Ridge said. His voice was rough with raw emotion.

Savannah didn't say anything as Ridge held her tightly against him.

"It's not Bunny."

At those three words, Savannah stopped breathing. She forced herself to swallow hard as she looked up at Ridge. His face was hard. His jaw was tight. The lines around his eyes and lips showed the stress he was feeling.

"How do you know?"

Ridge told her about what this guy named Kale had found out. Bunny hadn't spent money because she was on a yacht happily being petted by some douche from television.

"But if it's not Bunny, who is it?" Savannah felt the fear creeping back in. She had it under control when she knew the face behind it all. But now? She looked around at all the faces. It could be anyone.

Ridge felt her shiver and ran his hand up and down her back to warm her. "It's okay. We'll find out who's behind this. I'll keep you safe. I swear."

That was part of what Savannah was worried about. She wanted to be safe, but she wanted to be loved. She didn't want to be seen as a damsel in distress. She still had that nagging fear that Ridge was sticking around only to save her. But what happened after she was safe? Would he still want her then?

## 19

THE REST of the day was a blur as Savannah's house was cordoned off for the investigation. Kord had accompanied her upstairs to pack a bag and then she was escorted off the premises while everyone finished processing the crime scene.

Ridge had taken her back to his house and locked the doors. For the past hour, she'd been pacing while Ridge worked on sending his crew to another job site for a few days. They'd be back at Savannah's as soon as the crime scene tape was down.

There was the sound of footsteps behind her and Savannah turned around to see Ridge. His masculine face was filled with concern. "Sweetheart, is there anything I can do?"

Savannah let out a sigh and tapped her foot. "Let's go to dinner." The thought of getting out of the house perked her up. She was tired of feeling trapped. Trapped in her house. Trapped in Ridge's house. Trapped by fear. She was ready to be free. And to murder anyone who tried to take that away from her . . . again.

"I just put a pizza in the oven," Ridge said. The way his questioning eyes took her in told Savannah he felt her agitation.

"Then after dinner." Savannah walked over to Ridge and grabbed his hand in hers. "I can't let them take my freedom from me. I'm not going to stay locked up for days, weeks, or months on end until the person is caught. The man's dead. I'm not in danger anymore."

She could see Ridge hiding something from her when his eyes suddenly looked anywhere but at her. "What is it?" she asked.

"We don't know if the person who hired this man will just send another. So far Granger hasn't been able to find anything about the man who died today. He's a ghost."

Savannah put her hands on her hips. "And since when has this town been afraid of ghosts?"

Ridge finally cracked a smile. He took a deep breath and nodded. "We can go to Harper's for a drink after we have pizza. Half the town will be there and you'll be perfectly safe."

"So will you. I got your back, Ridge."

Savannah turned and as she was climbing the stairs she heard Ridge chuckle. Damsel in distress, her ass.

HARPER'S BAR WAS PACKED. No one noticed when she and Ridge slipped into the door and fought their way to the bar.

"It's time Shadows Landing had a mayor and there's no one more qualified than I. I'm a doctor and the head of the historical society. I'm tasked with protecting Shadows Landing's past and I am the perfect one to protect her future."

There were groans from the audience and she was pretty

sure Miss Winnie had just called the man talking a little prick.

"Who is that?" Savannah whispered as she looked at the man in loafers, khakis, a starched button-up shirt, dirt brown tie, and tweed jacket with elbow patches.

"Dr. Stephen Adkins," Ridge said with a roll of his eyes. "Although, he calls himself Stefan."

"What's he a doctor of?" Savannah asked, looking at him. He didn't look like any medical doctor she'd ever seen. Maybe pathology?

"He has a PhD in history. He's smart, but he's spent his whole life trying to leave Shadows Landing. He lost his accent and came back thinking he was superior. Education doesn't mean you're better than anyone else. Stephen doesn't see it that way."

Miss Ruby stood up and the room hushed. "We haven't had a mayor in our three hundred years and we don't need one now. We have a city council and it runs just fine."

Stephen scoffed and rolled his eyes. "Just fine? We don't even have a hotel."

"Young man," Miss Ruby said, and Savannah cringed.

"He's a dead man," Savannah whispered to Ridge, who smiled and nodded.

"Don't you talk to me as if your Yankee education suddenly made us all dumb. Unlike you, I have seen the charter that founded Shadows Landing. Our history is unique, but that's what it is—history. Our forepirates wanted Shadows Landing to be a safe haven. That's why we still have enough money for roads and upkeep with our low taxes. The money for this town is in the same account it's been in since the bank was built."

Ridge's lips brushed against Savannah's ear as he whispered, "The bank is next to the library, which used to be a brothel, and across from the courthouse so you could pull out money to bribe the judge and enjoy a tumble all in ten minutes."

Savannah snorted and then covered her mouth and nose with her hand to stop from laughing out loud.

"And I would love to see that document," Stephen said, stomping his foot like a child.

Miss Ruby smiled sweetly. "Maybe if you weren't such an asshole we'd give you the combination to the documents vault."

The whole bar laughed and Stephen turned red. "There's nothing in those documents saying we can't develop the town. That we can't bring in some national restaurants, some other banks, and some hotels."

"Actually, there is." Savannah recognized that heavy twang of Skeeter, who stood up with a beer in his hand. "It states that Shadows Landing should stay a sanctuary to its residents. All businesses must be owned by local residents and there is to be no more downtown expansion."

"There is no such thing," Stephen said with another roll of his eyes. "Pirates wouldn't have thought of fast food three hundred years ago."

"That's right, they didn't," Skeeter said but then smiled. "But the founding document calls for a review of the town rules and ordinances every one hundred years. The last review was done while you were up north. It was voted on and approved by a three-fourths majority town vote. So, in another ninety-three years you can challenge them."

"Here, here!" Miss Winnie stood up and thumped a large beer mug that looked to be filled with a Shirley Temple drink on her table. "I say we vote no to the mayor proposal and when my term is up on the city council, I nominate Skeeter to take my place."

"And if the measure does pass, I say we vote Skeeter for mayor," a young woman surrounded by countless children called out.

Skeeter blushed. "Thank you, Miss Lydia."

"Skeeter?" Stephen practically shrieked. "He didn't even go to college."

Lydia shifted the kid she was holding from one hip to the other and gave Stephen a glare that had everyone taking a step back.

"Uh-oh. Mommy has the Look. You're going into a timeout," a little boy with cowlicked hair said as his big brother pulled him close.

"Stephen Adkins, you have certainly lost your manners. You left Shadows Landing and don't think for one second we forgot that you never thought we were good enough for you. And when something goes wrong in this town, it's Skeeter who is the first one to show up offerin' to help. When Landry is on deployment, it's Skeeter, Turtle, Gator, and Junior at my house fixin' loose shingles, getting the gator out of the pool, or teaching Landry Junior how to ride his bike. It's not you. It's Skeeter who comes to the school and teaches the history of Shadows Landing. And it was Skeeter who helped Darcy and Wade find that treasure. A *Shadows Landing* treasure, which is exactly what Skeeter is to us. A treasure."

Everyone clapped and beer mugs were pounded on the tables. Gator put his fingers between his lips and let out a loud whistle. Skeeter turned redder than a beet but sent a sweet smile to Lydia.

"Skeeter! Skeeter!" the crowd began to chant.

"Skeeter for city council!" Harper yelled over the crowd. "Drinks on me!"

The place went nuts as Harper lined up over fifty glasses and began pouring beer after beer from the keg.

"Stupid idiots," Stephen muttered as he stormed out.

Ridge shook his head. "If Stephen didn't think everyone was beneath him and unbent enough to get to know people, I'm sure he wouldn't be such a bad guy. The trouble is he hated Shadows Landing growing up. Everyone knew that. He complained constantly. Since his return, it seems as if he hated not only Shadows Landing but everyone in it."

"Why did he come back?" Savannah asked.

"I think he thought he'd come back and everyone would bow down to his superior knowledge. He's a smart guy. But like I said, if he'd spent any time getting to know the residents, he'd see there're a lot of smart people here with knowledge in mechanics, arts, business, medicine, animals, history, and so much more. It's a shame really."

"Yo, cuz! I could use some help here," Harper called out.

"I'll help!" Savannah answered instead. The place was so alive and her fear was gone. Here, she could live. Here, she could be herself. Here, she could enjoy life.

"Start handing these out. Thanks, Savannah!"

Savannah grabbed three pints of beer and started on the far side of the room. Ridge grabbed some more and they worked together to get the free round of drinks handed out.

"I hear we missed the action," Ellery said after thanking Savannah for the beer. Ellery and Gavin were the last ones to get a drink as they had just arrived.

"Yes, it looks like Skeeter might be a politician."

"I was talking about you going all superhero and beating up the man attacking you," Ellery said before reaching out and gently touching Savannah's arm. "But how are you? I don't know if you know this or not, but my old boss attacked me and left me for dead. I understand the fear, the anger, and desire to forget all about it at the same time. Just know I'm here for you."

Savannah startled Ellery by throwing her arms around the woman's neck and hugging her. Because that was exactly how she was feeling. To hear that someone understood was the greatest gift Ellery could have given Savannah.

"Thank you. That helped more than you know."

Ellery hugged her back. When she pulled away, she told Savannah about a family dinner they were having in a couple days. "Will you two come?"

Savannah turned to look to where Ridge and Gavin were talking. "I'm sure we will, but I'll make sure Ridge doesn't have anything planned."

"Even if he does, you're welcome to come. I can pick you up if you need me to. Here, let me give you my number."

Ellery took Savannah's phone and entered her number as Gator took over the jukebox. Country music filled the bar as talks of the mayoral vote, Skeeter, and Bubba the alligator's latest antics filled the room.

Savannah took a deep breath as a smile naturally came over her face. This was *home*. This was where she belonged. She glanced over to where Ridge was now talking basketball with Quad Clemmons, who she'd learned was a standout high school athlete. Ridge talked to everyone with his full attention. He treated everyone with respect, from the oldest woman to the youngest little boy. Savannah's heart filled as the little boy with the cowlick came over and tugged on Ridge's shirt. Ridge bent down and scooped the boy up into his arms as he talked to Quad.

"He's a good one, you know," Ellery said quietly as if she didn't want to startle Savannah from her observations. She liked Ridge. She'd even been in lust with Ridge. But this was more. This was respect. This was trust. And when Ridge turned to her as if hearing her heart calling to him and smiled, Savannah knew this was love.

"Yes, he is." Savannah found the freedom of embracing her feelings comforted her like a warm blanket wrapping her in love.

RIDGE TALKED to Quad about the upcoming high school basketball season as he kept an eye on Savannah. She was talking to Ellery and had a happy little smile on her face that made Ridge feel better than anything else.

"Mr. Ridge?"

Ridge looked down and smiled at Lydia's youngest son, Leo. At four years old he was teetering between toddler and little boy. He still had chubby cheeks and thick legs that let him run all over, terrorizing his six older siblings and causing his mother to have an untold number of panic attacks.

"Yes, Leo?" Ridge asked as he bent down and scooped the boy up into his arms.

"Do you think that lady over there is pretty? My momma said she was and that she was your cigarette lover."

Quad bit his lower lip to keep from laughing as Ridge looked over at Savannah and smiled. "I think you mean significant other."

"That's what I said, Mr. Ridge. Is she your cigarette lover?"

"I'll let you in on a little secret since it's just us men talking," Ridge told Leo with very manly seriousness to his face. Even Quad stepped closer to make sure he heard the gossip. "I think she's the prettiest woman I've ever seen, and I hope she does become my significant other."

Leo nodded solemnly. "I swear I won't tell anyone but

my momma. She told me I'm never ever allowed to keep secrets from her."

"That's a very good rule," Quad told him. "And I'm sure Mr. Ridge agrees."

"Very much. Why don't you go whisper it to her now?" Ridge set Leo down and watched him bulldoze his way through the crowded bar. "Did you tell your mom everything?"

"Hell no," Quad laughed. "She'd send me out to pick a switch right now if she knew half the stuff I've done."

Quad looked nervously over at his mother. Quad's mother wore her black hair short and natural. Her dark skin was still smooth even in her late forties. She was in a suit, having just come from her job at the bank and didn't look like someone who could control a six foot, seven inch athletic high school boy.

"Your mom is so nice. She wouldn't do that," Ridge said with a laugh.

Quad's eyes went large. "Are you kidding me? She scares the bejeezus out of me. She gets this look and I tell you, it'll will make your balls shrivel up and drop off."

Ridge laughed and then looked over at Savannah.

"Man, you have it bad," Quad said, shaking his head. "That's the way all the girls look at me."

Ridge rolled his eyes and Quad laughed. "I'll tell your mom you're making fun of me."

Quad's laughter died instantly. "Not cool. Don't scare a man like that."

It was Ridge's turn to laugh. "Make sure you tell me when the first game of the season is. I think I'm going to take my girl home. Something your mom won't let you do yet."

"That's so cold," Quad chuckled. "I'll text ya the game schedule."

Ridge smiled at the people he passed but his eyes were locked on Savannah. As soon as he reached her he slipped his arm around her waist and pressed a kiss to her cheek. "Are you ready to go home?" he whispered into her ear. There was nothing better than the feeling of her in his arms.

"More than ready."

Ridge was sure even Mrs. Clemmons's famous glare wouldn't cause him to shrivel at this moment.

## 20

RIDGE OPENED the door to his house for Savannah as they walked into the kitchen from the garage. She turned on the lights and went to open a bottle of wine. She fit so perfectly here, in his kitchen and in his life.

The only thing holding him back from making a move was his worry that it wasn't the right time. And yet, the events of the past week had shown him that you had to live in the now because you never knew what was going to happen. If something did happen to him, would he wish he'd had even one day with Savannah? Yes.

"Savannah," Ridge said as he took down two glasses and set them on the island next to where she fiddled with the bottle of wine.

"Ridge," Savannah said at the same time as they both laughed.

"Go ahead," Ridge offered. He could admit to himself he was nervous and every second gave him the chance to come up with the best speech possible to make Savannah see him as something more than only a man who was good with a hammer.

Savannah was quiet as she poured the two glasses of wine and then handed him one. Ridge waited patiently as he thought of a million things to say to her but they all fell short.

"Will you spend the night with me?" Savannah finally asked.

Ridge almost sighed. He couldn't. It was torture to hold her when he wanted to tell her how he felt. What he thought of her. What he hoped they could have together. But he'd never deny her anything for as much as he was tortured to hold her, he was equally tortured not to have his arms around her.

"Of course. You're afraid to be alone after this week. I completely understand."

Savannah shook her head. "I'm not afraid to be alone. And I don't need comforting. I need you, Ridge. After the other night, you have to know how I feel about you. I don't want you to stop tonight. I want you, Ridge. All of you."

Ridge almost choked on his wine. Words fled from his mind as he set his wine glass down and stepped forward until they were toe to toe. Savannah nibbled nervously on her lower lip and Ridge reached up and brushed his thumb softly against it. When her mouth opened in a silent gasp, Ridge moved his thumb to her chin and raised her lips to his.

It started off slowly. A brush of the lips to give her time to back away, but she didn't. Instead, Savannah reached up and ran her fingers through the hair at the back of his neck and pulled him closer. Ridge didn't hold back. He used his body to guide Savannah's against the kitchen island as his lips never left hers.

Her hands moved from his neck to his shirt, and he

broke free of the kiss as she yanked his shirt off over his head.

"Ridge, tell me I'm not the only one who has these feelings." Savannah's hands were running down his muscled chest as she spoke. And while Ridge had to rein in his control, he heard the vulnerability in her voice.

Ridge reached down and cupped her cheeks in his hands. She looked up at him and he was lost. "You're never alone. Not with me. We can stop if you'd like. I should wait a while, give you time."

Savannah shook her head. "No, I don't want more time. I've had years of misery and loneliness. But with you there's only happiness. Even with all that has happened. It's taught me to never take tomorrow for granted."

Ridged nodded and instead of nerves he felt joy as he brushed his thumb over her cheek and smiled down at the woman who had his heart. "I'll never take you or our time together for granted. Savannah, I love you."

Tears filled her eyes and Ridge's nerves came racing back. Shoot, he should have waited to tell her. He was just living in the here and now and she was so beautiful as she opened herself to him.

"I'm sorry," he rushed to say.

Savannah grabbed his wrists as she barely shook her head in his hands. "Oh, Ridge. I love you too. With how my life is going, I just thought I didn't deserve such happiness. But I do. And so do you. I love you, Ridge Faulkner, with all my heart."

Ridge was sure his heart was going to swell right out of his chest, but sometimes words were not needed. This was one of those times. He tilted Savannah's face up toward his and kissed her reverently. But when her tongue slid across the crease of his lips, Ridge was lost.

He'd planned for a slow, sweet worshipping of her, but Savannah had other plans and he would not deny her. Her hand ran down his chest, over his abs, and then she unbuttoned his pants as he kicked off his shoes while fumbling with the buttons on her shirt.

The kiss became more demanding the longer it took to remove all their clothes. And by the time they were both naked, they were breathing heavily as he picked her up and placed her on the counter.

SAVANNAH DIDN'T EVEN NOTICE the cold stone against her skin when Ridge lifted her onto the kitchen island. She was too lost in the heat of the moment. The love in her heart and the passion they shared consumed her. Ridge was making love to her mouth with his tongue as he pulled her closer to the edge of the island and laid her back. His hands ran up her rib cage and cupped her breasts, his fingers rolling her nipples until she was arching off the counter.

Savannah moaned into his mouth as he leaned over her. His fingers wreaked havoc upon her senses before pulling back. She opened her eyes that she didn't realize she'd closed and saw Ridge opening the drawer of a built-in desk. He pulled out a condom and then turned to her with a questioning look.

In answer Savannah held out her arms to him.

"Love me, Ridge," she told him as he stepped between her legs.

"I already do."

RIDGE HAD TO LEAVE. Tinsley was at an art gallery that was

interested in displaying her work. Trent was busy putting the finishing touches on some pieces of new furniture that were being featured in some big magazine. Ryker was in Charleston. Gavin had patients. Ellery was at her gallery in Charleston. Wade and Darcy were still on their honeymoon, and Ryker's security team was coming any moment.

"Harper," he said as his cousin sleepily answered her phone. "Can you come over and stay with Savannah while I go to Mount Pleasant for a meeting I've put off as long as I can?"

Harper snorted. "Ridge, Savannah beat the shit out of an assassin and literally scared him so much he jumped out of a window to get away from her. I think she's fine. She's not a child nor is she a poodle that needs to be house sat."

"Maybe it's not for her," Ridge confessed even though Harper made him feel like a total heel for it.

"You'll have to leave her at some point. No relationship can work if you're attached at the hip every minute of every day."

Maybe she had a point, but he wasn't going to admit that to Harper. "As if you have relationship experience."

Harper sighed. "I know you're worried about her. I know you like her. I know all of that, but Ridge, her ex was a dick who didn't let her decide anything. So, how about this? You ask her if she wants me there. If she does, all she has to do is call me and I'll be right over. Deal?"

Ridge was quiet for a moment as he looked out of his office and saw Savannah sipping on her coffee. He hated it when he was wrong, but he was man enough to admit when he was. "You're right." Ridge let out a sigh and sat down in his office chair. "I just want to protect her."

"I know you do. Your intentions were good. It's just your execution that's sloppy," Harper told him.

"I can't wait until a man comes along and makes you all starry-eyed. It's going to be fun to see," Ridge said as he smiled and chuckled softly.

"Not going to happen. I like being in control too much."

"There is that dominatrix club—"

Harper snorted. "I also don't see me with a man crawling around on his hands and knees asking to be spanked."

"To each her own," Ridge said, laughing now.

"As long as he's not mine."

"You know, Granger —"

"Seriously?" Harper cut him off. "Granger is like a brother to us. Just, no. Eww. And stop playing matchmaker. Just because you're all lovey-dovey doesn't mean I need to be. I am happy for you. I like Savannah."

"Me too. I'll have her call you if she needs you. Thanks, Harp."

"What are cousins for?"

Ridge smiled as he hung up and walked to the kitchen. Savannah was looking out the windows while wearing one of his old T-shirts. The sun shone on her red hair, making it glow as if it were gold. It was an image he'd remember all day while he was away. Especially when Savannah looked up at him and smiled.

"I have a confession to make," Ridge confided as he leaned against the same island he'd made love to her on last night. "I asked Harper to come stay with you while I'm away today."

"Okay," Savannah said slowly.

"I was so concerned about protecting you that I didn't think to ask what you wanted. All my instincts say to protect you at all costs, but I forgot to ask you. I'm sorry."

. . .

SAVANNAH BLINKED. There were no words. Instead she sprang up, sloshing her coffee over the rim as she set it down and flung herself at Ridge. He instantly caught her as she squeezed him tight.

"Thank you," she whispered.

"You shouldn't thank me."

But she should. "I really appreciate it. You didn't have to tell me. But I'm so glad you did. We're learning this new relationship together, and I want nothing but honesty between us."

"Then I should tell you I'm scared to death to leave you." Ridge kissed her forehead and pulled her tight against his chest.

"I know, but I'm not, not anymore. I'm not afraid. I've been thinking about it. First I was so upset that I killed someone. But I didn't. I didn't push him out that window. And he was trying to kill me! Should I have let him so I wouldn't feel bad that he might be hurt when I was defending myself?" Savannah pulled away from Ridge. This had been on her mind most of the night. Well, when they weren't making love. "And what I've decided is I'm not sorry. He was a bad person who has killed people before and would continue to do so if I hadn't stopped him."

"You did nothing wrong," Ridge said, but she didn't need to hear it because she finally knew it.

"I know. And that's why I don't want Harper or anyone else here with me. I want to study up on Darcy's treasure so I can be ready for an interview when she gets home, and I can oversee the security installation too."

Ridge nodded, but he didn't tell her no. Instead, he pulled out his phone. "I'm texting you the security information Ryker sent me—names and photos of the people doing the installation. Make sure you have them teach you how to use it so you can teach me. And make sure you get two keys, know the codes, and so on. I want this to be your place for as long as you want it to be."

The way his voice trailed off, Savannah knew there was more he wanted to say but had stopped himself from doing so. "Honesty, remember. What else?"

"If you could, I'd appreciate a text or two from you today. Not because I want to know where you are, but because I just want to make sure you're okay."

Savannah rose up on her toes and placed a kiss on his lips. "I know. And I'll text you. Maybe even something extra special."

"I'd like that," Ridge said before bending down and kissing her deeply, then pulled away. "I have to go. I'll see you this afternoon."

"Love you."

"Love you too." And just like that, Savannah felt their relationship change. Not in a bad way. Just as if they took a step closer to something permanent. She waved goodbye as he drove off while her mind and heart processed the shift. Then with a smile, she closed the garage door and walked back into the house. It felt right. She was afraid it was too soon, but it didn't feel rushed. It felt right. Like she had a partner standing beside her now. She didn't have much time to think about it, though, as Ryker's security team showed up before she could finish her coffee.

## 21

THE SECURITY PEOPLE had gone over the system until Savannah was completely comfortable with it and could explain it just as well as they did. It gave her confidence as she closed the door on them and armed it.

Taking a deep breath, she felt powerful. She knew what she wanted and she was going after it. Savannah took her laptop out into the back garden. Her phone buzzed, an alert that the security camera sensed motion. No one was going to sneak up on her, that was for sure.

Savannah opened her laptop and got to work reading about the shipwreck and the treasure found, and was soon lost in the history of it all. She didn't know how long she'd been working when the phone buzzed again.

There was a notification of motion near the front door. Savannah tapped it and up came a live feed of the front yard and a second close-up view of the front door. Miss Winnie, Miss Ruby, and a man who looked to be in his late forties were getting out of their cars. Looked like it was time for a break.

Savannah arrived at the front door the same time they

did. "Good morning." Savannah smiled out to them after she opened the door.

"Oh, you poor dearie," Miss Winnie clucked. "You're nothing but skin and bones."

"Isn't Ridge feeding you?" Miss Ruby asked as they walked right on by and headed for the kitchen.

Savannah looked down at herself and was pretty sure she'd put on ten pounds since moving to Shadows Landing. She looked up and her eyes met the kindest pair of deep brown eyes she'd ever seen. The man wasn't overly tall. His black hair was in soft coils on the top of his head and the sides were shaved, making it seem as if they faded right into his umber skin.

"I hope you don't mind that I came along. I'm Reverend Floyd Winston," he said as he shook her hand. "I thought after going through what you did, you might want to talk about it."

Savannah didn't really want to talk about it, but this was a new Savannah. She was going to be open. Be trusting. Not hide things when they or she weren't perfect. In short, Savannah was going to be herself.

"That would be nice, thank you." Savannah looked into the kitchen where Miss Winnie and Miss Ruby were pulling out things from the pantry. "Do I need to help them?"

"Oh no. They're just making you a little something. Come, let's sit out in the garden and talk."

It FELT strange unburdening herself to a stranger, but Reverend Winston made her feel safe instantly. He wasn't judgmental, even when she told him about Ridge and her taking their relationship to the next level. Finally, she took a deep breath and let it out. "I think that's everything."

Reverend Winston smiled kindly and reached over to rest his hand on hers. "I feel very strongly you are where you're supposed to be. You're a very brave woman, Savannah. It's not easy leaving a relationship as you did, but you're spreading your wings now. You're taking control of your life and that should be commended."

The reverend paused, and she thanked him for listening.

"Have you heard the story of Shadows Landing?" he asked.

"I've read some of it. About how the pirates settled the town and turned it into a haven of sorts," she told him. She'd been reading about it this morning.

"That's right. And it's not just a haven for pirates. It's a haven for all who need it. You've found us just as you're getting ready to fly on your own, I have just the thing to help you take off."

"What's that?" Savannah asked as she leaned forward.

"What do you know about weaponry?" Reverend Winston asked seriously.

Savannah blinked. She'd expected a Bible study or something. "Weaponry?"

"Every Saturday morning we have a women's class at the church."

Savannah suddenly felt very stupid as she stared at the reverend. "You have a women's Bible study or a weapons class?"

Reverend Winston chuckled. "Both actually. Bible study at nine and weapons at ten." Savannah just stared. Her brain was having trouble processing it. "See, you know the town was founded by pirates. Well, so was the church. And while their men were off raiding the oceans, the women were left alone. Before the pirates left, they taught their women how to defend themselves. It's a tradition that continues to this day. The women of Shadows Landing are formidable."

"Oh, you have self-defense classes. I'd like that." Savannah smiled then as the door opened and Miss Winnie stuck her head out.

"Pie's ready."

"Good, I'll see you Saturday."

The inside of the house smelled like hot apple pie as she walked Reverend Winston to the front door.

"This smells amazing," Savannah told the two women after the reverend left.

"Homemade apple pie can fix anything," Miss Winnie told her.

"Even killing someone," Miss Ruby added.

"Now, we have to get going," Miss Winnie said, pulling out her phone. "Give us your number and I'll text us so we all have it. That way if you need anything you can just call or text us."

Savannah gave Miss Winnie her phone number as Miss Ruby cut a piece of the pie and placed a scoop of vanilla ice cream on top of it.

"Here you go," Miss Winnie said. Both Savannah's and Miss Ruby's phones beeped.

"Thank you both so much. I am going to take a photo of this and tease Ridge. He'll be jealous that I get hot apple pie," Savannah told them before she hugged both women.

"Men will do anything for some good apple pie," Miss Ruby said with a sly smile and a wink to Miss Winnie.

Um, okay. Savannah just shrugged off the strange comment as she showed them to the door. "Thank you again. I can't wait to eat it."

"You're welcome. Will we see you on Saturday?" Miss Winnie asked as they walked out the front door.

"Saturday? Oh, do you go to the self-defense class?"

They both gave each other that same sly smile again before Miss Ruby turned to her. "It's as unforgettable as a good apple pie. Hope to see you there."

"I think I will. Bye!" Savannah called out as the old ladies began laughing as they walked to their car.

Savannah closed the door and locked it. She headed to the kitchen and looked at the perfect apple pie and bit her bottom lip. Did she dare? Savannah looked out the window and saw the ladies driving away. She closed the blinds and took a deep breath before pulling her shirt off over her head.

Ridge wanted her to text him. Well, text him she would. She pushed down her shorts and stood in the kitchen in nothing but her bra and panties before looking around one more time and then removing them. Savannah eyed the island where they'd had the best sex of her life and now sat an apple pie and smiled. She knew exactly what she was going to send.

Savannah moved the pie and the plate with the slice on it to the edge of the island closest to the table where she set up her cell phone. She set the timer and then ran to the other side of the island and climbed up. She stretched out on her side with her head propped up in one of her hands. She tilted the pie up to cover her hoohah and used her arm and the plate with the slice of pie on it to cover her breasts. Savannah bit her lower lip right as the camera took the picture.

Savannah clambered down and nervously pulled up the picture. "Oh!" she gasped as she realized she looked like a naughty cover of a cooking magazine. And it looked . . . hot.

Okay, she could do this. Savannah didn't breathe as she quickly pulled up her text, attached the picture and wrote,

*Just lying here waiting for you to eat me.* Then she added the apple pie emoji, and before she could think twice, Savannah sent it.

Letting out the breath she'd been holding, Savannah set down the phone and pulled on her clothes while she nervously waited to see Ridge's reply.

Her phone dinged and Savannah almost tripped over her own feet to see what Ridge typed.

*Oh sweetie, you don't have to try that hard when you have good apple pie.*

What? Oh no, no, no, no!

Savannah's breathing stopped as she looked upward from the text to see it wasn't Ridge she'd texted but Miss Winnie and Miss Ruby. She was going to die. Right here. This was going to kill her when the assassin couldn't.

With shaking fingers Savannah sent them a text apologizing for sending it to them. Miss Ruby replied with a laughing face emoji and Miss Winnie with an apple pie emoji followed by a heart eyes emoji followed by an engagement ring emoji. Yup, Savannah was ready to die right now, this second.

Savannah groaned and buried her head in her hands right as her phone dinged again. Nope, no way was she going to look at it. She turned, found the open bottle of wine in the fridge, and was drinking straight from it when the garage door opened.


Savannah gasped and spun toward Ridge. Her face was red, her eyes wide, and the look she had was the same as if a child had been caught sneaking a cookie from the cookie jar. Ridge glanced around the kitchen and relaxed when he saw nothing out of place. But he smelled it. It smelled so good.

"Hmm, apple pie. I love apple pie."

Savannah groaned and tipped the wine bottle up to her lips and drank.

"Am I missing something? Do you have a strong dislike for apple pie?"

Savannah might have groaned again but he couldn't tell between that and the chugging sound.

"I take it Miss Winnie and Miss Ruby were here?" Ridge asked as he closed the door and set down his bag. "They know how much I love apple pie."

"They know way too much now," Savannah said, slamming the bottle onto the counter and using the back of her hand to wipe her mouth.

"Okay, I know I am missing something. What's going on? Did you get in a fight with two old ladies over apple pie?" Ridge teased but the look of horror on Savannah's face had his smile dropping instantly. "Oh my god, you didn't beat up two old ladies, did you?"

"No. It's worse," Savannah groaned as she picked up the wine bottle again.

"I don't understand. What could be worse than beating up two little old ladies?" Ridge asked slowly as she stepped to the other side of the island. It was hard not to reach for the slice of apple pie with melted ice cream on it.

Savannah picked up her phone and turned it toward him. "This! This is worse."

Ridge looked down and instantly forgot about the pie. There was a picture of a naked Savannah stretched out on his counter and it was the hottest thing he'd seen, and that was saying something considering what they'd done on that island the night before.

"Wow," he said, taking a deep breath. The thought of shoving the apple pie from the island and feasting on

Savannah definitely did more than cross his mind as he smiled at the picture. "This is so sexy."

Ridge finally looked up from the picture at Savannah's freaked-out face. Did she not think he'd like it? He didn't like it. He *loved* it! If he could, he'd print off a poster of it to hang in his office.

One look at Savannah's face made him realize she must be insecure about taking it. Maybe embarrassed. But she shouldn't be. "Sweetheart, this is amazing. Thank you so much for taking this for me and don't worry, no one else will ever see it. But if you want I can delete it."

"Too late now! You're not the only one to see it." Savannah took a gulp of wine and Ridge suddenly felt angry. He didn't want anyone else to see this. This was his. She was his.

"What do you mean I'm not the only one who's seen this? If my cousin walked in—" Savannah shook her head and groaned again. "Granger? Kord?"

"Worse," she said, covering her face with her hands. "Exit out and you'll see," she mumbled through her fingers.

Ridge clicked Done above the photo and suddenly he found himself in a group chat. Oh shit! He looked at the names and instead of being mad he burst out laughing. "You *sexted* Miss Winnie and Miss Ruby?"

"Don't laugh!" Savannah yelled through her fingers covering her face. "I'm mortified!"

Ridge looked down at the text and read it. First, he went instantly hard at her text and then he had to bite his lip to stop from laughing. He felt horrible for Savannah, really, he did, but he'd been so worried she'd sent it to her ex or to any man for that matter, but finding out it went to the two old church ladies had him biting his lip harder to make sure he wasn't laughing out loud.

"Does this mean I don't get to eat some apple pie?" Ridge finally asked as seriously as he could.

Savannah gasped, threw the dishtowel at him, and then broke down in gut-wrenching peals of laughter. Tears seeped from her eyes as she shook her head. "I can't believe I sent a nude picture to Miss Winnie and Miss Ruby!"

"Thank goodness you sent it to them and not me. I would have wrecked the car when I saw this." Ridge licked his lips as Savannah straightened up and wiped the tears of laughter from her eyes. "But now I find myself very hungry for some pie."

He reached out for her and she giggled. That giggling stopped when he reached past her and grabbed the slice of pie. Savannah gasped in indignation as he took a bite. "Mmm. But not as good as you."

"Oh!" Savannah threw another dishtowel at him and laughed.

"Come on, I want what you texted me."

"Not after that." Savannah giggled as she jumped out of his reach. Before long, he was chasing her around the house as they both laughed so hard they were out of breath.

"You caught me," she said when she could breathe again.

"And in the bedroom. Imagine that," Ridge said, leaning forward and brushing a trail of kisses up her neck. Savannah's head tilted to the side, and he kissed his way up to her ear as his hands cupped her breasts while he ran his thumbs over her pebbled nipples. "I think I should get a reward for catching you."

"Oh yeah. What kind of reward?" Savannah said. Ridge loved the catch in her breath as he teased her nipples and gently nibbled on her earlobe.

"Pie," he whispered before lowering her to the bed and taking his fill.

## 22

SAVANNAH'S HOME had been cleared, and Ridge had his crew back to work on her house after just two days off. Savannah was right next to him as she worked on her phone, preparing for her interview with Darcy the next week.

The night before had been amazing and it seemed impossible that there was still a cloud hanging over them, especially when they were so happy. But there was a cloud. A deadly one.

It had been quiet for two days. No attacks. No strange people snooping around. Nothing setting off the motion detectors except Bubba crawling through the yard that morning. And right about now, having Bubba as a patrol gator didn't sound too bad to Ridge.

The trouble was, as great as life had been those past two days, it wouldn't be permanent until whoever hired the hitman was taken care of. At the sound of someone turning into the drive, both he and Savannah turned.

"It's Granger. I wonder if he has any news," Savannah asked, echoing his thoughts.

"We can only hope." Ridge clasped his hand with hers

and they greeted Granger as a united front. "Have you learned anything?"

Granger's tightly pressed lips told him the answer. "Nothing. Fingerprints were removed or so altered there was no way to run them. This guy was a pro. We got his phone, but haven't been able to hack into it. I've called and begged the phone's developer to give us information on this serial number." Granger handed a sticky note with a long number on it to Ridge. "But they just laughed at me. I even got a court order from the judge, but it's not looking promising."

Granger paused and took off his mirrored glasses. Hard lines were set on his face, and Ridge knew whatever he was thinking he wouldn't like it. "Tibbie called. I found out Pepper has become *persona non* grata in both Atlanta and Charleston society after a sex tape was released. One she didn't take. Neither did the man she was riding while wearing her pageant crown. It was shot through a window, but it was enough for society to turn their backs on her. Tibbie said she heard Pepper was always just a follower of Ginger's. Now apparently she's in New York, trying to pitch a reality show. No one has really seen Ginger in almost a year. They say she's at some European spa getting plastic surgery."

"So, nothing to go on there," Ridge said with a sigh.

"Tibbie learned that everyone thinks Penn is a prick and they all love Savannah. Penn's lost some accounts after his cheating got out. But they still put up with him because he's making them money." Granger took off his hat and ran his fingers through his hair. "Right now all *legal* channels are failing."

"What does that mean?" Savannah asked as her grip tightened on Ridge's hand.

"It means my hands are tied. I can't *legally* access the

phone to attempt to find out who hired him. I am at an impasse on your case."

Ridge's gaze locked on Granger's. Granger didn't waver as he kept looking right at Ridge. "*Legally*, nothing more can be done at this point."

But *illegally*? Yeah, something could be done and he knew just the person to call. "Thank you for all you could do, Granger. I'm sure something will turn up."

"Let me know if it does." Granger slipped his sunglasses on, tipped his cowboy hat to Savannah, and left.

"What did all that mean?" Savannah asked as they watched Granger pull out of the driveway.

"It means Granger's hands are tied by the law so if we want info, we need to break the law. And he can't be a part of it."

Ridge was already pulling out his phone.

"How exactly are we going to break the law?" Savannah asked.

"We're going to have someone do it for us."

*I need your help,* Ridge typed and sent to Kale Mueez.

*I'm unavailable until tonight. Will call you then unless it's an emergency.*

Damn. Ridge wanted this taken care of now, but it could wait until tonight. *Talk to you tonight. Thank you.*

"Are you sure we should be doing this?" Savannah asked quietly.

"I'll do anything to keep you safe. Anything." Ridge kissed her to try to reassure her. "Kale is a friend of my cousin who is in the FBI. He's not dangerous."

Savannah nodded then and looked a little more relieved. "And you think he's good enough to hack this guy's phone?"

Ridge looked down at the serial number in his hand. "Let's hope so."

RIDGE HADN'T WANTED to go to Gavin's that night, but there he was. He would have preferred to be at home with Savannah in his bed. But when Savannah had come into his room dressed in a cute pair of shorts and a top and all excited about the family BBQ, he couldn't say no. It was time to let Savannah shine in her new home town. Her top was the color of sunshine and the setting sun made her hair glow. She looked like a goddess among the mortals.

"How are you doing?" Gavin asked, bringing him a beer.

Ridge took it and grunted. They were all standing out back at Gavin and Ellery's house. The river ran down behind them and a nice breeze was rolling off it and sending the smoke from the BBQ toward them. It made Ridge's mouth water as they waited for the BBQ to finish cooking.

"That well, huh? Wanting to hole up at your house with Savannah?"

"Exactly," Ridge admitted to his cousin.

"I know how you feel. It's natural to want to protect her."

Ridge turned to Gavin. It was hard to remember that he'd gone through something similar. Now he and Ellery were the picture of marital bliss. "How did you do it? How did you ever let her leave the house again after what you went through?"

"I told myself she needed to fly to beat her fears. I handled it because I knew I would always catch her if she fell," Gavin said softly as he stared at his wife, his face full of love.

"Thanks," Ridge told him as he looked back at where Savannah and Harper were laughing. He watched as Tinsley and Ellery joined them and relaxed. Savannah fit in with his family effortlessly and something about that made him fall for her a little more.

"So, this man is like a hacker genius?" Harper asked Savannah.

"That's what I got from it. He operates outside the law," Savannah told the Faulkner women around her.

"That is hot. Like seriously hot," Harper said, fanning herself as everyone laughed.

"Please, that's much more my speed. A dorky guy behind a computer," Tinsley told them. "You're a more muscled badass-on–a-motorcycle kind of woman."

Harper held up her hands. "You caught me. But come on, hacker boy sounds like a bad boy and that's much more my speed than yours."

Tinsley shrugged as if saying I don't know.

"Does he have a cool name?" Ellery asked. "Like Night Hawk or something like that?"

They all laughed again and Savannah shook her head. "Kale."

Tinsley and Harper instantly stopped laughing while Ellery cracked up even more. "Like a killer salad? Oh my gosh, I'm dying." Then she paused and looked at Harper and Tinsley. "Why aren't you laughing?"

"It can't be," Tinsley said to Harper, ignoring Savannah and Ellery.

"It has to be," Harper replied.

Tinsley turned to Savannah and asked, "Did he give you a last name?"

"Yeah," Savannah told them. "Easy, no Muse, no—"

Harper gulped. "Mueez?"

Savannah snapped her fingers. "Yes, that's it." She

paused and then looked at them. "Do you know him or something?"

"His sister, Abby, is married to our cousin, Dylan Davies. They're both like Special Forces or something," Tinsley said, looking curiously at Harper.

"So, a hot Special Forces hacker," Ellery said, nodding slowly. "Yup, totally Harper's kind of thing."

"But that's the thing. He was introduced to us as a grad student," Tinsley told them.

"And while he is hot, he's not Special Forces hot. Not a tattoo to be seen," Harper told them expertly.

"He is muscled, though. Maybe he's undercover?" Tinsley wondered out loud.

"His dad and sister are like superheroes. Of course, some of that has rubbed off, but he's definitely not a soldier," Harper said with confidence.

Savannah held up her hands. "Hold on. Why didn't Ridge know him?"

"Ridge didn't go to Dylan's wedding. He was the keynote speaker at some big conference that weekend. But Harper and I went and we met him," Tinsley told them.

"So, is he hot?" Ellery asked the important question.

"Totally," Harper confirmed. "But not bad boy enough for me."

All eyes turned to Tinsley. "Too young for us both. He's like twenty-five or something."

Ellery nudged Savannah. "Notice she didn't say he wasn't hot?"

Tinsley blushed as Savannah laughed. "Fine, he's hot. But my artsy side would make his brain explode."

The woman all laughed and Savannah's eyes drifted to where Ridge was joking with his cousins. He glanced over at her and smiled before his cousins started teasing him. Only he didn't look worried about it. Instead, he laughed and turned once more to give her a wink.

"Aren't they cute?" Tinsley smiled happily as she clasped her hands.

Harper rolled her eyes but didn't say anything while Ellery nodded her head in agreement. "He makes me happy. He makes me feel . . ." Savannah struggled to find the right word. "More."

But before she heard what the women were going to say, Ridge looked down at his phone and then looked immediately to her. "It's Kale."

"Go," Tinsley shooed.

"And then tell us everything!" Ellery called after her.

Savannah hurried over to where Ridge was holding the back door open for her. "One second, Kale. Savannah and I are just stepping inside."

Savannah went through the door into a kitchen that was cool with the house's air conditioning and filled with trays of food. "Hi, Kale. I'm Savannah. How is your sister, Abby?"

Kale chuckled over the phone as Ridge shot her a questioning look. "I didn't know you knew the family."

"Tinsley and Harper were just telling me about Abby's wedding to their cousin Dylan. They sound like a neat couple," Savannah said as her eyes didn't leave Ridge's face. She saw the moment he made the connection and rolled his eyes at himself as he shook his head.

"They are. They're out of the country at the moment on business. I'm sure they're having fun," Kale told them.

"The conferences I went to were never fun," Ridge said dryly.

"Eh. You're not overthrowing a dictator," Kale said, and Savannah couldn't tell if he was joking or not. "But anyway, what did you need?"

"We have a problem," Granger told him.

"A Bunny problem?" Kale asked and Savannah tried not to snicker.

"A someone-is-trying-to-kill-me problem," Savannah answered for Ridge.

"That's interesting. Why is someone trying to kill you?"

Savannah shrugged as if Kale could see her. "That's why I called," Ridge said, taking a deep breath. "The sheriff here is our friend."

"Granger Fox."

"That's right. You saw him and listened to him when you hacked my phone," Ridge explained. "Well, he's out of legal options to get some answers. We thought Bunny was behind the attempts of harming us, but after you told us she was on a yacht, we turned our direction to finding out who hired the man that tried to kill Savannah."

"What man?" Kale asked.

"We thought for sure Bunny was behind it, but a man tried to kill Savannah and he told her he'd been paid for it. We thought it was Bunny."

"What did the man say during interrogation?" Kale asked.

Savannah cringed. "Well, he kinda jumped out of a window to escape me and died."

"Gotcha," Kale said. "You need to find the contract and trace it back to who is behind it all."

"Exactly. The man has a phone on him, but Granger is out of legal options to unlock it," Ridge explained.

"Ridge, hand your phone to Savannah," Kale ordered and Savannah took the phone from him. "Smile."

She smiled but didn't know why. "Why would you have me smile?"

"I just took your picture. I'm going to run it through

some software to see what I can find on the dark web. And the wanted lists. People post the darnedest things on there. But usually when there's a contract out on someone, they don't use the person's name when they hire someone. They use a photo and a location. I already have your location."

"You can do that?" Savannah asked, surprised.

"I can do just about anything," Kale told her. "Now, tracing a contract might take a little while, so hang in there while I work on this."

"I don't suppose there's a way to get this information admissible in court?" Ridge asked. Savannah hadn't even thought about court. She just wanted to know who was behind this and why."

"Has there been any kind of court order?" Kale asked.

"Yes, Granger got one for the phone, but the company is stonewalling us."

Kale snorted. "No problem. I just need the phone's serial number, and I'll see what I can find and then send it to Granger."

"How is that admissible?" Savannah asked. She knew enough about law to realize this was seriously gray territory if not off limits completely.

"I'll send it from the company's email. It will look as if the company was simply following through on the court order. And I won't tell if you don't tell."

"You can do that?" Ridge asked, stunned.

Kale laughed again. "As I said, I can do just about anything. Send me the number and I'll get started. Stay safe and I'll call you if I find anything."

The line went dead and Savannah looked over to Ridge. "Who is that man?"

"At least he's a friend," he said as he shook his head.

"Do you really think he can find the person behind

this?" Savannah asked, torn between hope and not wanting to know. Part of her wanted to run and hide her head in the sand. The other part wanted to know who it was and kill them.

"I guess all we can do it wait and see," Ridge said as he reached for her and pulled her into a hug.

"And stay alive," Savannah said into his chest as he held her.

## 23

Savannah pushed her sunglasses up as if they were a headband. She looked up at the church as a couple of old ladies were leaving Bible study. Was she really going to a self-defense class with a bunch of seniors? Taking a deep breath, Savannah walked up the steps of the church. Well, some self-defense was better than no self-defense. Maybe they had pepper spray she could have.

Savannah entered the church and looked around at the beautiful stained glass. A grandma in a knitted cat vest came toward her. "Excuse me, where's the self-defense class?"

The woman blinked and then smiled. "Oh, weapons are in the armory. Go through those doors and take a left. You'll see it."

Armory? Weapons? The poor dear was so old she was confused. "Thank you," Savannah said to the cat lady before following her instructions.

Savannah turned left down the hall. At the end of the hall there was an open door. She could hear laughter and the sound of metal upon metal. Maybe they were knitting?

She'd ask the knitting group where the self-defense class was.

Savannah turned into the room and froze. The tap-tap-tap sound of metal upon metal wasn't two knitting needles, but two long, thin, and very sharp-looking swords being wielded by two women that were old enough to be grandmothers.

"Oh, good. You joined us," Miss Winnie said with a grin as she teetered over to her using a large pike as a cane. "How was the apple pie?"

Savannah blushed and Miss Winnie laughed. "What is this?" Savannah asked as women began to fill the room. Some were seniors, some were younger, and then she recognized Lydia with her eldest daughter who couldn't be more than ten. And even Tamika, the teenage waitress, came in.

"Welcome to our weapons class, Miss Ambrose," Reverend Winston said as he smiled at her upon entering the large room.

"This isn't self-defense," Savannah finally stuttered.

"It is and it isn't. I told you, women are the protectors of Shadows Landing."

Savannah looked incredulous. "But that was during pirate times. As far as I know, there aren't any more pirates raiding the shores of South Carolina."

"Doesn't mean we don't keep with tradition. Besides, it's a good workout and you never know when we must protect the flock. Are you ready to join us?"

Savannah looked over at Reverend Winston. He had to be joking, but then Tamika pulled out a giant cutlass, and it wasn't funny anymore. She and Lydia began to battle in earnest as the little girl picked up a dagger, slid what looked like a piece of cork on the tip, and then began thrusting at a self-defense dummy.

"I can see you're surprised, but we take our role of protectors seriously. Lacy just turned ten two weeks ago. That's the age they're allowed to start training. It's a rite of passage here," the reverend explained as he saw Savannah watching the little girl.

Savannah took a deep breath and nodded. "Tell me what to do."

"Lacy," Reverend Winston called out. The little girl immediately put her dagger to her side and approached.

"Yes, sir?"

"Today you have a new partner. Meet Miss Savannah."

"Pleased to meet you, Miss Savannah," the little girl said, looking up at her.

"You too." Savannah couldn't help but smile back at her.

"Would you please get Miss Savannah a beginner's dagger?"

"Yes, sir. Come with me, Miss Savannah. I took the one with the pink handle, but there's a really pretty one with a green handle that you'll love."

And with that the little girl reached over and took Savannah by the hand. She led Savannah to the far wall and slid open the large door. That was when Savannah learned that the church did, in fact, have an armory.

FIVE MINUTES LATER, Tinsley, Harper, and Ellery joined the class. Tinsley and Harper each wielded something large and mean looking while Ellery had a blue-handled dagger. Ellery, Savannah, Lacy, and another girl from Lacy's fourth-grade class were working with Reverend Winston on the proper way to use a dagger.

"Good, Ellery," the reverend praised. "Next week you can advance to throwing the dagger. You'll be up to boarding pikes in no time."

Meanwhile, Savannah was having a ten year old rolling her eyes at her. "Not like that, Miss Savannah," Lacy said with all the annoyance of a tween. "Don't be scared of it. The dagger is an extension of your hand. Use it like you would use a fork or a pen."

Savannah was having issues learning how to properly thrust with the blade. It didn't help that two ten-year-old girls were snickering at her.

"Don't grip it so hard," Ellery whispered. "It'll just tire your hand muscles. Like Lacy said, hold it with the same pressure as you hold a pen."

Savannah relaxed her grip and found it easier to maneuver the blade in the pattern Reverend Winston was teaching them. After thirty more minutes, class was called and those fierce warriors went back to senior citizens, grandmothers talking about grandbabies, kids talking about school, and adults talking about their jobs.

"It's surreal, right?" Tinsley asked as she showed Savannah the clean-up process.

"I thought it was a self-defense class," she said stupidly.

Tinsley smiled and nodded. "It is and it isn't. I took this class when I was a kid. After I left for college, I didn't come back until I was attacked in my home. Now I do this once a week and I also take a self-defense class in Charleston. You're welcome to come with me."

"I'd like that, thank you." Savannah took a deep breath and focused on herself for a moment. "I do feel more confident."

"Knowing how to protect yourself and others gives you that feeling. I'm glad you came."

"Savannah," Reverend Winston called out. "Good class. Usually you put your weapons back, but I'd like you to take yours home and practice. I have a feeling by next week's class you'll feel a lot more comfortable."

"Thank you. I enjoyed the class a lot." Savannah slipped the safely sheathed dagger into her purse.

Harper soon joined them, and together they walked outside.

"I've been thinking," Harper said as they crossed the street and headed to her bar together. "Do you think your ex could be behind this?"

"Penn?" Savannah thought about it as she'd been doing for days. "I thought about it, but I don't know why he would. He took almost all the money in the divorce. As per the judge's order, we both changed our wills and I never had life insurance. It's not like there's anything to gain. He didn't want this house, so I don't see him paying someone to kill me in order to get it. Actually, he wouldn't even get it, and he knows that. It's part of my new will and will go to my estate."

"Could he just be mad that you left him?" Tinsley asked.

"He never really cared if I went back to him."

"Then why would someone want you dead?" Harper asked the million-dollar question or at least the twenty-thousand-dollar question.

"I wish I knew. Hopefully, Kale will find something out."

RIDGE LOOKED over the work they'd completed on Savannah's kitchen and knew it was back on track now. The guys were doing great work and they'd even come in Saturday morning. They wanted to get a jump-start on the work that fell behind after the police had shut down the property for a couple days.

Ridge looked at his watch and saw that it was already four in the afternoon. "Okay, guys. That's good for today. Go home and spend some time with your families. I'll see you bright and early Monday morning."

Granger pulled up to the driveway as the guys were pulling out. Ridge walked over to his SUV as he got out. "So, I got this email from the phone company."

"Imagine that. I guess they complied with the order."

Granger's eyebrow rose, but he didn't comment. "There wasn't that much on the phone. Just a picture of Savannah and her address. I thought to ask Savannah if she knew who took this picture of her. It might give us a lead."

"Another lead may pop up at anytime, too," Ridge said cryptically.

"Until it does, I'm going to do my police work so I have enough evidence to put the person in jail for life," Granger told him before looking back to the house. "Is Savannah here?"

Ridge shook his head. "She texted me this morning that she's at the bar hanging out with Harper and Tinsley after the weapons class. That was five hours ago. I haven't heard otherwise, so I'm guessing she's still there."

"Can you find out?" Granger asked as he put away the paper printout of the email he'd received from Kale . . . um, the phone company.

"Sure." Ridge sent her a text that Granger was looking for her and a minute later, he had his answer. "She's helping Harper serve drinks at the bar. She said it's packed there."

"That's right. It's the big game between Clemson and South Carolina." Granger paused and shook his head.

"That's how stressed I am. I can't believe I forgot this holiday even as I drove down a packed street."

"It's because they changed rivals weekend from just after Thanksgiving to now. I still can't believe they did that," Ridge grumbled about the biggest football controversy to hit the state in years.

"Shoot, parking is going to be a nightmare."

"I'll meet you there." Granger got into his SUV and backed out of the driveway. Ridge looked at his watch. Four ten. The game started at six. It was tailgating time. Ridge ran home and grabbed his South Carolina T-shirt and then drove past Harper's house, but her driveway was already full so he went to Gavin's and parked.

Ridge walked as quickly as he could the couple of blocks to downtown. There were no spaces available as cars lined both sides of the road. Golf carts were parked on the sidewalk next to at least ten bikes and two riding lawn mowers. Ridge shook his head. He was surprised someone hadn't come on horseback.

Ridge pushed open the front door and was immediately assaulted by the noise. The room was clearly divided. Clemson fans on one side with all their purple and orange and South Carolina fans with their garnet and white on the other side. People were yelling taunts at each other across the room as the pregame show aired on the large televisions across the bar.

Harper was behind the bar, pushing out drinks as fast as possible while Tinsley delivered them. Both Harper and Tinsley were in South Carolina jerseys as some customers high-fived them while others dared to boo them. When they booed, their drinks suddenly went to another table.

"It's packed." Ridged nodded in response to Granger who had just come in behind him.

"I don't see Savannah." Ridge had to yell to be heard over the noise.

"There's your family. They have a table on the South Carolina side. Maybe they know where she is."

Ridge and Granger began to push their way through the crowd to the table where Trent, Ryker, Gavin, and Ellery sat with Edie Greene Wecker, their childhood friend who was now a widow.

"You brought the traitors," Trent said with a sly grin to Ridge as he finally pushed his way to the table.

"Huh?" Ridge asked as Trent nodded to Granger. It was then that Ridge turned to see Granger in a deep purple Clemson T-shirt. When he looked back at Trent, who was looking across the room. Ridge followed his gaze and there was Savannah looking every bit the Clemson cheerleader. She was in a denim miniskirt with the same purple Clemson T-shirt that Granger had on, but it was tied in a knot at her waist, exposing a strip of her smooth skin across her belly. Her high ponytail had orange ribbons tied around it.

"Oh no," Ridge whispered as Granger busted out laughing.

Right then, Savannah turned and saw him. Her eyes lit up, and she smiled broadly as she put a platter of chicken wings down at a table. Until her eyes dropped to his shirt, then her smile faded and she crossed her arms over the giant tiger paw on her T-shirt and shook her head.

This wasn't good. Ridge had heard of houses divided, but he didn't know if this relationship could work now. His cousins teased him as Savannah made her way over to the South Carolina side of the bar.

"I should have guessed after Harper and Tinsley pulled out their South Carolina gear. You were almost perfect,"

Savannah said with an exaggerated sigh before kissing him.

Ridge kissed her back. His fingers danced around the exposed skin at her waist, causing her to tense. He loved the feel of her against him. The way she fit against him. The way his . . .

"Go Cocks!"

Ridge pulled back as Gator yelled at the television.

"I have to get some more food out. I told Harper I'd help her. I hope you don't mind."

"Of course I don't mind. It's very nice of you to do."

Ridge still couldn't bring himself to let go of her.

"Then sit with your family, and I'll come join you once things slow down."

"Granger—" Ridge turned to find that his friend had left him and was now firmly over on the Clemson side high-fiving Skeeter. "Well, Granger has something to show you. We'll talk when things slow down."

"Did Kale find out who hired that man?" Ridge felt her go tense under his hands again. Only this time in fear.

"Not yet. He said he's working on it."

Savannah went up on her toes and kissed him quickly one more time. "I'll be back as soon as possible. Love you."

"I love you too. Even if you are a Clemson fan."

Savannah's laughter was music to him as she headed back to work. Now it was time to wait. Wait to see if she knew anything about that picture. Wait to see if Kale found out anything more. And wait to see if South Carolina could pull off the win.

## 24

SAVANNAH'S FEET were killing her. The game had just started and she had lost count of how many times she'd been back to the kitchen to get some deep-fried frog legs, chicken wings, pizzas, or burgers. Harper had told her that it was a big day. She'd brought in help to cook the food but hadn't found any waitresses. Tinsley had volunteered, and Savannah thought it would be a good distraction. Well, her aching feet were a great distraction.

Savannah ducked, dipped, bobbed, and weaved her way through the crowd, delivering food while Harper poured drinks and Tinsley delivered them. Both sides of the bar were yelling and screaming as the game went on.

Savannah jumped as someone grabbed her wrist. She put her hand to her chest when she saw it was Granger.

"Sorry," he yelled over the crowd. "I didn't mean to scare you. I wanted to see if you have a moment to take a break yet?"

He let go of her wrist and Savannah looked around to see if anyone else was about to order. It appeared as the start of the game had caused a shift of focus from beer and wings to football. She was sure she'd be swamped at halftime.

"Yeah, I think so. Let me just get Ridge."

"Meet me outside. It's too loud to talk in here." Granger saw her nod and got up from the table and began working his way to the front door.

Savannah was about to get to Ridge when she saw he was already standing and heading her way. He pointed to the front door and Savannah nodded. They both followed in Granger's wake and made their way out front.

Granger held the heavy door open for them, and when she took a step out into the fall air, Savannah felt completely relaxed. The door closed and the loud pounding noises fell to a dull whisper with the occasional muted cheer.

Savannah collapsed onto the bench next to the bar and groaned. "I haven't waitressed since high school. I don't remember it being so hard."

"I'll rub your feet when we get home tonight," Ridge said, sitting down next to her and putting an arm around her. He pulled her against him and kissed the side of her head.

"Promise?"

"Promise," Ridge chuckled as he squeezed her again.

Savannah looked at Granger and prepared herself. "What did you want to talk to me about?"

Granger pulled out his phone and held up the picture of her. "Can you tell me about this picture?"

Savannah looked at herself. It was a picture from her birthday party six months before she filed for divorce. "That's from two years ago. It was my twenty-sixth birthday. What you don't see are the two women my arms are around. They're the ones I found in bed with Penn."

"Who took the photo?" Granger asked as she leaned back into Ridge's embrace.

Savannah took a deep breath and looked skyward as if that would help her recall. She took the phone and really studied the picture. The events of that night flashed through her head. She saw at the bottom of the picture the faint glow of candles and remembered. "This was right before I blew out the candles on my cake. This could have been taken by anyone. There were close to one hundred people at the party Penn put on."

"Any guests who'd want you dead?"

Savannah shook her head. "I've been wracking my brain about that and can't think of anyone with a reason to kill me. Further, that picture was online within minutes of it being taken. That's how I recognized it. It was in all the society articles."

She saw Granger's lips tighten and put away his phone, and Savannah felt as if she'd failed him. This was his lead, and she'd just chewed it up and spit it out.

"It's okay. We'll get to the bottom of this one way or another," Ridge said as if trying to reassure both her and Granger.

Savannah looked up at Granger. "I'm sorry. I wish I could be more help. I hate feeling so useless."

"It's not your fault," Granger told her. His head turned to watch an SUV slow down as it drove toward them. "I will work—"

All of a sudden, Granger vaulted toward her as the sound of firecrackers went off. Granger grunted and slammed forward, landing on the flowers next to her as the *pop pop pop* sound rang out.

Savannah wanted to ask what was happening, but only a scream came out as Ridge pulled her off the bench, shoved her behind a car, and covered her body with his. "Stay down!" Ridge yelled as the sound grew louder as the SUV stopped. Glass shattered above them and Savannah realized it wasn't fireworks.

A second later, Ridge rolled off of her and crawled to Granger. He pulled at Granger's legs, drawing him off the planter. Granger groaned and cursed as he came to again. "Come on, Granger," Ridge yelled at his friend as he pulled him next to Savannah. "Put pressure on the wound."

"Shit," Granger hissed as Savannah shoved her hands against the bleeding hole in his side.

Savannah was still in a suspended state of disbelief. Someone was on the other side of the car shooting at them. Her heart pounded, her hands shook, but then there was Ridge. He grabbed Granger's gun from his hip, stood up, and fired. He didn't think twice. He didn't flinch as he stood up among the flying bullets and his hands were steady as he emptied the magazine.

"Mags. They're at the small of my back," Granger grunted as Savannah helped roll him onto his side. Gone was the nervousness. It was replaced with anger. Granger had jumped in front of her and had been shot for it. She reached under the back waistband of his pants and was surprised to find two magazines in a hidden belt at the small of his back. She never would have known they were there unless she felt for them. She pulled them out and handed one to Ridge who ducked behind her as the bar door flew open.

"What the hell?" Gator yelled as a shot was fired at the door. "No way, buddy. It's a commercial timeout and I ain't missing my game."

Gator pulled out a large hunting knife, and with a flick of his wrist sent it flying at the half-open window of the

SUV. Savannah heard glass shattering a moment before a barrage of heavy glass beer mugs went flying from the bar.

Ridge clicked the mag in place and began firing as the SUV tore off down the road.

Savannah wasn't watching, though. She had pulled up Granger's shirt and paused. A foot-long scar ran down his side. Right in the middle was a bleeding hole. Savannah looked on one side and then the other. "The bullet went through your side," she told Granger as she ripped her shirt off and wrapped it from one side to the other, pressing so hard she thought Granger was going to pass out.

"How bad?" Granger barely groaned as people began bursting out of the bar.

"Blood is a nice bright red and the wound is very close to your side. I think you got very lucky. Thank you, Granger. You saved my life." Savannah felt the tears pressing against her eyes as Ridge squeezed her shoulder in silent support.

"Couldn't let my friend's future wife die, now could I?"

Savannah swallowed hard as Harper, Kord, and Ryker were by his side. Tinsley ran out with a stack of napkins, lifted Savannah's hands out of the way, and cringed. "Sorry, Granger." And then pressed hard against the wound.

Granger roared as Ryker and Trent held him down, and Harper stroked his head softly as if to calm him as Ridge picked Savannah up and started looking her over for injuries.

Gavin had run by them a second ago but now reappeared with a black medical bag next to him. "Let me see."

Tinsley stepped back and Ellery gripped Tinsley's hand tightly in hers as they watched Gavin work. A young woman with golden skin and sun-kissed blonde hair pushed her way through to kneel next to Gavin. Together they worked side by side. It was as if she read his mind and handed Gavin what he needed before he knew it.

"Who is that?" Savannah whispered as Ridge worried about Savannah's bleeding knees.

"Sadie. She's Gavin's nurse." Ridge stood stiffly by and held her. It seemed like forever, but it was only minutes.

Gavin looked up and found Ryker. "Get your SUV. We're taking Granger to Charleston."

"We'll go with you," Ridge told them. "Savannah needs to be patched up."

"What?" Savannah only then looked down at herself. There were glass shards in her legs, and her knees looked as if she'd been in a bike wreck. And that wasn't counting her hands and arms. She'd gone numb as soon as Granger was shot and hadn't felt a thing yet.

Ryker took off running and seconds later his SUV slid to a stop. Kord was already running for his cruiser as Trent, Ridge, Gavin, and Gator lifted Granger into the back of the SUV. Gavin and Sadie climbed in next to him and Trent took the front seat.

"Come on. We'll ride with Kord," Ridge said, gently pushing his hand at the small of her back toward the cruiser with lights flashing.

"Let's go!" Ryker yelled out as Savannah and Ridge slid into the back seat of Kord's cruiser. Kord flipped a switch and sirens sounded as he took off toward Charleston with Ryker right behind him.

RIDGE HELD Savannah tightly against him. He'd seen the shards of glass sticking out of her legs and had instantly wanted to rush her to the hospital, but his friend had saved

Savannah's life and he knew his injuries were more severe. They had to make sure he was taken care of first.

They didn't talk during the whole car ride to Charleston. Kord was flying and Ridge didn't want to distract him. He also knew that Granger was like Kord's big brother. Kord's jaw was tight. His grip on the wheel was tight. He was struggling to keep his emotions in check.

He shot through downtown Charleston at a dangerous speed. Cars slammed on their brakes and some even jumped the curb onto the wide sidewalk to get out of the way. Ridge glanced behind him and saw that Ryker was no more than five feet behind them with his lights flashing and leaning on his horn.

Ridge held Savannah tightly and looked down at her. She was biting her lip so hard it looked ready to puncture. Silent tears streamed down her face. Her hands clutched her legs above her knees so hard her fingers were white, and she was cutting off circulation in her legs.

"Savannah?" he whispered questioningly to her.

"It hurts," she gasped and then bit back a sob.

"It's okay to cry, sweetheart."

Savannah shook her head. "Not when Granger is shot. Not when he saved my life. He comes first. Promise me you'll get him inside first."

"We will," Ridge promised before tightening his grip on her as Kord slammed on the brakes. They had finally arrived.

"Go get Granger!" Savannah yelled on a sob. Kord was already out of the car and Ridge nodded and hurried out as well.

A stretcher was already being rushed out from the hospital. Standing there in all her glory was Olivia

Townsend, directing doctors, nurses, and staff as if she were the head of the hospital.

She strode out behind them as everyone worked to get Granger loaded onto a stretcher. "You take the best possible care of him or I swear I will have the funding for the hospital cut by morning!" Her eyes calmly ran over each person one at a time. "Where's Savannah?"

"In the cruiser," Ridge answered as his heart ached watching his friend being wheeled into the hospital.

Olivia was already striding over to the cruiser. She opened the back door and immediately began ordering people around again. "We have another one. Get a gurney now! She joins Sheriff Fox in the secure area. No one, and I mean, no one gets through without being approved by me. Do you understand?"

"Yes, ma'am," a nurse agreed as Ridge rushed to help Savannah from the back of the car.

"You poor thing," Olivia said quietly as she held Savannah's hand. "Tinsley called me. She told me what happened. I'll make sure you're safe while you're here."

Ridge was shocked as Charleston police fell in to surround them. They were safe. For now. But someone was very tired of Savannah being alive. Ridge kept his hand on her shoulder as they were moved to the secure area. He knew he had to do something and fast.

## 25

RIDGE HAD HELD his breath as Savannah was stitched up. Six stiches here. Eight there. And then there was the horrible process of cleaning out the dirt, gravel, and glass from her hands, arms, and knees. She was such a mess they'd given her morphine along with numbing the area so they could work.

Ridge had kept his hand on her the entire time, but all Savannah wanted to know was how Granger was. "Please, go check. They're almost done here."

She was exhausted and in pain, but Ridge left her. "Trent," he said as he approached the small waiting room that had been put aside for them. "Can you sit with Savannah while I check on Granger?"

"Sure thing," his cousin said and stood up.

"Let us know, will you?" Ryker asked as he shot a look at Kord. The young man looked ready to break apart at any hint of bad news.

"I will."

"I'm coming with you," Olivia said in a tone that left no room for argument. She stood and straightened her pink pencil skirt and white blouse. Ridge nodded and Olivia joined him as they walked, security nodding their approval. They were on the approved list.

"How is Savannah? I would like to see her too," Olivia asked quietly as they walked toward the small nurses' station.

"In pain, but she's only concerned about Granger." Ridge paused and looked over at the tall knockout who had both beauty and brains. "Thanks for doing whatever it was you did to get us a secure area."

"Your sister can be quiet fierce when she wants to be. I believe she's the one who made it happen. She called Ellery's friend, Mrs. Elijah F. Cummings."

Ridge chuckled at that. The old woman was the grande dame of Charleston society. "What did Tibbie do?"

Olivia grinned. "What *didn't* Tibbie do? She had the president of the hospital and the hospital's top surgeons and doctors out of their game watch parties and here in under fifteen minutes. I just made sure everyone was ready for Sheriff Fox and Savannah."

"I think you did more than that, and it's appreciated," Ridge told her as they stopped at the empty station.

"It sounds silly, but I like your family and your town. After helping Wade and Darcy, I feel as if I'm a small part of it all somehow. And I won't take an attack against my family sitting down. Now, what more can I do to help?"

"I'm about to do something illegal," Ridge finally said. He knew the second he saw Savannah hurt he knew what it was. He was going to kill the person behind this. "Keep me out of jail."

Olivia looked and him and gave one brisk nod. "I'll do my best."

"Can I help you?" a nurse asked as she came out of a room.

"We want to check on Granger Fox," Ridge told her.

"He's waking up from surgery, but I'm sure you can see him for a minute."

"How is he?" Olivia asked.

"Luckily, the bullet missed the critical organs. The surgeons got him all cleaned up and now he'll start recovery. It's not fast, but he will fully recover."

"Thank you," Ridge told the nurse who pointed out the room Granger was in.

Ridge and Olivia approached the door and heard a doctor talking. Ridge pushed open the door slightly and quietly they walked into the room.

Ridge heard a small gasp from Olivia and looked at her. Her eyes were wide and Ridge turned to follow their direction. Granger was on his back and was mostly nude except for a sheet over one leg and his privates. And on full display were two wicked-looking scars from his car accident in college.

"Get her out of here," Granger snapped as the doctor moved and Granger caught Olivia staring at his scars.

It seemed to snap Olivia out of it. "I will not leave until I have news I can report to your friends. They're all worried about you."

The doctor looked to Granger who nodded as he yanked up the sheet to cover his full body. "He's very lucky. No vital organs were hit. His rib is cracked, though, and that's going to be a slow, painful healing process. We're going to keep him here for a week to make sure no infection sets in so we won't have to debride the wound."

"Thank you," Olivia told the doctor as she took a step

closer to Granger. "We're all thankful you'll be okay. Is there anything I can get for you or do for you?"

"Yes," Granger snapped. "Get out."

Olivia nodded and spun on one heel before leaving.

"Granger." Ridge shook his head. "She's trying to be helpful. She's the one who got you in here so quickly with the chief of surgery."

Granger ran a hand over his face and then looked up at the doctor. "Is that true?"

"From what I've gathered, a woman named Tinsley called Mrs. Cummings who called the hospital. Tinsley also called Miss Townsend. When I wasn't here fast enough, it was Miss Townsend who called next. I've been threatened a lot in my life but . . . Let's just say, her threat got me here in five minutes."

Granger grumbled to himself, and Ridge saw that he knew he was going to apologize. "How do you feel?"

"Like I've been shot."

"Speaking of which, the state police want to talk to you, but Miss Townsend told them they weren't allowed to until morning. Is that your wish?" the doctor asked.

"Damn," Granger groaned. "Now I'm really going to need to apologize. Keep everyone away except for whoever Miss Townsend approves."

"Yes, sir. There's a call button. We'll be checking on you in thirty minutes."

The doctor left and Ridge took a seat. "You saved her, you know. I'll always be in your debt. I don't know what to say."

"It's my job. Plus, I like Savannah," Granger said as he shoved the sheet back down. "Is she okay?"

"Few cuts and scrapes, but okay."

Granger looked down at his scars and shook his head. "I mean, at least the scar will just blend into the others."

"It's not as bad as you think it is," Ridge finally said. "Stop focusing on that and focus instead on the fact that you just saved Savannah's life. You, my friend, are a hero."

Granger rolled his eyes. It was going to take a lot more than Ridge telling him his scars weren't bad for him to believe it. Granger's scars were so much more than surface marks. The women he'd been with had scarred his heart.

"Screw legalities. I want this person," Granger finally said.

Ridge pulled out his phone, called Kale, and handed the phone to Granger.

"What's up?" Ridge heard Kale answer.

"The bastard shot me."

"Granger?"

"Yup," Granger affirmed. "And the bastard shot me. Find him. Any way you can."

"I just did."

Ridge froze and Granger's eyes shot to his. "Who is he?"

"So, here's the thing. I can't find the contract yet. But I found out the *why*, which leads me to the *who*," Kale explained.

"Wait," Ridge interrupted. "Let me get Savannah. She needs to hear this."

"Okay," Kale said. "How did you get shot, Granger?"

Ridge left Granger telling Kale about the shooting as he hurried down to Savannah's room. "Granger is doing well. Nothing major was hit. Full recovery in time. He'll stay here for a week to make sure there's no infection and it's draining properly."

"Thank goodness," Savannah said. Her whole body seemed to finally relax.

"I'll tell the others," Trent said as he stood.

"Wait," Ridge told his cousin. "Help me move Savannah. We need to see Granger."

"Why?" Savannah asked as Trent moved a wheelchair close to her bed.

"Because we're on the phone with Kale, and he knows why and who wants you dead."


SAVANNAH DIDN'T BREATHE as Trent and Ridge helped her into the wheelchair. Trent grabbed her IV stand and Ridge placed a blanket over her lap before he got behind her and began to push her down the hall.

"Here they are," Granger said as he smiled at her when she entered his room. Ridge and Trent positioned her right next to Granger who had a sheet pulled up to his armpits. She reached out to him and he took her hand in his.

"Thank you for saving my life." Savannah had found it was hard to talk. Her eyes were filled with tears but she refused to shed them. It was time to get down to business and find out who was trying to kill her.

"You're welcome," Granger said gruffly. He moved in his bed as he handed the phone back to Ridge and his sheet dropped. He quickly yanked it up, but not before Savannah saw the scars and the dressing for the bullet wound.

"It's okay. You don't have to hold up your sheet," Savannah whispered to Granger who seemed so tired his arms were shaking.

She could tell Granger was fighting it. "I won't look. I promise. Look at me," she said to him as she pulled away her blanket to reveal the fifty-some stitches she got along her knees and legs.

"I'm sorry," Granger whispered back.

"For what? Scars? They're just life stories."

Granger let his sheet drop to where it pooled around his waist, but Savannah didn't stare. She turned to Ridge who was holding the phone. "Kale, it's Savannah. What have you found out?"

"So, I haven't been able to find the actual contract yet, but it's only a matter of time before I find that communication," Kale told them.

"I thought you found out who was behind it?" Savannah felt completely dejected. Were they really at step zero still?

"I did. Just not with evidence." Kale paused and then asked, "Savannah, how many bank accounts do you have?"

"Um, checking, savings, and a small investment account. Why?"

"Are any of your accounts at Ocean Waters Bank in the Caribbean?"

"No," Savannah answered quickly. She knew her face mirrored the confusion she saw in Ridge's. "Why?"

"Because according to what I've found, you have eleven million dollars in that bank."

The only noise was the medical equipment. That didn't even make sense. "I'm sorry, what?" Savannah finally said.

"What does your ex-husband do?" Kale asked, but Savannah knew Kale must already know.

"He's a venture capitalist. I'm sure you know that. Please, just tell me what this is about." Savannah was running out of patience. She felt her heart beating hard, and it caused her stitches to feel like they were throbbing.

"It'll make sense soon. I promise," Kale told her. "What do venture capitalists do?"

Savannah let out an agitated huff of air. "He finds small companies or people who have a good chance of going big if only they had enough money behind them. He scouts them and then writes up a business plan for them that will take them to the next level. Then he gets money either from his firm or from investors to make his business plan work. The small company grows and the investors get their money back plus interest. Some of them become equity partners and then get a percentage of sales as well."

"So, your husband was a general partner who takes money from limited partners to invest in companies?" Kale asked.

"Right."

"And what if the company fails?" Kale asked.

"That's part of the risk," Savannah explained. "It's why it's called venture capital."

"When you were married, did he ever mention Heart Stone Medical Company?" Kale asked her.

Savannah nodded. "Yeah. It was a huge account that he raised millions for, but then the warehouse burned down and the owner died. The company folded. It was a huge hit for Penn's portfolio. He was worried he'd get fired for it. He was working on this deal during our divorce. He used it as a reason to pay me less."

"Can you guess how much he raised for it?"

"I don't know," Savannah told Kale. "I remember it being more than ten million. Why?"

"I bet I know," Ridge said grimly. "Eleven million dollars."

"Ding, ding, ding. We have a winner," Kale said.

Savannah shook her head when she saw Trent and Granger had gotten it. And then it hit her like a truck. "The same amount that's in my name in a foreign bank. He embezzled it? That son of a bitch!"

"That's right," Kale told them. "It was all a shell. The man who died technically did own Heart Stone Medical, but he was an eighty-six year old widower with dementia. His daughter swears he never started that company. She'd never heard of it, and he didn't have any papers for it. He certainly wasn't of sound legal mind to start the company eight months before he died."

Savannah thought she'd be sick. "Penn killed him." She pressed a hand to her stomach to try to keep it from revolting against her. "Like he's trying to kill me. An accident. The man died in an accident, right?"

"Faulty electric work," Kale told her, and then Ridge was there rubbing her back as he tried to calm her.

"And the money?"

"He couldn't put it in his name because his company runs regular searches on their employees. And he didn't put it in your married name. He put it under Savannah Ambrose the day after you signed the divorce papers."

"His company would never find it," she said. "It's brilliant, but he can't get it either. It's in my name."

"Except—" Kale began, and Savannah had a bad feeling she wasn't going to like what he was going to say. "Except if you die. The account is payable to Penn Benson upon your death."

"I'm going to kill him," Ridge snapped behind her.

Savannah was shaking her head. Through the nausea, through the rage, and through the pain, she knew exactly what she wanted to do.

"I need everyone to think I'm in the hospital, and then I need to sneak out and get to that bank." Savannah looked over at Ridge and saw him smile slowly.

"You're going to steal it from Penn."

"How could it be stealing if it's in my name?" Savannah asked sweetly.

## 26

RIDGE BLINKED. Was it stealing? "Trent, will you ask Olivia to bring everyone back here? I think we need some help with this."

"Sure thing," Trent sent Savannah a wink and Ridge rolled his eyes at his cousin.

"Savannah," Granger said after Trent left. "Can I have a moment alone with Ridge?"

Savannah looked surprised but then nodded. "I just need a push."

Ridge looked questioningly at Granger who glanced down at his bare chest. Ah. "I'll just push you out into the hall and you can wave the group down." When Ridge made it out into the hall, he leaned down and kissed Savannah. "He wants to get covered."

"Oh," she said understanding. "I'll keep everyone here until you're ready for us."

"Thanks, love." Ridge bent and kissed her again before hurrying back into the room.

"Get this blasted thing on me," Granger grumbled as he tried to figure out the dressing gown.

"What can I do?" Kale asked over the phone. "Besides finding evidence?"

"I hate to admit it, but I need help," Granger said, sounding completely pissed off about it. "Can you send Walker?"

Walker Greene had been one of their best friends growing up. He'd turned into a DEVGRU man until a mission went horribly wrong—the same mission that had left his sister, Edie, a widow. Walker was injured and in hiding when Gavin turned to their cousin, Layne Davies, for help. A wedding later and Walker was now teaching other soldiers and law enforcement officers at an elite school in Keeneston.

"I know someone better and who's available right now. Walker is out of town with the Davies brothers looking at equipment to buy for the school," Kale said.

"Send him here and I'll deputize him," Granger said, his voice harsh with pain as Ridge made him move to slip his arm into one of the sleeves.

"You don't need to worry about that. If you can get Savannah out of Shadows Landing, you all can meet up on the island," Kale told them.

Granger let out a sigh as Ridge lowered him back into bed now covered in his gown. "Want me to let them in?"

"Yeah. Let's see if we can get Savannah out of town."

"I mean, I can make it happen if you can't," Kale told them as Ridge opened the door. The number of people had grown. Olivia pushed Savannah into the room. Behind them were Kord, Ryker, Trent, Tinsley, Gavin, and Ellery.

"Harper had to stay at the bar. It's packed and the state troopers are there," Tinsley told the room. "Though I think they might just be watching the game."

Ridge moved to stand next to Savannah again. He rested

his hand on her shoulder as he faced the room. "I have Kale Mueez on the phone. Here's what we've learned."

Ridge gave a summary and then turned to Olivia. "Can Savannah cash out the account?"

"Yes. It's in her name, so she should be able to access it. The trouble is, those funds are illegally obtained money. I wouldn't touch them without an immunity agreement in place so Penn's company doesn't come after her as a co-conspirator."

"Can you help me with that?" Savannah asked Olivia. "I can give the money back to the company."

Olivia was quiet for a moment. "How well do you know the president of the company?"

"Really well. He and his wife were very supportive of me during the divorce. They have a daughter my age that I still talk to," Savannah told her.

"Okay. I need an FBI agent, a federal judge, and the president of the company to get this all wrapped up. You'll need someone with federal authority with you when you retrieve the money so they can take possession of it for evidence."

"I've got that all covered," Kale's voice said calmly over the phone. "I'll send all the information to your phone."

"You don't have—" Olivia started to say but was interrupted by her phone. She looked down and her eyes went wide. "How did you do that? My number is unlisted."

Kale just chuckled as if she'd said something funny.

Ryker cleared his throat. "I can get you out of the hospital and to the island without any customs. You can take the yacht."

"Thank you," Ridge told his cousin.

"No dead bodies. I swear if someone dies even near my boat I'll kill you."

Ridge and his cousins laughed. Their cousin Wade had pulled a dead man onto Ryker's speedboat and Ryker had sold it instantly, claiming it had death cooties.

"What about Penn?" Savannah asked. "And what about the man who tried to kill me?"

"I've been thinking about that," Kord told them as he looked around the room. "What if he thinks Savannah is here and no longer guarded. He can tell the assassin and we can catch him in the act. Hopefully, Kale can find the communications and we catch not only the assassin, but also Penn on a charge a lot worse than embezzlement."

"Solid plan," Granger said, nodding his head.

"But how will he know about Savannah?" Ellery asked.

Ridge felt Savannah go stiff as she inhaled sharply. "Because the hospital can call him again as my emergency contact."

Ridge shook his head. "No. Then he'll want to see you."

Savannah looked up at him and actually smiled. "Exactly. He will rush in here and find me in the lockdown area. I'll be upset, of course, and I'll tell him it's because a police officer was shot. Then I'll tell him they hope to move me down to a regular room in a couple days. A regular room with no security."

"And a nurse can tell him that visitors are limited and she'll call him when you're moved. That will give you time to get the money," Ridge added on. "I don't like it. I don't want him near you, but this could work."

"But you're in a wheelchair," Ellery pointed out. "You can't go running around."

"I'm fine," Savannah told them. "They're pumping me full of antibiotics to prevent infection. As long as I keep the wounds nice and clean, I was going to be discharged tonight. I'm just stiff from where the stitches are pulling and the skin is scabbing. Nothing will stop me from doing this."

Everyone was quiet as they all looked at Savannah. It was as if they were gauging if she were strong enough to pull it off.

"Well, you can't walk into a bank wearing that," Tinsley told them.

"I'll have my assistant get you clothes so you can rest." Ryker was already pulling out his cell phone. "My boat will be ready in an hour," Ryker said a minute later. "I'll pick you up at the back door in the commercial delivery zone."

"Let's get you back to bed and have the hospital call Penn," Ridge finally said, giving in to the plan.

TWENTY-TWO LONG MINUTES. That's how long it took Penn to rush to the hospital after he was called. The Faulkners were all in Granger's room and Savannah had been moved to the room next door. Kord stood guard between her room and Granger's. And that was after Olivia had whipped the hospital security into something resembling a swat team. They were at every door and the one outside the wing she and Granger were in had a clipboard with names on it. It was a short list. Doctors and nurses only. Penn's name wasn't on it. A nice nurse would get him through "just this one time."

That nice nurse was an FBI agent with a camera hidden in her ID tag. Somehow the Keeneston connection had gotten a quick team assembled to cover things in Charleston. FBI Agent in Charge Peter Castle was dressed as a doctor and would also come into the room to video Penn. He'd deliver the news that she was to stay in the secure ward for a couple more days.

They had Savannah looking worse than she felt with some fake blood and some makeup for bruising. They needed to convince Penn she would be there for a while. So when he walked in with the FBI nurse, Savannah pretended to be asleep.

"Here's your wife, Mr. Benson. I'm so sorry," the nurse said.

"Is she going to be okay?"

"The next few days will be the most telling," the nurse said in hushed tones. To Savannah it sounded as if she were at death's door. "I'll give you a moment with her as soon as I take her vitals, but then you'll have to leave. I'm sorry. I shouldn't have let you in in the first place. It's a secure area and your wife can't be exposed to any germs right now."

Savannah made a groan of pain and felt the nurse come to her bedside. "Mrs. Benson," she said gently, "your husband is here. Isn't that great?"

The nurse slipped on the blood pressure cuff and turned it on. Savannah blinked open her eyes as if she were having trouble focusing them. "Penn? Is that you?"

"Yes, pet. I'm here."

Penn moved to her side and pulled up a chair so he could sit next to her. He took one bandaged hand in his and the nurse stopped him. "I'm sorry, no touching. We're guarding against infection," the nurse told him, and Savannah was so grateful she was there. She'd keep Savannah safe from Penn.

"Sorry. Oh, pet. What happened?"

Savannah wanted to punch him. Instead, she grimaced. "Wrong place at the wrong time. They've told me the drive-by was meant for the police officer who was shot and I just happened to be too close. I was cheering on my Tigers at a bar. It was supposed to be a fun night out, and then I don't know what happened."

Savannah heard the heart monitor speed up. She wasn't faking the stress she was feeling. "Oh, Penn. It was so scary. I thought I was going to die."

"What has the doctor said?" Penn asked.

"And who are you?"

Savannah looked over Penn's shoulder at Agent Castle dressed in scrubs and a white coat. Penn stood up and held out his hand for the doctor.

"I'm her husband. Is she going to be okay?"

"Nurse, did you let him in? You know it's authorized personnel only." Agent Castle ignored Penn as his coworker sputtered about how sad it was and that he should be able to see his wife. Agent Castle turned to Penn then. "You'll need to leave after my report."

Penn nodded. "Is it that serious then?" he asked, his voice dropping as if he were concerned.

"We don't know yet. Right now, my main concern is keeping infection at bay. If she's holding steady in three or four days, I can move her out of this ward and into a normal room without the extra security. Then you won't have any hassle seeing her. If you leave a number with the nurse, we'll call you daily to let you know how she's doing," Agent Castle told him.

"I can't stay with her?" Penn asked, and Savannah really wanted to punch him. He was probably enjoying the fact she lay there injured.

"Sorry. It's not in her best interest, and this ward is in a complete security lockdown. But, if she improves and becomes stable, we'll move her when a room opens up."

"What could kill her?" Penn asked. "I mean, what are you so worried about?"

Yeah, so he could kill her. Savannah had to school her features to appear as if she were falling back asleep.

"Embolism, infection, stroke, heart attack, to name a few," Agent Castle told him. "She's very vulnerable right now. If there's nothing else, say your goodbyes and the nurse will walk you out. Make sure she has the best number to reach you."

Penn came over to her and looked down at her. Savannah kept her eyes closed. "Goodbye, pet."

Savannah heard him blow her a kiss and then the FBI nurse was walking him out of the room. Agent Castle shut the door, but didn't say anything as he looked around the room. "Okay, you're all clear. I wanted to make sure he didn't leave behind a phone or anything he would have to come back for."

Savannah yanked off the extra bandages that had been added for effect. "Thanks for staying with me. I felt safe with you here."

"I have an agent who will tail him from here, and I have another agent planted at his hotel."

"Thank you," Savannah said as she worked to sit up in bed. She was sore and the numbing medicine was wearing off, but she was able to get up and walk now. It just wasn't comfortable. "I believe I have a boat to catch."

"Here's my number. If you need any help, just call," Agent Castle said, handing her his card. "And I'll see you when you get back in town. I'll be here to help bring these guys down."

The door opened and Ridge stood with the rest of his family. Olivia brushed by them and smiled at Agent Castle before turning to Savannah. "You're all set. You have immunity from the FBI, the state of South Carolina, and the president of the company. He sends his most sincere regrets that you've been involved. He really is a nice guy and thinks very highly of you. He also sends his thanks for returning the money."

"Are you ready?" Ridge asked as he brought in a bag from a local boutique.

Savannah was banged up. She was hunted. She'd been unknowingly involved in a massive embezzlement scheme, but she wasn't down for the count yet. She had one more play to make. "Let's go."

## 27

RIDGE WOKE up with his arms around Savannah. They were in a stateroom on Ryker's yacht and it was heading toward the Caribbean as fast as it could go. They'd reach the small banking island northwest of the Bahamas in a day and a half. They'd already spent a good amount of time on the boat and expected to arrive that night. Ridge had to hand it to his cousin. Ryker loved luxury and speed. And right now that was perfect.

"Are we there yet?" Savannah asked sleepily.

"Our ETA is around midnight tonight," he told her. "We'll sneak ashore in the small skiff as the yacht goes back out to sea. We'll get a hotel room and then grab the money as soon as the bank opens. I've already talked to the captain and agreed to a meeting place and time."

"You think Ryker would mind if I never got off the boat again? This is pure heaven."

Ridge got out of bed and opened the curtain. Outside was nothing but beautiful, sapphire blue water. "Ryker was right. This is so much better than flying. Plus no one is checking your passport so long as we're careful. No way for Penn or his associate to know you're not at the hospital."

"And it gives me time to heal."

Ridge turned back to her and sat gently down on the queen-sized bed covered in a white and navy comforter. "How are you feeling?"

"Very sore," Savannah admitted. "I need to take my medicine too."

"Well, Ryker is Ryker. We have a captain and a small crew on his boat. I'll tell the chef we're ready for breakfast. Do you want to eat out on deck or in here?"

"On deck. I have one day to enjoy this and I'm going to do just that," Savannah said as she held out her arms and fell back against the bed.

IT SEEMED the discomfort had grown during the morning as Savannah moved around, but after her medicine and some stretching, she felt somewhat better. She grimaced when she got up and began walking, but after a couple steps her body relaxed into the achiness and it became bearable.

They'd spent the entire day relaxing, talking, and pretending that everything was fine. They were just a normal couple on a date. On a yacht. With a chef. And a steward. Running from someone who wanted to kill her. On her way to pick up eleven million illegally obtained dollars. So, yeah, just a perfectly normal date.

But the warmth of the sun, the wind, the ocean breeze, and time with Ridge when they didn't need to constantly be on guard had more healing power than the hospital. So by the time the sun had set and the stars shone in the night sky, Savannah was ready to go.

Ryker's assistant had gotten her a pair of ultra-light black linen pants that were not only cool enough for the hot weather, but also hid all of her wounds. She paired it with a long-sleeved khaki tunic. It was very chic with the statement pieces of jewelry that had also been included. While fake, they make her look like she was part of a wealthy family on vacation.

Savannah very carefully packed those clothes for the next day before she slid her feet into her sandals. That night she was in a maxi dress that reached the ground. She lifted it up to her thighs as she climbed onboard the small skiff.

They didn't turn on the boat's lights as Ridge took the wheel. They began to make the twenty-minute boat ride to shore and Savannah felt her whole body tighten in fear. Would they be stopped? What would happen if they had to show their passports?

"Tell me again why we are going to this huge hotel?" Savannah asked. She had to raise her voice to be heard over the motor as Ridge expertly handled the boat.

"It's just where Kale said to meet our contact."

"And this contact can get us into and out of the country?" Savannah asked for probably the fifth time today.

"That's what Kale says, and he hasn't given me any reason to doubt him."

Savannah wrapped her arms around herself and watched the coastline growing closer and closer. Bright lights lit up a beach dance club, and as they got close enough, she could hear the music and see people dancing.

"This is the hotel," Ridge told her as he slowed down and cruised past the dance club part of the resort.

"This looks like a five-star hotel," Savannah said quietly even though they couldn't be heard over the music.

"There's the private marina Kale told me about."

Savannah looked into the shadows and saw the marina. It was small, but solidly built with soft glowing lights. As they approached the one open spot on the dock, the shadows moved.

"There's our contact," Ridge said. He tried to remain calm, but Savannah could hear the tension in his voice as they approached. The man pulled off his baseball cap and suddenly Ridge cursed in surprise. "Holy shit. I don't believe it."

Savannah was reaching for anything she could use as a weapon when the man grinned and waved at them. "What's up, cuz? How was the trip?"

"Cuz?" Savannah whispered as her hand wrapped around the small fire extinguisher as Ridge just shook his head.


"DYLAN"—RIDGE laughed as he tossed the rope to his Keeneston cousin—"what the hell are you doing here?"

"My brother-in-law said you needed some help. You know me, always willing to illegally invade a country for family."

Ridge turned to Savannah to see her face full of confusion. "Savannah, this is my cousin, Dylan Davies. He's married to Kale's sister, Abby." Ridge turned back to his cousin. "Does Abby know you're here?"

"Who do you think knocked the guard out and scrambled the security monitors?" a woman's voice said from the shadows. A second later, Abby emerged in a black sequined mini dress. Her bright blue eyes stood out among the dark hair cascading down her back. "Hi, I'm Abby Davies," Abby said to Savannah as she held out her hand to help Savannah out of the boat.

"Savannah Ambrose."

"And I'm Ridge Faulkner. I'm sorry I couldn't make the wedding," Ridge told her as he hopped out of the boat and shook hands with Dylan.

"Don't worry about it. This is way more fun. Come on, Sebastian has a suite for us. I ordered room service and it should be there soon," Abby said, motioning for them to follow.

"Who's Sebastian?" Savannah asked.

"Sebastian Abel. He owns the hotel. He's the one who gave me the codes needed to shut down the cameras for a little while. He's also giving us an off-the-books room," Abby explained as she led the way down the docks as if she owned them as opposed to sneaking into a foreign country.

"I think Ryker knows him," Ridge said to Dylan who nodded.

"Probably. Power and wealth, they all stick together," Dylan said.

"But what about the FBI agent we need to witness me getting the money?" Savannah asked. Ridge laced his hand with hers, trying to calm her. He could tell she was very worried. He was too, but Dylan and Abby didn't seem worried, and that helped keep him calm.

"I'm doing it," Abby said cheerfully. "I'm your cousin, after all."

"You are?" Savannah asked, her voice full of doubt.

"Well, your boyfriend is my husband's cousin." Abby shrugged. "Close enough. Dylan and Ridge will stay outside the bank and keep their eyes open for anything suspicious. You and I, cousin, will go into the bank and withdraw the money."

"You're FBI?" Savannah asked, and Ridge knew Abby didn't miss the doubt in her voice.

Abby shook her head. "Hell no. That's the Parker branch of the Davies family. They're all FBI. I'm CIA. Well, when I feel like it."

"When you feel like it?" Ridge had to know more.

"Let's just say I'm part-time. But my signed account of the money transfer and my escorting the money to Agent Castle will be legal. Plus, as a CIA agent who is 'undercover,' the courts don't demand my name, and I won't be called to testify."

"That's genius," Savannah said, and Ridge felt her relaxing. She turned then to Dylan. "Are you CIA?"

Dylan shook his head. "Nope. Special Forces. When I feel like it," he said, echoing his wife's words. "Now it's mostly what I'd call private contract work. Like helping you."

They stopped talking as they entered the opulent lobby of the beach resort for the wealthy. A quick elevator ride up to a floor that only had four rooms on it, and then they were at their suite. Only calling it a "suite" didn't quite do it justice. A marble entranceway opened up into a massive living room and kitchen area with a dining room table big enough for twelve people separating the two rooms.

The far side of the living room, dining room, and kitchen area was a wall of sliding glass doors that opened onto an enormous balcony with full-sized sofas, chairs, and a hot tub.

"Your room is to the left. Ours is on the other side of the kitchen," Abby said right before the bell rang. "That's room service. Why don't you put your stuff away and meet us on the balcony. We'll go over tomorrow's plan before bed."

Ridge followed Savannah to their room and almost ran into her as she stopped to stare at the pure luxury. A giant king-sized bed. A sitting area. A large marble tub with a sunroof over it so you could sit in the tub and open the window to feel the ocean breeze while relaxing. And that was before she saw the shower.

Savannah looked at the clock and then looked at him. "I could stay for an extra day or two, what about you?"

They both laughed, then he kissed her. They spent most of the day kissing on the boat, but since they began preparing to sneak into the country, things had been tense.

Just like every time he kissed her, he instantly wanted more. Having Savannah in his arms was heaven. "Come on. Let's get this meeting over with so I can have you all to myself."

Savannah sighed. "Sounds good, but I don't think she's really CIA."

Ridge laughed as he opened the door to their end of the balcony. "I don't either. But whoever they work for, they're on our side."

## 28

THERE WAS no way Abby Davies was CIA. First, she looked way too upset that she didn't have to shoot anyone as they made their way into the bank the next morning. And second, Savannah didn't think a CIA agent would hand her an arsenal of weapons to carry as if she were an agent. Call her old-fashioned, but she'd never seen a cop hand a civilian two guns, four knives, and a stun gun. Savannah felt completely weighed down as they walked into the bank through the private entrance for high net worth clients.

"Breathe," Abby said with a bored look on her face. She was dressed similarly to Savannah in an understated outfit well suited to the very wealthy. "Dylan said everything is clear outside. Everything is fine. It's just another bank and another withdrawal. You've done this a million times in your life. Got it?"

Savannah forced herself to breath. "Got it."

"Miss Ambrose," a man in a black suit with smooth ebony skin said smoothly as he greeted her. He seemed to sail across the polished floor toward her. "It is so lovely to finally meet in person."

"Thank you," Savannah said, smoothly slipping into the perfect-wife persona she'd used at all of Penn's dinner parties. She looked at the man's nametag with just the tiniest flick of her eyes. "Javon."

"This morning you said you wanted to withdraw your money? I hope we didn't disappoint you in any way," Javon said with a touch of worry as he led the women to his private desk.

"Oh no!" Savannah immediately went full Southern belle. "Don't you worry about that at all. You've been so wonderful, Javon. It's just that my cousin," Savannah said, motioning to Abby, "and I have always longed to do some yachting. A boat that we must have came up for sale. It was nerve wracking trying to get a deal made. Darn Londoners were trying to steal it out from under me. But, I was able to get it on the condition I pay with cash within three days. My nerves are shot, Javon. Until I have that money and hand it over for the title, I'm likely to have a breakdown." Savannah laughed at herself and patted Javon's arm.

Apparently used to dealing with wealthy clients, Javon nodded understandingly. "So, would you like the full amount in cash or a bank check?"

"Cash," Savannah said sweetly. "Thank you, Javon."

"We offer a security service for hire if you'd like," Javon said as he began typing on his computer.

"Thank you, we have someone with us. Someone very discreet. I'm sure you understand," Abby said, speaking for the first time.

"Oh, I do. Our bank is known for its discretion. There," Javon said, not looking up from the computer. "I have the order in and they'll be packing up the bags as we speak. Now, I have some papers for you to sign and of course, I need to see your passport."

"Of course," Savannah said, pulling it from her purse. Her heart stopped beating, and she forgot Abby's instructions on breathing as Javon looked over it and entered something into the computer. Then he closed it and handed it back to her.

"We're all set. Just sign these, please, Miss Ambrose."

Savannah didn't even look at the papers. She just signed them and handed them back. Her hands were sweating, and she was struggling not to bounce her leg. "Would you be a dear and give me a copy of all the paperwork? Both the papers opening and then closing the account?"

"Not a problem," Javon smiled and hit another button. A printer somewhere began to print. "Oh," Javon said as his brow furrowed, and he leaned closer to the computer.

Savannah shot a nervous look to Abby who barely shook her head and then took a deep breath as if reminding Savannah to breath. "Just this morning you opened a new account online and made a cash deposit. Do you mean to close that as well?"

"Yes," Abby said with a roll of her eyes. "I told you that you'd need that money to hire a crew. Why did you deposit it?"

Savannah forced herself to laugh. "I am so sorry. Please tell me I didn't make a mess of it all?"

Javon smiled as if he really wanted to roll his eyes. "Not at all. We're happy to keep this account open, or I can close it as well."

"Close it, please," Savannah said embarrassed. "I shouldn't have done it. I don't know what I was thinking! But, can I have all the paperwork on that as well? I'm sure my accountant is going to have a fit."

"Of course." He tapped some more into the computer and Savannah went through the signing of forms again before Javon stood up. "I'll be right back with your copies of the paperwork."

Savannah and Abby were quiet until Javon was out of earshot. Then Abby was talking to Dylan through some communication equipment Savannah couldn't even see. "Someone made a cash deposit in a new Savannah account this morning."

Abby turned to Savannah and smiled as if nothing was wrong. "Dylan is on the lookout and will pull the car right up to the exit when we give the go-ahead. Ridge is already calling Kale."

"It's Penn. He's here."

Abby was quiet for a second. "You're right. It's Penn. Kale found a plane ticket for him. He left Charleston last night. His departing flight is tonight."

Abby froze all of a sudden. "Got it." She leaned down into her bag and pulled out a large sunhat and plopped it onto Savannah's head.

"What are you doing?" she asked.

"Dylan spotted Penn at a coffee place across the street from the private entrance. He must have been inside ordering because he wasn't there five minutes ago. We need to make sure you're not seen."

Savannah worked quickly to pull her red hair up and under the hat as her hands shook.

"Don't worry, he can't hurt you. If he tries, he'll be dead before he has a chance."

That stopped Savannah's hands from shaking because the way Abby said that left her feeling very secure. "Sunglasses?"

"Use mine," Abby said, handing a pair of black, large-framed glasses to Savannah who grabbed them as if they'd save her life. "No, don't take him out. Great idea. We're finishing up here."

"Taking him out sounds good to me," Savannah whispered and Abby grinned.

"I'm happy to oblige if you really want."

Savannah couldn't tell if she was joking or not.

"Dylan is going to put a tracker on him. Then we'll know where he is at all times. Here comes Javon. Don't look at the papers here. We'll look them over on the boat," Abby whispered. "Now smile."

Savannah swatted at Abby and giggled.

"Here's all your paperwork, Miss Ambrose." Javon handed her a large packet of papers that she slipped directly into her bag. "And here comes your money. I have the full receipts for both accounts in the packet."

The two women stood. "Thank you so much, Javon. I'm sure I'll be back soon. You've made this such a wonderful banking experience for me."

"I'm so glad, Miss Ambrose. You have my email. Let me know if I can help in any way."

Savannah shook his hand, then walked from the table back out the way she came with Abby and five bank guards, three of whom were carrying two giant duffle bags apiece, each with the bank's name on it. A little too obvious, but nothing could be done about it right then. Savannah was careful not to walk too fast, and when one of the security guards opened the private door to the back parking lot, she saw Ridge behind the steering wheel of a black SUV with heavily tinted windows and kept her head down. The large floppy hat hid her face from view of the coffee shop where Penn was sitting.

"Here you go, ma'am."

"Thank you," Savannah said when the guard opened the back door for her.

Ridge got out of the SUV and opened the tailgate. "Can you place them in the back, please?"

The guards placed the bags of money as directed while Abby climbed in. Ridge walked casually around to the driver's door and got in.

"Where's Dylan?" Savannah asked, her voice breathless as she dared to look at Penn, sheltered by tinted windows, sunglasses, and her hat. Her body turned to ice as he looked up and winked at the waitress. She wanted to scream for that innocent woman to run as far as possible from him.

"Did you forget to breathe?" Abby asked as she nudged Savannah.

Savannah sucked in a breath once Penn was out of sight.

"Dylan is placing a tracker on Penn. He said he'd meet us at the boat. How did it go?"

"There were two accounts," Savannah blurted even though Ridge already knew that. Her head swam, her vision blurred, and her heart felt as if it would leap out of her chest.

Abby yanked off Savannah's seatbelt and shoved her head down. "Deep breaths," she ordered as she rubbed her back. Savannah stared at the floor of the SUV from between her knees as her body gradually stopped shaking and the roaring in her ears began to fade away.

Ridge pulled up to the hotel and parked the SUV in the reserved space Dylan took it from this morning. "Everyone grab as much as you can carry without looking like pack mules," Abby told them as they got out. "And leave the keys under the floor mat."

They hadn't even pulled all the duffle bags out when

Dylan arrived. "We're up and running," he said, picking up two bags.

Savannah picked up her and Ridge's bag of clothes, but before she could grab Dylan and Abby's, Dylan took it in hand. "I got it. Don't want to risk setting anything off. Let's go. I'm looking forward to seeing the fam."

RIDGE TOOK a sip of Ryker's bourbon as they all sat on the deck after dinner. They were well on their way to the United States by now. They had called Agent Castle before they'd gotten too far offshore that morning. He'd told them his agent had called and checked in with Penn. He immediately pulled plane records when Ridge told him Penn was on the island with them.

"He must have slipped out the back of his hotel. I wondered why we hadn't been able to get eyes on him today. I'll have my guys ask around at the conference. Let me know when you're closer to Charleston," Agent Castle had said.

Ridge didn't tell him about the second account yet. Kale had been called away, whatever that meant, and was just now getting to work on trying to find the source of the five hundred thousand dollars in the second account. At least that's what he told Abby when she'd checked in with him via a satellite phone.

They'd spent the day enjoying the weather together as they rested in the sun and talked. Abby told them about her overprotective father, and Dylan added his own stories. Then Ridge got to tell Abby all about the history of Shadows Landing. It was as if they were in this little bubble of happiness and couldn't be touched while on the open water.

They were safe. And for twelve more hours or so they had no worries.

"Ready for bed?" Ridge quietly asked Savannah after they'd all had a couple drinks. When she nodded, he stood. "I think we're heading to bed. Thank you both for all your help."

"It's our pleasure," Dylan said as he wrapped his arm around his wife, who nodded her agreement.

Ridge and Savannah left them snuggled together on the deck and headed to their room. Ridge was torn. After today, all he wanted to do was strip Savannah naked and keep her in his bed forever. The thought of her being in danger when they got back was too much.

Ridge sat down and watched her as she began to get ready for bed. The way she tugged her hair loose and shook it out. The way she stripped out of her clothes and tossed them on the back of a chair. And when she turned, completely nude, toward him, he stopped breathing.

"You know, I'm not supposed to get my stitches too wet. Want to help me shower?"

"Anything to help," Ridge said with a smile as he followed her to the bathroom, losing clothes along the way.

---

## 29

RIDGE COULDN'T DECIDE if he wanted to get back to Charleston or not. Part of him wanted to so that he could finally move on with the woman he loved. But the other part of him wanted to never leave the boat. They could hide away somewhere in the ocean as if they were the only two people in the world.

Ridge watched with a mixture of dread and excitement as the marina in Charleston came into view. The wind blew his shirt against his body as he stood at the front of the yacht, watching.

Savannah came up behind him and silently slipped her hand into his. "It's almost over."

Ridge wrapped his arms around her and pulled her against his side before leaning down and kissing her. Soon it would just be the two of them with no fear. Ridge knew Savannah would grow and spread her wings even more then. He couldn't wait to see what she'd do when she was no longer in danger.

"Okay, it's time to get out of sight," Dylan called from behind them.

"Let's finish this," Savannah said, her face tilted back as she looked into his eyes.

"I'll always have your back. I love you." Ridge gave her a quick kiss and took her hand in his as they went below deck.

"So, Agent Castle has an unmarked van waiting for us. We will turn the money over to him, along with the recordings and copies of the papers you received. I heard from Kale that he's still been unable to find where the second account came from," Dylan explained. "Kale said to turn it over, and he'll keep working on it. The plan is in place to call Penn as soon as you're back in the hospital. Abby will be in the bathroom of your room with you, so you'll never be alone. Cameras are all set up and ready to record the whole thing."

Abby nodded and reached out to take Savannah's hand. "I can put on a red wig and be in bed instead of you."

Ridge wanted to say yes, but Savannah shook her head. "He saw me when he shot Granger in the drive by. He'll know it's not me the second he sees your face. I don't want to risk him getting off by being cautious and professional enough to make sure he kills the right person."

The yacht slowed and Ridge knew they were in the harbor now. Abby reached into her bag and pulled out a short black wig and handed it to Savannah. "It's go time."

SAVANNAH HANDED over the money and paperwork in the large van with no windows and the normal seating removed. The only seating was a bench that ran along one side. It had *Thumbs Up Plumbing* written on the side, and at first glance looked as if it would fall apart from the rust. But the inside was redone and there were even metal rings on the floor to secure prisoners.

"So, this half a million isn't part of the money embezzled from Penn's company?" Agent Castle asked.

"We have no idea where it came from. But no, it's not part of that embezzlement scheme," Abby answered.

"We'll take it in as evidence, but if we can't find that it's from illegal sources, it's yours," Castle said with a shrug as the truck bounced along the old streets of downtown.

"Mine?" Savannah asked with shock.

"It was in your name. So yeah, it would be yours," Castle reassured her.

"I never thought about it. But knowing Penn, I'm sure it's illegal."

Castle nodded in agreement. "We'll wait and see. In the meantime, my men located Penn and are tracking him." He turned to Dylan and told him, "That tracker you put in his luggage is working perfectly. Thank you for that."

"When do you think the hit man will come after me?" Savannah asked, finally voicing the question that had been weighing on her mind since they'd come up with this plan.

"The nurse is going to tell Penn he can come anytime since there isn't security in that wing. This is all conjecture, but I believe Penn will come to see for himself. We will make sure it looks like a walk in the park. We hope the man will make his move tonight. We're going to tell Penn exactly when the fewest people will be around in hopes that he conveys that to his guy. If not then, I expect it to be tomorrow. We'll stress accidental death from secondary causes is still a risk, but only for the next two days in order to put some pressure on him to move quickly."

"Penn's conference ends today," Savannah told them. "He'll be back in Georgia soon."

"Not to worry. We can arrest him in Georgia just as easily as here," Castle told her. "He won't get away with this."

Savannah took a deep breath as the van slowed to a stop at the maintenance entrance to the hospital. They were all in gray overalls with a large thumbs-up logo on the chest pocket. Savannah got out with her black wig and a baseball cap pulled low along with Abby, Dylan, Ridge, and Agent Castle all in various degrees of disguise. They worked quickly carrying in "tools" as they made it into the building and out of sight.

They quickly shed their overalls and tools. Savannah handed the wig to Abby who stuffed it in a bag that she called her little bag of tricks. Dylan called it the boom bag. Savannah got the impression whatever was inside could probably level the entire hospital.

Abby and Dylan slipped into scrubs, Agent Castle put on a doctor's white coat, and Ridge helped Savannah get into a hospital gown and into her wheelchair. Being busy was good. It kept Savannah from thinking too much. But all too soon she was in her room, Penn had been called, Ridge was sitting next to her, and Abby had turned the bathroom into her office. And by office, she really meant kill room.

"Penn just pulled into the parking lot. He doesn't have his tracker with him, but the security cameras picked him up," Dylan told her when he stepped into the room. He kissed Abby and sent her a wink before turning to Ridge. "Come with me, cuz."

Savannah's heart began to beat wildly as her nerves kicked into overdrive. Abby also gave a wink. "You got this. I'll be here with you," she said before turning off the bathroom light and leaving the door open enough to see out. Abby wore black scrubs and seemed to just disappear from view.

"Thanks," Savannah said, knowing her new friend would hear her.

Ridge bent down and his kiss lingered on her lips as if he never wanted to pull apart. It felt like goodbye. "You'll do great. We're all around you. I've always got your back. Remember that. I love you, Savannah."

Savannah took a deep breath as she cupped his cheek in her hand. "Thank you, Ridge. I love you too. So very much."

Ridge leaned down and this time the kiss was more passionate before he pulled away and left without turning around. Only Agent Castle remained in the room. "All the audio and visual cameras are working. I'll be across the hall. Dylan and Ridge will be next door. We all will be able to see and hear you. Just play up how tired you are and downplay how good the staff is."

"Got it."

Savannah took a deep breath as Agent Castle stood next to her, staring intently at his clipboard. She closed her eyes and focused on her breathing. Slow and steady. Breathe in one, two, three. Breathe out one, two, three.

"How is she doing?" she heard Penn ask five minutes later.

"We needed that intensive care room for another patient, so she was moved before I wanted her to be," Savannah heard Castle say as he moved away from her side. "She's still in danger of what we call secondary risks. Were you told she'd developed an infection?"

"Yes," Penn said gravely. "I hated that I couldn't see her."

"I know. It looks like we have the infection under control, but we always worry about blood poisoning, heart attack, stroke, and embolism." Castle paused and looked down at his phone.

"I have one more patient I have to see. The night nurse will call me if there's any change. Fingers crossed the next forty-eight hours goes smoothly. If so, she'll be all clear. After that infection, I'm worried her body is in a compromised state. But, she's a fighter. And now she has you to fight along with her."

"Is that you, doctor?" Savannah mumbled.

"Yes, Mrs. Benson. I just gave her some medicine that unfortunately makes her rather drowsy. She'll be out until the last check of the night around four in the morning. That's when they'll wake her up to draw labs. So you might want to talk quickly. And there's no security in this wing, so just ignore the visiting hours. You can stay as long as you'd like."

"Thank you, doctor," Penn said as Savannah batted open her eyes. Agent Castle walked from the room and across the hall where she knew he'd be watching. "How are you feeling, pet?"

"Woof, woof," Savannah said, letting her eyes slide closed. "Meow."

"Savannah, wake up," Penn said, and Savannah fought a gasp when his hand tightened around her wrist. He shook her and her eyes popped open.

"Penn? Is that you? You're all fuzzy-looking."

"Do you need me to call the nurse?" Penn asked.

"Nah, I haven't seen her in forever. I don't think she's here." Then Savannah sniffled. "But you're here. That's so sweet of you, Penn. Thank you for not leaving me alone." She let her voice trail off as her eyes began to slide shut.

She heard Penn walking around the room. Then he pulled a cord and her machine began to go wild. Warning bells rang repeatedly.

"Penn, can you answer the phone?" Savannah murmured.

Finally someone came in and she heard Dylan's voice. "Do you need something?"

"I think this messed up," Penn said.

Dylan silenced it. "I'm just an orderly. I'll see if I can find the nurse. Between you and me, it might be a while. Is it an emergency?"

"I don't think so. I think a wire fell out, but I don't know how to fix it."

"The nurse will be in when she can. There's only one nurse on the floor and they're finishing up their shift change. The night nurse is something to look at, but that's when you actually see her. You didn't hear it from me, but she tends to nap most nights." Dylan scoffed and Savannah could practically hear his eyes rolling.

"Will my wife be taken care of? Do I need to transfer her?" Penn asked as he tried to hide the glee from his voice.

"She comes around every hour on the hour. Sets an alarm. Nothin' ever happens on this floor so I'm sure your wife is fine. Need anything else, bro?"

"No, thank you for helping quiet this. I'd hate to wake my wife up."

"No problem. Have a good night."

Savannah heard Dylan leave the room and then felt the tightness of Penn's hand around her arm. "Wake up!" he snapped.

Savannah's eyes popped open. "Oh, no. Did I oversleep?"

"No, pet. I just wanted to thank you for all you do for me. Goodbye, pet."

Savannah felt her heart stop. Was he going to kill her himself?

"Goodbye, Penn. Have a wonderful day at work. I'll clean the house in just a moment." And then she closed her eyes.

She heard Penn let out a huff as he pulled out his phone. "Savannah?"

Savannah didn't move. She heard a photo being taken and then he was texting. Before she could pretend to be awake, he was leaving.

"Savannah," Ridge said and her eyes popped open. "He's gone."

"So, now I wait for someone to kill me."

"I'm afraid so."

ABBY STAYED HIDDEN in the bathroom. Agent Castle stayed across the hall monitoring all the hidden cameras. Dylan was similarly in the room next door. And Ridge sat by her side holding her hand, but they didn't talk. Savannah couldn't. She didn't know what to say. She was overwhelmed that this could be the last time she was with him and yet was at a complete loss of words.

The sun had just set. Her nerves couldn't decide what to do. Relax or get worse. "Potential suspect spotted coming up the stairs."

Ridge squeezed her hand. "I love you."

"I love you too," she whispered desperately as Ridge hurried from the room. But not before she heard him tell Abby, "I'm trusting you with the life of the woman I love."

Then there was silence. She could hear the swirling of the air conditioner. She felt every ounce of the weight of the bulletproof vest she had on under her gown. It felt as if it were pressing every breath from her body. And then there were the footsteps. They were practically silent as the rubber soles of the shoes came into the room.

There he paused, and in the darkness of the room, the

bright screen of his cell phone lighting up was seen even through her closed eyelids. She'd been afraid of breathing too much, but instead her breathing stopped. Her lungs burned, but she couldn't make herself inhale.

Then she heard rustling and felt his hand moving to hers. His grasp was warm, strong, and steady as he took hold of her hand. She felt the pressure of him sliding a needle into her port and then it was suddenly done—the pressure and his hand. Just gone.

Savannah's eyes popped open and the man was fighting Abby who had him in a headlock. He was kicking and trying to pull her hair. Savannah didn't think. The red haze of anger was back.

"How much am I worth?" she yelled as the room filled with people. "No, don't!" she yelled at Abby who instantly loosened her hold to prevent him from blacking out.

"The other guy was paid twenty thousand. How much were you paid?"

The man lunged, dragging Abby with him. His hands reached for a knife and then he was just inches away as Dylan and Castle leaped forward. Savannah was on her knees on the bed and the second she saw him narrow his eyes before he lunged, she'd reached under her Kevlar vest.

*Zap!*

The man stopped. The knife dropped as Savannah held the stun gun the size of a lipstick container Abby had given her against the man's arm. Then, just for fun, she pressed the button again. The man dropped to the floor and farted.

"Abby, you didn't," Dylan groaned.

"It was the best stun gun to hide on her," Abby defended. The man farted again. Loudly. "Sorry. Dylan's cousin developed this. It was a practical joke, but it's actually a very good stun gun."

*Bruumpht.*

Savannah snorted as she tried to not laugh like an eight year old boy at someone farting. Dylan let out a huff. Abby snickered. Agent Castle broke out laughing. And Ridge wrapped his arms around her and kissed her.

## 30

DYLAN USED the man's finger to unlock the phone before the FBI hauled him away. While Dylan worked, Ridge stayed with Savannah as she changed. The worst was over. All they had to do was pick up Penn. Then this nightmare would be over.

There was a knock at the door and Savannah's eyes shot to Ridge's as she pulled out that small stun gun again. "Who is it?"

"It's Kord. Can I come in?"

Ridge and Savannah both visibly relaxed. "Come in," Ridge told him.

"I'm so happy to see you both. Agent Castle told me they caught the assassin and that you both can go home. I'm your ride."

"Thank you for coming all the way from Shadows Landing to get us," Savannah said as Ridge slipped his hand into hers.

"Ready to go home?" Ridge asked her.

"More than ready." When Savannah smiled at him, he

saw his whole future in her face. He couldn't wait to get home and wake up tomorrow together, with nothing holding them back. No danger, no ex, nothing but love and potential.

"How's Granger?" Ridge asked as they headed out of the hospital room.

"Recovering really well. He'll come home in two days. Walker has already asked his wife to come evaluate Granger. They'll be arriving next week and staying for a week so she can show Granger exactly what kind of physical therapy he needs to be doing."

Ridge nodded and turned to Savannah to explain. "That's how our friend Walker met Layne Davies. She's a doctor of physical therapy and specializes in gunshot wounds, especially for military personnel. She was a keynote speaker for a convention here and Gavin went to get her help. Walker gained a wife and the Faulkners gained the Davies family."

"Your cousins, like Dylan?"

"And aunts and uncles. Our families had been estranged because of some pettiness on my great-grandmother's part. But thanks to Walker and Layne, we're all family again now."

Ridge and his small group stopped where Dylan, Abby, and Agent Castle stood with a team of FBI agents. Dylan turned to them and nodded. "Agents verified hours ago that Penn was at the hotel. His location has just moved. He appears to be leaving the hotel."

"Are you picking him up now?" Ridge asked as he held Savannah closely to him.

"Leaving right now," Dylan told them with a wink. "It'll be fun. We'll come straight to your home in Shadows Landing afterwards, Savannah."

Savannah nodded next to him and Ridge felt her take a deep breath. "That's good. We'll see you there."

"Be careful," Ridge told his cousin. "Aunt Tammy would kill me if anything happened to you."

"Don't worry about a thing. See you all soon. I've been dying for some barbeque. Abby hasn't had any, so I thought we could grab some from The Pink Pig and Lowcountry Smokehouse for a late dinner tasting."

"We can make that happen," Ridge told his cousin before shaking his hand and pulling him in for a quick thump on the back. Dylan wasn't really a touchy-feely guy, but Ridge needed to express more than he could with a handshake. "Thank you for all your help."

"You're welcome. See you soon."

They followed Kord out to his cruiser and slid into the backseat. Savannah wasn't talking as she kept her eyes directed out the side window, but she did reach for Ridge. He laced their fingers together as Kord talked about what was going on in town and how everyone was doing. He asked about their trip and Ridge answered for them both. It was clear Savannah was in her own world, and Ridge wanted to give her the time she needed.

"Savannah's house or yours?" Kord asked Ridge as they grew closer to Shadows Landing.

"Mine, please," Savannah answered, finally coming out of her thoughts. It had been an overwhelming week and while she knew others would think it was silly, she was worried now that the threats had been taken care of, Ridge might find the dinner-planning, fall-decorating, social-chair Savannah boring. Also, now that the threat was gone, there was no reason for her to stay at Ridge's house. She loved him, yes. But they'd just started dating. She was just now coming into her own.

She saw Ridge look at her and then at Kord, and she knew Ridge was going to talk to her as soon as they had some privacy. Kord pulled into her driveway and Savannah's eyes went wide. Ridge's crew had completed so much in only a couple of days. Her window was fixed. Her kitchen was completely framed and covered so her house was protected from the elements.

"Wow, I can't believe how much they've gotten done," Savannah said as they waited for Kord to let them out of the backseat.

"I had two crews working so it could be livable for you."

Savannah's heart sank even when she didn't want it to. Here she was at her house because she didn't want to push Ridge into a relationship, but having him get her house ready so quickly made her feel that maybe he was rethinking their relationship. Savannah took a deep breath and physically shook her head as she got out of the cruiser. She was being silly. She was inventing problems where they weren't any.

"Kord, do you think you could grab a bunch of barbeque for the team when they show up?" Ridge asked as he took out his wallet and handed Kord some money.

"You're sure you don't want me to stay until everyone arrives?" Kord asked.

"It's okay. I'm actually starving," Savannah told him. And she really just wanted a moment alone with Ridge. They needed to talk and she didn't want to have to play hostess too.

Kord took the money, and as he drove away, Savannah led Ridge onto the porch. "Thank you for asking Kord to get dinner."

"I could tell you wanted to talk," Ridge said, giving her space, for which Savannah was equal parts grateful and angry. She wanted his arms around her, but she wanted to stand on her own two feet as well.

"I do. I learned the hard way there should be no secrets between couples. That I should trust and be trusted completely. And because I love you, I trust you with my feelings."

"Savannah, you have my love. Do you doubt that?" Ridge asked, and she gulped. How did she put this so she didn't hurt him, yet express her fear.

"No. I just don't know what to do with myself right now. We fell in love under intense and unusual circumstances. I'm afraid of making the wrong move and messing it up," she admitted.

Ridge was quiet for a moment and then reached for her. Savannah exhaled and moved into his arms. He wasn't mad. The way he was looking at her told her he understood. "I don't want you to be worried about being anything other than yourself. Always be honest with me. I'd rather you feel momentarily uncomfortable by talking to me so that we can resolve what's worrying you, than having you try to hide it or second guess yourself. Trust me to tell you the truth. Trust me to support you. Trust that my love for you encompasses not only your outstanding qualities, but also the ones you or I might not like. I love you, the whole you. All your feelings, all your quirks, everything."

Savannah gasped. "Quirks? You mean there's stuff you don't like?"

Ridge grinned. "I don't like that you wear a nightgown to bed, but I can live with it if it means I have you in my bed." Savannah busted out laughing and swatted him. "So, what's worrying you?" Ridge asked.

Savannah was no longer scared that Ridge would be angry. She should have known he was different. He talked, he shared, and he listened. Savannah was going to trust in their relationship enough to be completely herself. "I think we're moving too fast. I was equally afraid you'd ask me to move in with you or you wouldn't ask me to move in with you. If you asked me to, I'd feel pressured to say yes when I want to stand on my own two feet first."

"Okay," Ridge said slowly. "I understand things have happened fast. If it makes you feel better, we'll slow it down. I love you, and I want to be with you. Any way you'll have me. What is it you want, Savannah?"

"I'll tell you what I really want," Savannah said, feeling empowered. She'd taken a risk and told Ridge what she felt and he wasn't upset. Instead, he was listening to her. "I want to flip this house over the next month and sell it. I want to use the proceeds to finish my bachelor's degree in design and try my hand at starting my own interior design company."

Savannah held her breath as she watched Ridge listening. Then he nodded. "I don't know how much help you want, but the second floor above Tinsley's art gallery is empty. I bet she'd rent it out to you at a very reasonable price. And then, if you really want—and no pressure—you can always use some space at my architectural firm in Charleston. I'm never there, but it's in Ryker's building and has a secretary."

"You'd let me use your office? And you wouldn't mind me going back to school?"

"I'd let you use anything of mine. And why wouldn't I support your dreams?"

The look of confusion on his face made Savannah kiss him. "I love you. I'm so excited!"

"I love you too," Ridge said against her lips before taking her with his mouth again. His lips were warm, soft, and demanding as he pulled her to him. Savannah placed her hands on his chest and curled her fingers into him. She felt his heart beat, she felt his muscles tense, and she felt the man she loved.

"Someone's been a naughty little pet."

Savannah didn't have time to respond. Ridge shoved her behind him, sending her rolling down the wooden steps of the porch. Pain shot through her as she curled into a ball trying to protect her head. One. Two. Three. Four. Five. Six. Seven. Eight. She counted as the breath was shocked from her body with every step she fell down.

She stopped bouncing with a hard crash to the walkway. Everything hurt. Her lungs burned as she fought the panic and forced herself to realize she was still breathing. Her eyes focused on the setting night sky and then to the sounds of a fight.

"Ridge!" she thought she yelled, but it was really just a ragged gasp for air as she saw Penn and Ridge fighting.


"SAVANNAH, RUN!" Ridge ordered as he ducked the knife Penn swung at him.

He saw her get to her knees and begin to crawl away. Penn did too. He swung the blade at Ridge, but Ridge blocked it, sending it onto the porch. Ridge followed up with a punch to the stomach, causing Penn to double over. When he went to knee Penn in the face, Penn grabbed his leg and fell backward.

Ridge was yanked forward as he and Penn crashed to the porch floor. The house shook as the battle resumed. Ridge had the upper hand and slammed a fist into Penn's cocky face. Penn rolled, sending Ridge tumbling to the side as both men scrambled to their feet. Only this time, Ridge wasn't fast enough.

Penn grabbed one of the potted plants. As Ridge tried to stand, Penn slammed it onto his head. The last thing Ridge saw was Penn jogging down the stairs toward Savannah. Then everything went black.

## 31

SAVANNAH HAD JUST DRAGGED in her first full breath when she felt a hand slide into her hair from behind. The hand fisted her hair and yanked her backward. Savannah screamed, although it was weak even to her ears because she was so short of breath.

"What a surprise I got I when I emailed Ocean Waters Bank and found out my accounts had been withdrawn and closed. Somehow I'd cashed them out the same day I made a deposit. Where's my money, pet?"

Penn yanked her up to her feet by her hair and spun her to face him. Savannah would have been fearful, but the moment she saw Ridge unmoving on the porch she lost her mind. Her heart broke and the anguished cry that tore free from her throat sounded like a dying animal. "Ridge!"

Savannah was so focused on Ridge she didn't see the hand flying toward her. The slap had her eyes watering and her cheek feeling as if it were about to explode. The scream died as her head snapped to the side with the force of the hit.

"Focus now, pet. Where did you put my money?"

Savannah's hand was resting on her stinging cheek. Tears had stopped halfway down her cheek as anger replaced her pain. "Go to hell!" Savannah spit in Penn's face and braced for what was coming.

Penn didn't disappoint. The punch to her stomach knocked her to the ground, gasping for air once again. He grabbed her hair and began to drag her back toward her house. "Let's go inside where we won't be disturbed, pet."

"That money belongs to your firm. I gave it back to them," Savannah said as soon as they reached the steps. Lying on the patio was the knife Penn dropped. If she could get her hands on it, she'd kill him.

"You did what?" Penn snapped as he threw her onto the steps. The edge of the steps hit her hip and ribs, sending shooting pain through her body.

"I gave it back in exchange for your firm's agreement not to file charges against me."

"Eleven and a half million dollars?"

Savannah shook her head. "Eleven million. The exact amount you embezzled."

Savannah sat up and inched her way up to the next step. She looked over to Ridge and saw blood on the back of his head in the glow of the porch lights and gasped. She made a move to run to him, but Penn grabbed her shoulders and threw her down onto the porch away from Ridge. And away from the knife.

Savannah inched her way back from Penn as he stood menacingly over her. "What about the half million?"

"I kept it."

"Where is it, pet?" Penn's voice was so slow and cold it sent chills down her spine. She backed farther away from him, her hand stopping when she hit her purse—the purse that had the small dagger in it from the weapons class.

Penn took a step away and kept his eyes on her as he bent down to pick up his knife. A sick smile spread over his face as he stalked her. Savannah scrambled backward, her hand slipping into her purse and closing around the dagger's cold handle. Penn raised the knife and Savannah yanked the dagger free.

Penn laughed as he swung toward her arm. Savannah rolled and pulled the blade from the leather sheath. In the move little Lacy had taught her, she blocked the swinging attack from Penn. His eyes went big for just a second in surprise before he laughed again.

"Ever heard of dying from a thousand little cuts?" he asked and swung again. This time a tiny cut appeared on her shoulder. She'd been able to block the worst of the attack. "Where's my money, pet?"

"Don't you mean *my* money? It was in my name, after all."

Savannah dove to the side and rolled up against the house. With the house to her back and her dagger in hand, she used the wall to help herself stand on shaking legs.

"You've always been so stupid. You could never see the endgame. And you messed it all up just like you messed up my entire life," Penn spat.

"Screw you, Penn. You messed up your own life. You lie, cheat, and steal and then blame me for it. I deserve that money for putting up with your sorry ass for as long as I did. *I* screwed up *your* life?" Savannah faux laughed. "You won't be half the man you are without me. You can't even climb the corporate ladder without me. Do you know your boss offered me a job today? It was always me, Penn. Without me, you're nothing but a criminal."

"A rich one. See, pet, there's a really nice life insurance policy I took out on you two months ago. I would have had twenty million to start my new life, but since you had to screw it all up, I'll have to settle for ten million instead."

"What life insurance policy? I would have found it." Savannah didn't believe him. Someone would have found it.

"I don't know how you found these accounts, but I was even trickier with the life insurance because it was my fallback plan. You always thought you were so much smarter than me, didn't you? Do you have any idea why I delayed the divorce?"

"To torment me," Savannah said. There was no question about it.

Penn shook his smug-looking head. "No, because for the past twenty months, Savannah Ambrose has been in Switzerland establishing residency. As soon as the divorce here was finalized, Savannah and I re-married in Switzerland. Two months ago, Savannah Benson took out an insurance policy worth ten million dollars with a bank there. A life insurance policy naming me her beneficiary. At least this bank doesn't share any client information."

"What are you talking about? I've never been to Switzerland." Savannah knew he wasn't lying by the look of victory on his face. She wanted nothing more than to wipe that smirk off his face.

"The night you caught me was all planned. Haven't you wondered where Ginger is?" he asked. Ginger, of one of her supposed best friends who she'd caught him with in bed that fateful night. The friend who so closely resembled her that everyone thought they were sisters. The one Tibbie said was in Europe.

"That's identity theft," Savannah whispered as the pieces were falling into place. That's why he dragged out the divorce. So the fake Savannah would have the means to secure the life insurance and then he'd kill the real Savannah Benson, file the claim, and he and Ginger would be ten million dollars richer. "Why embezzle? You had to know you'd be caught."

"As if that's the first time I embezzled. I've taken a lot more and I haven't been caught. I'd been stealing money for years. I bought a house in your name in Switzerland three years ago. Ginger and I visited every year. I told you that you never see the long game. But then I had to push you over the edge to get you to file for divorce. Then you tragically die of an accident, leaving me free and clear to claim the insurance money no one knows about. I wouldn't be a suspect in your real death because I'd have nothing to gain. Just a rundown house I didn't want."

"But you underestimated me," Savannah said with a smirk of her own. She loosened her grip on the handle of her dagger just the way Lucy taught her as she got ready to fight for her life.

"I did. I admit it. I don't know if it was you or the inept hit men I hired. Either way, here you are. You'll die tragically while visiting the family home. Ginger used your passport to enter the country last week. We're all ready. She's my alibi to show I've moved on. It was only you who hadn't. We had to change things up, but the new narrative is that you're desperate to get me back. You've hurt yourself in cries of attention. I have the hospital logs showing where they had to call me. Being the nice guy that I am, I came. You begged me to come back into your life, but I refused. I'd moved on with Ginger. So, to get revenge you pick up a random guy. Things go bad and you both die. He'll murder you so I can get my insurance payout, and then he'll commit suicide,"

Penn said smugly as he tossed a glance at Ridge, still lying unconscious where he had fallen.

"The police will be here soon. They know you stole the money," Savannah warned him.

Penn shook his head. "No, they won't. Ginger is occupying that deputy you sent for food and my decoy has the FBI morons fooled. It's just you and me, pet. I'll wrap this up, and Ginger and I will be out of the country before anyone can stop us. They might know I stole some money, but they won't think I murdered you. Not with your boy toy here."

No, she couldn't be alone. She had to keep him talking. Help would come soon. Dylan, Abby, and Agent Castle weren't stupid. As soon as they saw the decoy, they'd come for her. She had to stall Penn and save Ridge.

"What I don't understand is where the five hundred thousand came from," Savannah told him, hoping to keep him talking.

"I took an advance from some not so nice people in Atlanta to cover my next scheme. Again, you messed everything up. But you can fix it. I just need you to die."

Everything seemed to happen in slow motion. Savannah kept her eyes on Penn, not on the knife, just as she'd been taught. She saw the second Penn pulled back his arm ready to stab her.

Savannah reacted instantly. She didn't pull her blade all the way back. Instead, she jabbed it forward as she leapt toward Penn, using her body weight and momentum to drive the dagger into his stomach. With a sickening feel, the blade gave way as it tore through his clothes and skin before sinking in.

·  ·  ·

THE THROBBING in Ridge's head was the first thing he noticed as he came to. His eyes were closed and he heard talking. His mind registered that he was lying facedown on something hard.

*Open your eyes.*

Ridge felt as if he were lifting two garage doors when it was really just his eyelids. A hazy light assaulted his eyes as he tried to focus on what was underneath him. Everything was blurry as he tried to remember what the hell happened.

His brain tried to start up, but it felt like a flooded engine slugging its way to turn over. He blinked his eyes again and turned his head just a bit. The pain helped wake him up as he found his eyes slowly coming into focus. He was looking at a house. He was lying on a porch. The engine sparked and his brain came to life. Savannah. Penn. The potted plant.

"The police will be here soon. They know you stole the money," Ridge heard Savannah say. She was trying to be strong, but he heard the fear in her voice. He heard the way it shook just a little as she tried to challenge Penn.

As they talked, Ridge struggled onto his hands and knees. His eyes felt like they were bruised and his head screamed in pain. The pain made him nauseous. But he turned his head and saw a knife in Penn's hand. Penn's back was toward him, his menacing stance blocking Ridge's view of Savannah.

Ridge grabbed hold of the porch railing and hauled himself up. His vision made it appear he was on a tilt-a-whirl ride, but there was one thing he saw clearly. He saw Penn pulling back his hand with the knife in it as he said, "I just need you to die."

Ridge bent down and grabbed the heavy terra cotta pot planted with a mix of mums and lamb's ears. The pot had to weigh fifty pounds as Ridge fought off the dizziness and stepped forward.

Savannah screamed, Penn stumbled back, and Ridge slammed the pot onto Penn's head.

SAVANNAH SCREAMED as Penn's knife sliced the side of her arm. He stumbled back and then her eyes went large. It wasn't because of her knife sticking out of his white dress shirt with red blood blossoming from the wound. It was the sight of Ridge slamming a massive plant container over Penn's head.

Penn dropped to the ground and Savannah cringed when he landed face first, sending the dagger deeper into his body. "Ridge!"

"You're safe," Ridge said as he swayed as if he were drunk. Suddenly he stopped swaying and crumpled to the ground.

"Ridge!" Savannah screamed again as she kicked the knife from Penn's hand before bounding over him to get to Ridge. She dropped to the ground and pulled his head into her lap. "Ridge, can you hear me?"

Sirens sounded off in the distance, but Savannah couldn't hear them over her sobs. Ridge was alive, but he wasn't waking up.

"Savannah!" Abby was by her side pulling her away as Dylan examined Ridge. Savannah finally looked up and saw that her front yard was suddenly filled with people. Abby helped her stand. Dylan and Gavin were on either side of Ridge. Agent Castle had Penn flipped over and was administering CPR. Kord handed a screaming Ginger over to an FBI agent.

Savannah made an animalistic-sounding growl as she

pushed Abby's hands off of her and vaulted down the stairs. Kord saw her running toward them and jumped back. Ginger was screaming at her, but Savannah didn't hear it. All she heard was the sound of her fist connecting to Ginger's nose and the satisfying crunch it made.

"You bitch!" Ginger cried as she grabbed her nose.

"What's going on here?" Agent Castle asked, coming to stand beside Savannah. Savannah was breathing hard and she wished she could punch Ginger again.

"She hit me! Arrest her!" Ginger ordered.

"Is that what happened?" Agent Castle asked the FBI agent.

"Nah, she tripped getting out of the police cruiser. This is Penn Benson's accomplice. I found her in possession of a forged passport stating she was one Savannah Benson along with her own driver's license stating her identity as one Ginger Pettit."

"Yup, saw it too. Just fell all on her own," the agent said to Castle. "Deputy King here told me she was trying to prevent him from getting back to the house. That's how he discovered her identity."

"Is that so?" Castle asked as he put a steadying hand on Savannah's arm. He could feel her tension and her desire to go after Ginger again.

"I mean, I know ladies can't resist me, but here's one new to town looking very similar to the woman at the center of Savannah's divorce. She wanted to take me someplace private, so I let her. Only when she went for Prince, I went for her bag and discovered the passports. I arrested her and immediately came here where I called Gavin for medical help as you all arrived."

"Wait," Castle said. "Who's Prince?"

Kord looked down at his pants. "You know. I'm the King so he's my Prince."

Savannah snorted as Castle shook his head.

"You don't have anything on me!" Ginger yelled as Castle told his agent to detain her.

"I have everything on you," Savannah called out. "I have the identity theft, the insurance fraud, Switzerland, everything."

She smiled as Ginger's face turned whiter. Then Savannah's smile grew as Ginger actually did slip and fall, going down hard onto her knees before being shoved into the back of an FBI vehicle.

"Savannah," Agent Castle said seriously as he held onto her arm. "Penn's dead. I don't know if it's from the dagger in the stomach or the head wound. I'll need your statement."

"I'll call Olivia for you," Kord told her before sending her a wink. "Nice punch."

"I don't know what you're talking about," Savannah said with virtuous innocence.

"I know this was self-defense. But to preserve any case I have against Ginger, I need to keep you and Ridge separate until I get both of your statements," Castle said gently to her.

"But," Savannah turned to see Gavin working on bandaging an unconscious Ridge.

"I will keep you updated on him, I promise."

"Ridge!"

Savannah turned to see Tinsley racing for her brother. Tears were streaming down her face as she fell to her knees next to him while Gavin worked. Dylan and Abby left Ridge to Gavin and Tinsley's care and walked over to join Savannah and Castle.

"How is he?" Savannah asked.

"He's unconscious. Probably has a nasty concussion. But his vitals are strong," Dylan assured her.

Abby looked upset as her lips were pressed tightly together. She shifted from foot to foot with her hands on her hips. Dylan pressed a quick kiss on her forehead and then guided Agent Castle over toward Ridge.

"Are you okay, Abby?" Savannah finally asked when the men were out of earshot.

Abby stopped moving back and forth and her frown deepened. "Am *I* okay? I'm the one who made the call to go after the GPS tracker instead of coming here with you. Ridge is hurt and you could have been killed. I should be asking if you're okay."

Savannah took a deep breath, and when she let it out, she smiled. "I am. I'm good. In fact, I feel great. As soon as I know Ridge is okay, I'll finally be free."

Savannah saw Abby relax slightly. "I'm still sorry I wasn't here."

"You want to do something about it?" Savannah asked suddenly.

"Anything," Abby told her.

"Ginger Pettit. Get whatever evidence the FBI needs to put her away for a very long time."

Abby's lips twitched into a grin—a grin that literally sent chills down Savannah's back. Abby was so nice and outgoing, but that smile told Savannah there was another side to Abby that Savannah hoped to never cross.

"On it," Abby pulled out her phone and as she walked toward an unsuspecting Ginger, Savannah heard her say, "Kale. Get me everything on Ginger Pettit. She was pretending to be Savannah in Switzerland. I need it ASAP. I'm going to have a little chat with her in a moment."

Damn. That woman was scary when she wanted to be.

SAVANNAH HAD WATCHED as the still unconscious Ridge was loaded into the back of an ambulance. Gavin had turned and gave her a nod before climbing in and sitting beside Tinsley. That was the last news she'd had on Ridge in the last two hours.

Now she sat in Kord's office with Agent Castle and Olivia Townsend. Olivia had made the last agent storm off, nearly in tears. Thirty minutes ago, Agent Castle came in to take the fleeing agent's place.

"We want an update on Ridge's health, then we'll continue," Olivia said with finality as she leaned back, crossed her long legs, and pulled out her phone. She didn't even look up as Agent Castle sighed.

"Just a few more questions—" he tried to say, but Olivia held up her finger and slowly wagged it back and forth as she never took her eyes off her screen. "Fine."

"You're so cold and it's so hot," Kord told her when Castle left the room.

"That's so sweet. I bet your girlfriend loves your sweet talk." Olivia sent him a wink.

"As if one woman could keep me down. Though I bet you could."

Olivia smiled at him. "You wish."

Kord winked at her and then looked down at his phone. "Hey, you think you can quit twisting Castle's balls and get us out of here by eleven? Granger's nurse just texted and wants to get together at this club in Charleston."

"My, how quickly I'm tossed aside," Olivia said dryly. "How is Granger?"

"He's doing really well. Although he can't wait to get

home. They're only letting him go in a couple of days since Layne will be there to stay with him."

The door opened and Agent Castle walked back in. "Ridge is awake and is in the process of giving his statement to an agent. He has a concussion, and he had to have some stitches. He'll stay overnight at the hospital. If there're no worsening signs of trauma, he'll be discharged tomorrow afternoon."

"Then here is my client's full written testimony, already signed." Olivia slid a thick packet of paper over to Castle who looked ready to scream.

"I have questions," Castle said again.

"And there are your answers."

Savannah just wanted to get to Ridge, but she trusted Olivia to protect her so instead of saying anything, she just sat back and waited patiently as Castle read her statement.

"If I have more questions . . ."

"Then my client will be made available to you at a convenient time to answer them." As Olivia stood, Savannah did too. "I'll drive you to Charleston."

"Thank you." Savannah reached out and squeezed Olivia's hand before smiling at Castle and sending a wink to Kord. That had been two tough hours of questioning, but she knew it was to make a case against Ginger and clear herself of murder so it was worth every second. However, there was nothing she wanted more than to see Ridge.

"ABOUT TIME YOU WOKE UP."

Ridge's eyes fluttered. The air smelled of disinfectant, and he heard the steady sound of machinery. "Granger?" He turned his head and groaned as Granger came into focus. He was in a button-down shirt and athletic pants, seated in a wheelchair with various tubes coming from him. That was when Ridge noticed he had an IV in his own hand as well.

"That's right. And the FBI is here to talk to you. I'm sitting in as well. Want me to bring in your lawyer?" Granger asked.

"Olivia is here?"

"Nope," Granger said with a slow grin. "Olivia is with Savannah. Ryker sent Olivia's boss. I've never seen a man with a stick so far up his—"

"Sheriff, I see you're talking to my client without me."

Ridge smiled because the man did look like he had a literal stick up his ass. His back was ramrod straight and there was not a single hint of amusement anywhere on his face. In fact, he was rather wrinkle-free. Ridge guessed it was due to his lack of smiling even though he was probably in his sixties if his white hair was any indicator.

The next two hours were the longest of Ridge's life. He was pretty sure he fell asleep through some of the interrogation. He told his attorney, Mr. Hendrix, what had happened and Hendrix had taken it from there. Ridge gave his statement, answered some questions, napped a little, and then signed his statement. Finally everyone cleared the room and he was left with just Granger.

"Any word on how Savannah is?" Ridge asked. He couldn't wait to hold her, but the FBI agent had told him they weren't allowed to be together until they'd both given their statements.

Granger chuckled to himself as he shook his head. "Kord called on his way here to pick up my nurse for a date. He said they were delayed because Olivia made an agent cry, but that they're on their way here now."

"Already here," Savannah said, rushing into the room. His heart pounded as he opened his arms and Savannah crawled into the tiny bed with him. "Oh, Ridge. I thought I lost you! I love you so much."

She eased down gently beside him and rested her hand on his heart. She looked so tired that all Ridge wanted to do was to shut out the world and hold her while she slept. "You're safe now," Ridge whispered as he ran a hand over her hair and then down her back.

"Shouldn't you be in bed, Sheriff?"

Ridge turned to look at where Olivia stood in her pencil skirt, heels, and blazer, looking like a stern mother hen at Granger.

"It's still my case," Granger said stubbornly as he crossed his arms over his chest and transformed himself into a pouting child.

"I know it is and then the big, bad FBI came in and tried to take it from you. Well, we'll make sure you get all the credit." Ridge could feel Savannah's body shaking with silent laughter as Olivia grabbed Granger's wheelchair and began to turn him toward the door. She spoke to him as if he were a child. "But the *little* sheriff won't be able to fight for his case if he's not rested up."

Savannah snorted in laughter and tried to hide it by burying her face against Ridge's chest.

"But, I'm not ready to leave," Granger complained. "And Kord stole my nurse."

"And yet we are leaving anyway. Say your goodbyes, and I'll help you into bed."

Ridge was biting his lip so hard there were tears in his eyes. Granger was normally tough as nails. Ridge hadn't ever seen this side of him before, but he had a feeling the pain killers were playing a rather large role.

"Goodbye. I'll check in on you tomorrow," Granger called out as Olivia wheeled him from the room.

Ridge looked down at the woman in his arms. "I love you, Savannah."

"I love you too."

And when she tilted her face up to his, Ridge leaned down and placed his lips on hers. It was more than a kiss. It was a promise of their future.

---

## 32

TWO MONTHS—SAVANNAH had done it all in two months. She'd shaken hands with the buyers of her house and handed over the keys. The house Ridge had helped her renovate was finished a month before, and for the past month she'd used the house as her showpiece. She'd had Olivia sell the house in Switzerland and used the money to finish work on this house even while putting most of it in savings. Savannah had worked on designing every detail. Getting every color just right. And then with a little help from both Ridge and Trent, she got her house featured in two magazines. Not for interior design, but it was still shown with her name attached to it. One was for country renovations and the other was for custom furniture Trent had made for her, including her own porch bed swing.

"Enjoy your house," she told the new owners before leaving the bank and heading down Main Street.

Her phone rang and she looked to see it was the sheriff's station.

"Hello?"

"It's Granger." Granger was fully healed now and had served as a protector of sorts for her. There had been no more pushy FBI questions. She'd been cleared of Penn's death, and while the five hundred thousand had been taken into evidence against an Atlanta loan shark, she wasn't prosecuted for any of Penn's crimes. On the other hand, Ginger had been. Her attorney advised her trial would not go well when he saw the video of Abby's interrogation. Apparently there were whispered words that weren't caught on tape, Ginger screaming and crying before spilling her guts. Ginger had taken a plea deal the second Abby left the room and her attorney had arrived. She'd get out in twenty-five years if she behaved.

"I'm about to walk by the courthouse," Savannah told him.

"Good. I need to see you."

Savannah pulled the phone away to check. Yup, Granger had hung up on her. He was a man of few words but she'd never had a better friend.

As she approached the courthouse, the front door opened and Granger stepped outside holding a large envelope.

"Savannah Ambrose?" Granger asked.

"What? Am I in trouble? I got all the permits you told me I had to get for the house remodel."

Granger signed a piece of paper and handed her the envelope. "You've been served."

"Served with what?" Savannah asked, and she felt like throwing the envelope back to Granger.

"Don't know. Let's find out."

"I don't want to find out," she shoved it back at him. "You open it."

Granger took it with a shrug and tore it open. Thick folded papers came out and he opened it. His head nodded slightly as he read the top letter, but he didn't say anything as he skimmed the rest.

"Well?" Savannah was practically shaking. Nothing ever good came from a sheriff serving you papers.

Granger held up a finger to tell her to wait as he finished reading. "It's from an attorney in Switzerland."

Savannah's stomach plummeted. Her legs began to shake and she swayed slightly as she tried to regain her breath. "What does he want?"

"It appears after Ginger married Penn in Switzerland as you, he got that insurance policy on Savannah Benson." Granger paused and looked up at her.

Savannah nodded. "Ginger pretended to be me so they could get the life insurance money after they killed me. I know."

"What you don't know is that it appears that, at the same time and to avoid suspicion, Penn also took out a life insurance policy with one Savannah Benson as the beneficiary. After you were to die, he could easily change the beneficiary to Ginger and no one would think twice about it."

"But I didn't die."

Granger smiled and flipped to the last page but didn't give it to her yet. "No, you didn't. And the policy was paid up for the entire year. The insurance company's lawyers were able to identify you as Penn's wife via the marriage record in the United States. They also found the divorce decree making Savannah Benson, Savannah Ambrose of Shadows Landing."

"Right. I know. But he told me he'd change his will and

his life insurance beneficiary." Savannah looked at the papers he was holding and then nodded. "I get it. These are the cover-their-butts paperwork so they don't have to pay out the insurance."

Granger's lips turned up into a smile. "They read the transcript of the trial and know the marriage in Switzerland was null and void. Therefore, they determined Ginger wasn't the beneficiary. His actual wife was one Savannah Benson, now Savannah Ambrose. However, they had to verify that your actual divorce decree says nothing about life insurance proceeds. You might have agreed to it verbally, but he didn't agree to it in the decree and it's the decree that the lawyers are looking at. Therefore," Granger said handing her the last page, "this is for you."

Savannah took the paper. Life insurance proceeds were listed along with an amount and her eyes went to the bottom where a check was attached for a Savannah Ambrose, formerly Savannah Benson. Savannah blinked and then blinked again. "A million dollars," she gasped.

"And now that you've been served with this, it's all yours. I would recommend walking right back into the bank and depositing that."

Savannah screamed something unintelligible and flung her arms around Granger. She could still hear him laughing as she ran for the bank.

"SAVANNAH!" Ten minutes later and one million dollars richer, Savannah was yanked from cloud nine at the sound of her name being yelled. Savannah looked across the street and saw Darcy waving to her. After getting back from their honeymoon, Darcy and Wade had quickly become a pillar of their lives right along with the rest of the family and the town. "Will you be at weapons class on Saturday?"

"Wouldn't miss it!" Savannah called out. She wanted to tell everyone what had happened. The most ironic windfall ever, but first she had to tell Ridge.

"I hope they'll let us use the pikes this time. Or at least the cutlass. I mean, I donated some of those."

Savannah laughed and shook her head at her friend. "As soon as we master throwing the dagger, we'll be moved up. Want to practice with me tomorrow?"

"I'd love to!" Then Darcy wrinkled her nose in thought. "Maybe we should have Lacy come and teach us after school gets out." Yeah, they'd ask a fourth grader for help.

Savannah waved goodbye to Darcy and hurried down the street to where Turtle held a ladder with Junior standing on the top of it. Her heart sped up at the sight. They were there for her and this had nothing to do with Penn. This was all her doing.

The two men were bickering as she approached and Savannah rolled her eyes. "Guys, what's the matter?"

"It needs to move one more inch," Turtle told her.

"I'm telling you, it's straight," Junior said as he looked down the ladder at Turtle.

Savannah took a step back and looked up. "You're both wrong. Shift the top to the right a half of an inch and it'll be good."

Junior did that and Savannah clapped. "It's perfect!"

A couple minutes later Junior was off the ladder and the three of them took a step back and looked up. Hanging off a black wrought iron hanger and freshly hung on the corner of the building was a white sign with navy blue letters outlined in gold that read *Designs by Savannah*.

"It looks great," Tinsley told her as she came out of her gallery and looked up at the sign.

Savannah squealed, jumped up and down, and then scared the two men by wrapping each of them up in a hug. So much had changed in two months. Shoot, so much had changed in the past ten minutes. Savannah now had enough money to fund her new company and she'd just enrolled in college to finish her degree. She'd spent Thanksgiving with the Faulkners and felt as if she had a huge family of her own. She and Ridge had been dating and were so incredibly happy. This was what freedom and happiness felt like. It felt like love, family, and community.

"See you at weapons class?" Tinsley asked as her phone began to ring.

"See you then," Savannah said before Tinsley hurried inside to get the phone.

It was only when she was alone and looking up at her new sign that Savannah let her smile slip. And money couldn't fix it—even a million dollars.

Two months ago she'd told Ridge she wasn't ready to move in together because it was happening too fast for her. She wanted to spread her wings. The fears brought on by her past had disappeared after only two weeks of dating Ridge. Ever since then, she'd been dropping hints that she was ready. And after two months, there wasn't even a question about what she wanted and that was Ridge. She was his and he was hers and she was ready to be together in all ways.

Ridge had done exactly what she'd asked of him. They'd dated. He hadn't pushed. He hadn't asked her to move in with him. He hadn't brought up marriage. In fact, he helped her move all her things into the extra rooms in her office three days earlier. For the foreseeable future, Savannah was going to be living in her office.

Savannah had gotten desperate three weeks ago and begun mentioning marriage to him. Ridge hadn't run scared. He'd listened and then nodded, but didn't say anything. But no more. Savannah had her own company and she'd sold her house. She did all that herself. She reached her goals with his support, but on her own. So today she was going to tell Ridge that she wanted him in her life forever.

Savannah opened the door to the upstairs unit and ran up the steep staircase she'd painted white to make it look less claustrophobic. She used her key to unlock the office door. Inside was a prime example of her decorating style, but it was her temporary bedroom in the back she was in a hurry to get to.

Savannah started to undress as she made her way back. She'd clean up later, she told herself as she kicked off her shoes and pulled off the ocean blue fuzzy sweater she'd been wearing. She would change into something pretty and then find Ridge and tell him everything. About the sale, about the money, and most importantly about how much she loved him and wanted to be with him.

Savannah pulled her tank top off and let it drop in the hallway as she turned into her room. She was looking down at her jeans as she unbuttoned them and rushed straight into a hard body.

She didn't need to look to see who it was. She knew every inch of Ridge's body and even then, she would have known it was him by his smell alone.

"Ridge! I was just coming to find you. I have so much to tell you."

Ridge dropped his hands from where he'd caught her

and took a seat on the edge of her bed. "Really? Why don't you finish undressing as you tell me?" He smiled and it went straight to her heart and then straight down to her . . . "Savannah, why are you staring at my lap?"

When she brought her eyes back up to his face, she saw him grinning back at her. What was she going to tell him? Whatever it was, it could wait.

She unhooked her bra, let it fall to the ground as she stepped toward him. His smiling face transformed into one of desire as he licked his lips in anticipation. He opened his legs and she stepped between them. With a flick of his fingers and a push of his hands, Savannah was bared to his gaze and to his touch.

THERE WAS nothing better than feeling Savannah under his hands. Ridge touched every inch of her. Tasted every inch of her. Loved every inch of her. And soon they were naked, breathing hard, and very satisfied as she lay in his arms.

Their lovemaking had grown more and more intense as they fell deeper and deeper in love over the past two months. Ridge couldn't get enough of Savannah.

Reluctantly, Ridge got out of bed. "We have the celebratory dinner for opening your company in thirty minutes. We better get going."

Savannah threw off the covers. "Oh my gosh, how did I forget about that?"

Everyone was gathering at The Pink Pig for a huge dinner. Savannah had invited practically the entire town. Even Earl from Lowcountry Smokehouse agreed to set foot in enemy territory so long as Savannah agreed to host her next event at his place and Darius agreed to go to that one.

Ridge pulled up his pants and slipped his sweater over

his head. He ran his fingers through his hair and tucked the loose strands behind his ears as he watched Savannah dress.

He'd given her the space she wanted. He offered his support and love to her as she set out to reach every goal she'd set for herself, and Ridge couldn't be prouder of her. Savannah spun around in the long-sleeved ivory sweater dress that hugged all her beautiful curves. She fluffed her hair and Ridge loved the way her cheeks were still pink from their lovemaking.

Savannah looked him over, and with a saucy grin, let her eyes linger on his pants. "Is that a hammer in your pocket or are you just glad to see me?"

Ridge looked down at his tented pants and stuck his hand into his pocket. "I'm always glad to see you. I love you, Savannah."

"I love you too." Savannah smiled sweetly as she came forward and placed a sweet kiss on his lips.

"Before we head out," Ridge started to say, "I have to tell you how proud I am of you. You knew what you wanted and you went after it. I love seeing you grow and flourish as you discover what I already know."

"And what is it that you already know?"

"That you are the most incredible woman in the world. You're smart, talented, kind, compassionate, and a true friend." Savannah blushed even deeper and Ridge felt as if there was no way to completely convey his feelings for her. "I'm so lucky to have you in my life."

"Oh, hush and take out that hammer. We're going to be late to the party." Savannah laughed before she kissed him hard and deep.

"You asked for it," Ridge teased as he pulled his hand from his pocket.

.  .  .

SAVANNAH COULDN'T CARE LESS if she was late to her own party. Ridge was her whole heart and hearing him talk was enough to make a girl ruin her mascara in all the fun ways.

Savannah licked her lips thinking about all the ways she was going to show Ridge how much she loved him when he pulled his hand from his pocket. It wasn't his hammer. "Ridge?" she asked as she saw the navy blue velvet box in his hand.

Ridge took a step back and went down on one knee. Savannah gasped and her hands started to shake as he slowly opened the box. There sat a beautiful emerald-cut diamond engagement ring and Savannah knew she was ruining her mascara in the best way possible.

"Yes!"

"I haven't asked you anything yet," Ridge said with a smile.

"The answer to you is always yes, Ridge." Savannah swiped at the tears as Ridge's smiled widened. She watched through blurry eyes as he pulled out the ring and held it up to her.

"Savannah, my heart knew you were for me the first time I touched you. Our souls met and they've been entwined ever since. Your passion, your love, and your kindness feed my soul. I can't imagine a day without you in it. Will you marry me?"

Savannah had been holding her breath, afraid she'd miss a single word Ridge said. Her body was physically reacting to him as she felt as if she vibrated with energy. Her whole body shook as she looked into his eyes and said, "Yes. It would make me the happiest woman in the world to be your wife. I love you, Ridge."

Ridge let out a relieved sigh as he slipped the ring onto

her finger. "I could hear you say that a million times and never get tired of it."

Savannah gasped and laughed as she bent over to cup Ridge's face in her hands. She kissed him then and when she pulled away she finally told him about the other million in her life before they proceeded to completely ruin her mascara, which caused them to arrive an hour late for her own party.

# EPILOGUE

"YOU WANTED a wedding in two weeks, you got a wedding in two weeks."

Savannah looked around Harper's bar in wonder. Harper stood in a plum bridesmaid's dress with her arms crossed and her long hair hanging down her back. Savannah thought she'd cry and ruin her mascara—again. She's ruined it twice the night before—once before the rehearsal and once after the dinner. All in the best possible way.

The ceiling of the bar was covered with strings of pretty lights and gauzy white fabric. The normal lighting was covered in greenery and flowers to make hanging floral arrangements. The left side of the bar was set with tables for dinner and the right was a dance floor. Gator, Turtle, Junior, and Skeeter were part of a country band that she and Ridge had hired to play the reception.

"This is beyond my wildest dreams. Thank you all so much." Savannah hugged Harper before hugging Tinsley and Trent who had all helped decorate.

"Did you find someone to help you tonight so you can enjoy the party?" Savannah asked Harper. "I want you out on that dance floor with me."

Harper nodded. "I finally got around to putting an ad in the paper and hired someone yesterday. Tonight's her first night at work. It's trial by fire."

Trent snorted. "It'll be a snap. Skeeter, Turtle, and Gator will be busy playing music instead of sitting at a bar."

They all nodded. That was true.

"Evie! Can you come out here for a minute," Harper called toward the kitchen.

A woman who looked to be in her late twenties walked out to join them. Her hair was a bright sunshiny blonde that stood out against her form-fitting black V-neck sweater. Her eyes were a brilliant blue and were framed by the loose bouncy curls of her long hair. She smiled at them and clasped her hands to her chest. "Oh, you're stunning! Congratulations."

Evie wrapped Savannah into a quick, but touching hug. The kind that left a smile on your face.

"Savannah almost-Faulkner, this is my new employee, Evie Scott," Harper introduced before doing so with Trent and Tinsley.

"You sure you can handle all of us and all the Davies?" Trent teased.

"Not all," Tinsley said with a disappointed frown. "Cousin Jackson can't make it. Aunt Paige said he's out of the country."

"Yeah, but Suze Bell told me she got a text from him today saying he'll be here in ten days to stay at her new cottage. So at least we'll get to see him then and if he stays long enough, you'll be able to meet him," Harper told Savannah.

"Well, I'm all ready," Evie told them. "I can't wait to meet everyone. I'm new to town so what better way to become a part of it?"

Harper took Evie into the kitchen for some last minute instructions. People were beginning to arrive at the church across the street. Tinsley and Trent both hugged her before they hurried to the church to get ready for Savannah's entrance.

"Harper, time for you to go!" Savannah called out. Harper hurried from the kitchen, and as she ran by Savannah gave her a wink.

Tinsley was serving as Savannah's maid of honor while Harper, Ellery, and Darcy were her bridesmaids. Lucy was a junior bridesmaid. After all, if it hadn't been for her, Savannah wouldn't have known how to handle the dagger that saved her life.

The bar door opened and there stood a tuxedo clad Granger Fox. "They're ready for you."

He held out his arm for her to take. With each step closer to the church, Savannah's pace quickened. She couldn't wait to start her life with Ridge. Kord greeted her with a low whistle as she heard the music from outside the church. Kord and Granger were ushers for the wedding.

"You sure you don't want to run away with me?" Kord asked and then pretended to be wounded when she just laughed.

"Did the nurse come?" Savannah asked as Granger took his place at the other door.

"Nah, she wasn't the one. But my one is out there somewhere," Kord told her.

Granger rolled his eyes. "Don't worry, he didn't come alone."

Kord smirked. "You see this smile? It's because I have a date. You see his frown? It's because he doesn't."

Savannah giggled as they teased each other until she heard the sound of the music she and Ridge had picked for her walk down the aisle. Kord and Granger looked at her, and when she nodded they opened both doors at the same time Savannah took her first step toward the rest of her life.

RIDGE DANCED with his wife under the soft lights. He hadn't stopped smiling since she'd said, "I do." But all too soon they were separated as the women swooped in and had to have all the details on the proposal. And then Uncle Miles from Keeneston held up a bottle of very good bourbon and wiggled it at Ridge.

"I'll be right over there," Ridge whispered to Savannah.

"Newlyweds. You're so adorable," Aunt Morgan, Miles's wife, sighed.

"I don't know, I say they get better with age," Aunt Gemma said, looking at her husband, Ridge's Uncle Cy, across the room.

The male Faulkner cousins stood with the Davies uncles and male cousins as Ridge joined them. Evie lined up tumblers and Miles poured a toast before they all held up their glasses. "To Ridge and Savannah."

"Cheers!"

"What I want to know is if I won the bet," Ryker asked with a smirk.

Walker, who was born and raised in Shadows Landing but married to a Davies, pulled out his phone. "Let's see. I keep everything on a text loop. Back in Keeneston, we have an app for betting on personal lives," he said as he began to scroll.

"Ryker, you did say two months," Walker said as he read through the texts.

"It hurts to be so good." Ryker grinned before taking another taste of his bourbon.

"But in this case, it hurts to lose so badly," Walker said with surprise and then laughter. "You didn't win."

Ryker's eyes narrowed. "Who did?"

"I did." They turned and looked at Harper. Evie took the bottle of bourbon from Miles and poured Harper a tumbler full of the amber liquid. "Nice try, boys," Harper said before silently toasting them and shooting the bourbon before snatching the cash from Walker's hand.

Trent watched as Harper walked away. "How did she win? Ryker said two months."

"Yeah, but don't you remember I told you the more specific the better?" Uncle Cade said, looking over Walker's shoulder. "Harper guessed the day of the wedding."

The men groaned.

"I do not like losing," Ryker said, pulling out a twenty. "Twenty on Harper getting married next."

HARPER COULD STILL TASTE the bourbon as she danced with all her cousins. She'd heard Ryker place a bet on her getting married and wondered if she could bet against him. She wasn't the marrying type. She was married to her life here at the bar. She loved it. This was her place. These were her people.

She'd never met a man who could hold a candle to the happiness she found there. Plus, there wasn't what you'd call a big selection of men in Shadows Landing. She'd dated all the available ones and there hadn't been any chemistry. For all her toughness, she wanted love.

Harper looked around her bar. This love. The love between family. The love between her aunts and uncles. The love Gavin and Ellery, Wade and Darcy, and now Ridge and Savannah had found. Harper sighed with deep feeling as her eyes landed on her Great-Aunt Marcy and Great-Uncle Jake Davies. They sat together, his hand holding hers, as they talked to friends and family. Decades of marriage and they still looked as madly in love as any newlyweds.

And until a man did that for Harper, there would be no wedding. And considering she was thirty and had never found it, she was pretty sure Ryker would lose his bet.

"Harper?" Great-Aunt Marcy called out. "Come sit for a moment." Harper noticed that the crowd had cleared from around Marcy as she joined her. "Jake, be a dear and grab that bottle of bourbon from Miles, would you?"

"Why?"

"Because it's my favorite and he didn't offer me any. So snatch it from him and tell him he can have it back when he finds his manners."

Harper tried to stifle her laugh. Uncle Miles had been in Special Forces, yet Marcy still treated him as a young boy.

"Yes, dear." Jake leaned over and kissed his wife's cheek. "Stay out of trouble while I'm gone."

Marcy grinned. "One, he knows better. And two, I still enjoy that view." That time Harper did laugh out loud. There were many layers to her great-aunt. "I wanted to ask you a favor, dear."

"Sure, Aunt Marcy. What is it?" Strange how two years ago Harper had only heard of Aunt Marcy and now she was the most stabilizing force in all their lives. Harper looked over to her parents and grandparents who were talking to

Jake and some of the aunts and uncles from both Keeneston and Shadows Landing. It was good seeing them all come together as one family. And they owed that to Layne Davies and Marcy Davies.

Marcy took Harper's hand in hers and then patted it. "You know your uncles have that little school of theirs, right?"

Harper nodded. "Right. But I don't know how I can help teach soldiers about Special Forces tactics."

Marcy waved her hand as if shooing a bug. "Oh no. It's law enforcement too. Anyway, I met this nice young boy at the café one day. He spent a week at the training center. We ended up having many meals together. He was so nice I made him an apple pie."

"That was nice of him. And you. Your apple pie is the greatest. Just don't tell Miss Winnie or Miss Ruby."

Marcy patted Harper's cheek. "You're such a sweetie." No one had called Harper a sweetie in . . . well, ever. "So, it turns out this nice young boy just moved to Charleston a month ago. He doesn't know a soul, bless his little heart."

Harper's stomach dropped. *No, Aunt Marcy, please don't*, she thought.

"And I told him my beautiful niece would be happy to show him around. He likes to get out of the big city and I told him about Shadows Landing, but I'm afraid I might have jumbled the pirate history a little. Anyway," Marcy pulled a piece of paper out of her purse and handed it to her. "I told him you two could get together next Friday. He told me he has that night off. Since I just met Evie and she said she'd take the Friday evening shift, you can show little Dare around town."

Well, crap. No getting out of this one.

Harper unfolded the piece of paper and saw *Dare Reigns,*

*Palm Meadows Island Resort Bar, 6:00 p.m.* written in Marcy's spidery handwriting. "There's no phone number." She needed to call and cancel this . . . this . . . she didn't know what this was.

"Oh dear. I knew I forgot something." Marcy blinked at her and it was supposed to look innocent but Harper was pretty sure Marcy was gloating. "You'll do this for me, won't you? He's just a nice young boy."

Harper knew when she was beat, so she gave a little smile. "Sure, Aunt Marcy. I'll show him around next week."

"Thank you, dear. Oh, I see that nice sheriff over there. I want to go say hello to him. Love you, sweetie."

"Love you too." Gosh, she was a sucker. Harper would go and get this meet-and-greet over with. Show some twenty-year-old kid around Charleston and be done with it.

"Come on, Harp," Tinsley yelled from the dance floor. Harper slipped the piece of paper into her bra and joined the party.

RIDGE LEANED DOWN and kissed his wife as they stood in the middle of the dance floor. It had been a magical night. Love surrounded them as he'd promised to cherish his wife forever. In her eyes, he saw a lifetime of love.

Savannah traced her hands from his shoulder to his neck and used them to pull down his head. "I have a treat for you at home," she whispered into his ear over the music.

"Oh, yeah? What is it?"

"Apple pie," Savannah whispered.

Ridge grinned. He still had the picture of Savannah and an apple pie on his phone. "A literal or a figurative apple pie?"

Savannah took a step back and crooked her finger at him. "You'll just have to find out."

Savannah laughed and Ridge took her hand. Together they ran through the cheering crowd and toward their future.

THE END

*Forever Devoted*

*Forever Hunted*

*Forever Guarded*

*Forever Notorious*

*Forever Ventured*

*Forever Freed (coming January 21, 2020)*

*Shadows Landing Series*

*Saving Shadows*

*Sunken Shadows*

*Lasting Shadows*

*Fierce Shadows (coming April/May 2020)*

Women of Power Series

*Chosen for Power*

*Built for Power*

*Fashioned for Power*

*Destined for Power*

*Web of Lies Series*

*Whispered Lies*

*Rogue Lies*

*Shattered Lies*

*Moonshine Hollow Series*

*Moonshine & Murder*

*Moonshine & Malice*

*Moonshine & Mayhem*

# ABOUT THE AUTHOR

Kathleen Brooks is a New York Times, Wall Street Journal, and USA Today bestselling author. Kathleen's stories are romantic suspense featuring strong female heroines, humor, and happily-ever-afters. Her Bluegrass Series and follow-up Bluegrass Brothers Series feature small town charm with quirky characters that have captured the hearts of readers around the world.

Kathleen is an animal lover who supports rescue organizations and other non-profit organizations such as Friends and Vets Helping Pets whose goals are to protect and save our four-legged family members.

Email Notice of New Releases

https://kathleen-brooks.com/new-release-notifications

Kathleen's Website
www.kathleen-brooks.com
Facebook Page
www.facebook.com/KathleenBrooksAuthor
Twitter
www.twitter.com/BluegrassBrooks
Goodreads
www.goodreads.com